Kathleen Pope is a St. Paul, Minnesota, firefighter who is just beginning to recover from having her heart ripped out by her ex-girlfriend. Belladonna Ward is a newly graduated Master of Accounting and Finance from Houston who has fled her mother's constant nagging about her life being easier if she would just hurry up and get through her "gay phase". The first ice storm of the year teaches Bella she has a lot to learn about walking across slick parking lots with sacks of groceries, but luck gives her a break when it's Kathleen that's standing in front of her when it happens. Kathleen drives her to an emergency room where each starts having feelings for the other in the worst way. More than just sparks, an entire electrical storm is brewing!

A HOLLYANNE WEAVER NOVEL

In loving memory of Sofía Lupíta Elena Santiago de Vasquez, a victim of hate.

#MI22ION

UNITED IN THE WAR AGAINST VETERAN SUICIDE

National Suicide Prevention Lifeline
https://suicidepreventionlifeline.org/
Call 1-800-273-8255
(Veterans, Press **#1** After Connecting!
Or Text to **838255**)

YESTERDAY OVER 20 VETERANS WERE LOST TO SUICIDE.

According to the best study we have right now, each day over 20 veterans take their own lives. But together we can win the war against veteran suicide. Join #Mission22 to let our vets know they have an army behind them.

http://www.mission22.com/#ourcause

Other Titles by HollyAnne Weaver:

LEAVING AFGHANISTAN BEHIND
THE PLAID SKIRT
AFTER SASHA
COMING OF AGE

Coming soon from HollyAnne Weaver
and Shadoe Publishing, LLC:

FURTHER INTO FIRE

HOLLYANNE WEAVER

FALLING INTO FIRE

Copyright © August 2017
by HollyAnne Weaver
Published by Shadoe Publishing

ISBN-13: 978-1975654047
ISBN-10: 1975654048

Copyright © August 2017 by HollyAnne Weaver

All rights reserved. No part of this book may be reproduced, stored in a retrieval system or transmitted in any form or by any means without the prior written permission of HollyAnne Weaver or Shadoe Publishing, LLC, except by a reviewer who may quote brief passages in a review to be printed in a newspaper, magazine, or journal.

HollyAnne Weaver is available for comments at hollyanneweaver618@gmail.com and https://hollyanneweaver.wordpress.com as well as on Facebook, or on Twitter @HAWeaver618. Check out her new website at www.hollyanneweaver.com if you would like to follow to find out about stories and books releases or check with www.ShadoePublishing.com or http://ShadoePublishing.wordpress.com/.

www.shadoepublishing.com

ShadoePublishing@gmail.com

Shadoe Publishing, LLC is a United States of America company

Cover by: Cover design for this book was the brainchild of Marie Sterling. Thank you so very much!

FALLING INTO FIRE

PUBLISHER'S NOTE

This is a work of fiction. Names, characters, places, and incidents are the product of the author's imagination or are used fictitiously, and any resemblance to actual persons, living or dead, business establishments, events, or locales is entirely coincidental.

The publisher does not have any control over and does not assume any responsibility for author or third-party Web sites or their content.

FOREWARD

I met Nöel Stensbeck here in Minnesota. Her girlfriend's name was Sofía Santiago. She's 33 years old now, and originally from Texas. She'd met the love of her life there in 2006. Sofía was of Mexican and American Indian descent, and grew up in Albuquerque. Sofía was a year and a half younger than Nöel. They were both raised Roman Catholic.

Sofía never had the courage to tell her parents that she was gay, knowing that they were extremely biased against homosexuality. Nöel's parents knew she was gay, but were completely unsupportive although she really didn't care that much. At least Nöel's sister was okay with her. Anyway, Nöel didn't let it ruin her life.

They were sitting at home in their apartment in San Antonio where they were going through their respective Master's programs at UTSA one Saturday afternoon and Sofía's family showed up on their doorstep for a surprise visit. It was more of a surprise than they knew. They asked them in, of course, but they couldn't very well conceal the fact they were together anymore since there were photographs all over the apartment of the two of them doing everything imaginable around town and out on vacations. Not to mention it was a one-bedroom apartment. They finally told them that we were lesbians and that they were in love and had been for quite some time.

Shit hit the fan big time and all Sofía got was the lecture on how she was going to straight to hell and she was going to be excommunicated. They also didn't like the fact that Nöel was Caucasian and involved with their daughter. The entire time they'd been together, Nöel and Sofía attended Mass regularly, staying very devout even though they disagreed on the Vatican's stance on homosexuality, but had shown no outward signs to anybody from the Church. All their friends knew and Nöel's family, but that was it. And of course, Nöel's mother always thought it was a phase that would pass. That afternoon some pretty ugly things were said and things were thrown inside their apartment by Sofía's father. He did a lot of damage to the inside of the apartment.

Nöel was always very afraid for Sofía because she was unable to let go of the pressure of her family. The surprise visit came during May 2010, after they'd had been together for four years and living together for two. Exactly one week later to the day, Nöel came home to find that Sofía had succumbed to the pressure and taken her life.

Nöel went through some serious depression. About a month later she voluntarily committed herself to a center for treatment for a month. She became functional again, but couldn't stand another minute in Texas. So she took all the money she had, loaded her car with her clothes, their cat, and all the photos of her and Sofía, and left for Minnesota, since Minnesota is a very gay-friendly state. I actually met Nöel at the wedding of Rod, a man I worked with, and his partner Howard.

To this day, Nöel struggles daily. Even after years of therapy, she can't get into the swing of life. She's actually dated a few women here, since there's a large and openly supportive gay community here (not to mention support for them from the community in general), but she can't ever make it past the second or third date because she can't let go of Sofía.

Nöel and I email periodically. She listens to me missing Becky and I listen to her about Sofía. One day, maybe, one of us will heal properly. For me, I would give up my own healing if it would give her my energy to heal her. Gladly

I wrote this book in memory of Sofía, and had it printed and bound to give to Nöel for Christmas. I worked hard on it to get it done in time, but it was also therapeutic for me to keep my mind off my own woes and troubles. We met up after work on the 26th, and I gave her the printed and bound book. She broke down crying, holding the book to her chest, sort of rocking back and forth for about three hours. I was sitting on the couch with her with my arm around her, just watching TV. She finally fell asleep like that. I covered her up with a blanket laying her down flat on the couch, and grabbed another blanket and a pillow and slept in front of her couch there on the floor, just in case she needed anything.

When I got ready to publish the book, I emailed her and asked her if I could. She said of course, it was mine. I explained to her that no, it was hers. I'd tried telling her that the night I gave her her copy. I wasn't giving her just the paper document. I kept the copyright, but it basically was my present to her. In the cover, there is a dedication to her old girlfriend, which reads "In loving memory of Sofía Lupíta Elena Santiago de Vasquez, a victim of hate." I also told her I wanted to keep the dedication in the book when I published it, which made her very happy.

HOLLYANNE WEAVER

CHAPTER ONE

"Owww!" I heard, immediately followed by the sound of groceries spilling out all over the frozen parking lot. I ran towards the noise and found a woman lying beside her car, the right rear door open, her purse and groceries on the ground. It was past dark and the lights in the parking lot cast an eerie glow.

"Are you alright?" I asked her. "You look like you took a damn nasty fall there."

"I don't know. It hurts pretty badly. I'm not sure I can move my right ankle, and my ass is throbbing," she fairly well cried.

"Just lay there for a minute and get your wits about you. I'll pick up your things," I said as I started gathering up her groceries and putting them back in the bags. I put them on the seat alongside her purse. I put her keys on the roof of the car.

"You're very kind, but you don't have to do that. Really."

"It's no big deal. I'm sure you'd help if it happened to somebody else. Do you think you can stand up?" "Truthfully, you're first person in my life that has ever stopped to help me. Not that I've needed it much.

Certainly not like tonight."

"Here, just wait a second." I closed the rear door and got right up by her torso. I grabbed her arms and put them around my neck. "Now, just see if you can put any weight on your legs. Let me lift you."

"No, I'll be alright in just a minute," she said pulling back from me.

I stared at her a minute, then pulled out my badge with my ID card. "Kathleen Pope, St. Paul Fire Department. Completely dependable; you don't have to be afraid of me, and I'm certainly an expert on a couple of things. One, how to carry people. Two, I can see by the way you're lying that you're hurt. Trust me on this one. Okay? Now give me your arms and let's try and get you up." I put her arms back around my neck and this time she didn't try resisting me but grabbed ahold.

"Let me pick you up and then put the weight on your legs and ankles after I have you up," I said to her, and tried as gently as I could to lift her up. As soon as I moved her past about forty-five degrees she screamed. I was right. She had done something disastrous to her right ankle. It was just at the wrong angle when I first saw it. I picked her all the way up and held her with my arms around her, keeping her weight off her legs.

"Now, let your left leg drop down and hit the pavement. That's right. Can you support yourself at all that way? Good." I turned her slightly so that she was standing on her left leg and holding onto the roof of the car.

"Don't move until I get back. I mean it, don't move. I'll just be a second." I had started my SUV with the remote starter when I first cleared the store, so it had been running for about fifteen minutes now. I drove it around to where her car was and parked, leaving a space between us, the passenger's side facing her. Then I jumped out quickly and went around to her side.

"This will be a whole lot easier if I knew what to
call you. 'Hey lady' is sort of crass." "Oh,
Belladonna Ward. People usually call me Bella."

I opened the passenger door on my SUV, then went over to Bella. "Let's get you loaded. Remember, don't lean on your right leg at all. Let me do the work."

"What do you mean? Where are we going? I'll be alright, just help me get in my car, if you would. Please."

"Horse shit. You're messed up. And where we're going is the emergency room. I know everybody that works there and I guarantee you VIP treatment."

"I really don't think I need to go."

"Well, who's the expert here and who's the girl who just did a wheels up landing on ice in the parking lot, huh? Let me get you in my car, I'll get your purse and lock yours, and then we'll take off. It's not like you can do much to me, you're out of action."

I could see Bella's shoulders slump and a huge cloud of icy breath leave her lungs into the crisp winter air. Today had been the coldest day of the season so far with a high of minus four degrees Fahrenheit, and it was probably back down to about eight or ten below right now. It was the Friday after Thanksgiving. Bella was shivering despite having on a heavy coat, boots and gloves. I'm sure lying on the cold ground contributed to that.

I got her into my SUV with her feet toward the center of the front and her body leaning back against the door on her left side. I walked around and got in and drove us to the ER. After I got there I left her in the truck and went inside. It would be hard for her to sit as well, and I suspected besides her ankle she may have cracked her tailbone. Or at least bruised it. I got a couple of people to get a gurney to the doorway then I picked her up and helped her limp in on her good leg while fully supporting her weight.

"You know for your size Kathleen, you're incredibly strong."

"I work out a lot. You have to if you carry two and a half inch hoses full of water fifty to a hundred feet. They're heavy."

"I guess," she giggled, then grimaced for having done so. Yup, she was in pain. I got her lying down on her left side on the gurney, and gently pulled her right leg up beside her left one. Her eyes were scrunched together tightly, and she was breathing through clenched teeth.

I reached down and moved her beautiful brown hair out of her eyes and off her face. "Hang on for just a little bit, hon, and let me get you checked in. Do you have insurance?"

Bella nodded her head in assent.

I picked up her purse from where I'd placed it at her feet and handed it to her. "Go ahead and give me your driver's license and your insurance card and I'll take care of everything." Bella fished through her purse and removed the two cards from her billfold, handing them to me. Before I went to the triage and admitting desk, I helped her sit up slightly and got her out of her coat after removing her gloves. Then I reached down and rubbed her forehead lightly. I'm not sure why, since I don't usually get all touchy-feely with people I don't know well.

It took about fifteen minutes to get her checked in much to the glares of many people in the ER waiting room. 'Who was this person to walk right in and get taken back?' I'm sure they were thinking. Oh well, deal with it. When they rolled the gurney back to the exam area, I went with Bella instead of waiting in front. I wasn't lying. I knew almost everybody working there from the many times I'd been through, because of the job.

It took about thirty minutes for Dr. Sridaran to come into our room. "Well, young lady, Kathleen here tells me you took a very nasty spill to the ground tonight. That's too bad. But we'll take a look and see what you've done, and then we'll decide what to do after we take a couple of pictures, okay?"

Bella nodded her head. Since I'd gotten her into my truck she hadn't said one word. Her pain was obviously getting progressively worse. Before Dr. Sridaran left the room, he took the penlight out of his pocket and asked Bella to look at him. "Stare straight ahead. Don't move your head and don't move your eyes." He shone the light directly into each of her eyes and she did as told. "Well it doesn't look like you have any concussion, so how about while we wait for the x-rays we get you a little something for pain. On a scale of one to ten, with ten being the worst, how much pain do you feel right now?"

"I'd have to say a ten at this very moment."

With that he left the room. About five minutes later, Maggie, a nurse, came in. "Oh, hi Kathleen. How have you been? I haven't seen you since last spring." She swabbed Bella's arm and gave her the injection she brought with her.

"Not too bad. Business has been good, unfortunately. Too good lately."

"I know what you mean. I know you like what you do but it must be a mixed bag. Thank goodness for your perfect job but it's also a shame things burn down."

"Pretty much the truth," I laughed. I looked over at Bella's face. Her eyes were already starting to become more relaxed.

"That must have really been some really nice feel-good juice they gave you. You already look a little better. Do you feel like it?" I asked her.

"Yeah. A little bit. You know you don't have to stay here with me."

"Sure. Who do you want me to call for you? Family? Friends?" I asked as I pulled my cell phone out.

"No. I don't have anybody. I just moved here from Houston this month. For work. I just graduated last summer."

"Then I'll stay with you and that's the end of that. Do you want some ice chips?"

"No. Well, actually, that sounds nice."

Bella was starting to really relax now. They must have given her something pretty potent. I went down the hallway right next to the nurses' station and got a cup of ice. When I got back, she had nodded off to sleep.

I rubbed her cheek with my fingertips. "Sweetie, open your mouth and take some ice. C'mon now. Open up." Without opening her eyes her lips parted enough for me to get some ice into her mouth. She munched on it until it was gone, then opened her mouth again. She did this about four or five times, then stopped. I put the cup down.

An orderly came in to take Bella to x-ray. He was well over six feet four and obviously exercised vigorously. "Hey, hey, hey, Kathleen. What's up, baby?"

"Hey Tony, buddy-bear. How's my big hunk of flaming man flesh?"

"I thought you didn't swing that way," he laughed.

"I don't, but if I ever switch teams you'll be first on my list," I laughed back.

"Good to know, girl. Good to know. Who's your friend here?" he pointed to Bella who was fast asleep at this point.

"She fell on the ice right in front of me at the grocery store tonight. I'm helping her out. I think her ankle's broken. Maybe more."

"Ain't it just like you, takin' in strays left and right. Don't worry, I'll get her down and back in a jiffy and I'll take extra special care since she's with you."

"Many thanks, Boudreax."

"You bet." With that he unlocked the wheels to the bed and rolled her down the hallway. She was gone about forty-five minutes. When she got back to the room, she was definitely not asleep. She had a terrible look on her face.

"Well, did they get any pictures good enough for your yearbook?"

"Oh, my God! They moved me in ways that I couldn't even imagine. And Kathleen, first I just have to say thank you a thousand times for helping me tonight. You were right. My ankle's broken. And... So is my tailbone. Seems like you mentioned something about that on the drive over. It wasn't so much I didn't trust you. I mean, for a stranger I do feel totally comfortable with you. Maybe because you're a woman. Maybe because you're a fireman. Firewoman. Whatever."

"Actually, we prefer firefighter, regardless of gender. Have forever. But most people don't know to call us that. We don't mind in any case."

"Well anyway, I would never have been able to push down on the accelerator. I would have been stuck in the parking lot. I'd have eventually had to call 9-1-1. And my groceries would have been all over the ground. Look at me. I'm a mess."

"You want some coffee? I can go get us a cup if you want. Or tea? Or ice water?"

"If you wouldn't mind I'd love a cup of coffee. But are you sure you don't have to be somewhere? It's starting to get really late."

"I'm off shift until at least Sunday. I already was off today and tomorrow. I'm supposed to work Sunday, but we'll see. And time I've got plenty of. Tinkerbelle only eats hard food so she's not waiting for me to get home to feed her."

"Tinkerbelle?"

"Striped silver American tabby. She's my little baby."

Bella laughed at that. She was looking better than she did when we first came in. She was at least lying flat in the bed now. Maybe better wasn't the right word. Maybe less uncomfortable would be a better description. Maybe higher than a kite was more accurate.

"I'll be right back. Hold tight," I said on the way out. It only took two shakes to get back with two cups of coffee.

"Are you sure it's okay for me to have this?" asked Bella.

"Don't sweat it. We're not tourists here. We're homeys." That made Bella really laugh. She put her free hand down against her hip when she laughed.

"Stop that. Don't make me laugh. I hurt."

"I would imagine. You're going to have to sit on one of those stupid donut air cushions anywhere from three to six weeks I imagine.

Everybody you work with is going to make fun of the girl from Texas getting acquainted to Minnesota winters."

"Oh, aren't you nice. I said I came here from Houston. I went to school at Rice. Who said I was *from* Texas?"

"Cut the crap. Not only are you from Texas but you're actually from Houston."

"What makes you think that?"

"Because you say 'YEW'-ston' and don't pronounce the leading 'H'. Gotcha!"

Bella laughed again, grabbing her side. "I told you to stop that!"

"Okay, I'll try. I will. Terrible coffee, isn't it?"

"I admit it's pretty bad. But it's coffee. And I'm so glad you brought me some. I think you must have the kindest heart I've ever met."

"Now you're going to make me blush," I told her.

"I think you've got a perfect haircut for a female firefighter. It's short enough to keep it out of your way at work but long enough to make you really pretty. And I love where it's darker blond on bottom, almost like a light brown and almost honey blonde on top...."

"I think you've had too much painkiller, and it's starting to make you babble."

"No, really..." she trailed off. Then suddenly she put the cup up to her mouth and started sipping almost like she came out of a trance.

If only she really would look at me like that. Just the thought of it gave me a smile. I finished my cup off and threw it in the trash just as Dr. Sridaran came back in with the cart to give Bella her cast.

"Oh, no. No, no, no, no, no... I want one of those removable casts. Get that away from me!" she practically shouted.

"Well, I hate tell you this. You didn't just fracture it. You broke it in multiple places. We're going to wrap it tightly then cast it. And it's going to hurt like a mother. In a week, you'll go to an orthopedist, and he'll do it all over again. But the second cast will probably last for two or three weeks. Then you get one more, and it'll last for the rest of the time. When you get the third cast you may, and listen to me carefully when I say, *may*, be able to get a removable cast."

Bella breathed a deep sigh and covered her eyes with her hands.

"And just exactly how am I going to walk around on the ice in a cast? I don't seem to be able to do it without one as it is."

"Well, for starters you're going to use crutches. They have non-skid tips on the bottom that should help a little. Don't worry, people have been living in Minnesota for a long time now and we've seemingly gotten by. Where are you from anyway?"

"Why does everybody ask me that tonight? Doesn't anybody that was born here ever fall on the damned ice?"

"It's not that. You just talk funny."

"Talk funny? Not me, don'tcha knoow," she said with a giggle.

Everybody laughed at that. The girl had a point. We did have a way of talking ourselves.

They got her foot in a cast and it had to set for thirty minutes or so before she could move it. Then they helped her up on the side of the bed. She tried walking a little bit with the crutches they had brought to her. It helped but she still was very awkward, partly because she hurt so badly in so many places from the fall, partly because she wasn't used to using crutches. Thank goodness it was a Friday night and she didn't have to go to work in the morning. Or I assumed that. She looked more like the business type.

"Bella. You have to go into work tomorrow?"

"Nope. Thank goodness. I don't have very much paid time off, since I'm brand new. But I do have short term disability and this would definitely qualify. I could probably take off two or three weeks I imagine. Maybe I can do a lot of work from home."

"How about this, then. You can barely walk. You have nobody in town to help. How about I bunk on your couch tonight. Just for a night. I'm not forcing my way into your place. Although I'm told it's a sweet neighborhood."

"What do you mean sweet neighborhood?" she replied, furrowing her eyebrows at me.

"When the guys took your car back to your place they put your groceries up. I hope you don't mind. They're completely trustworthy. They wouldn't touch anything, I promise you," I said, hoping she'd be okay with the fact I'd just made a decision while she was back in x-ray without actually being authorized.

"You took my car home already? And put up my groceries?"

"Well, when Mike called he said he just put the cold food in the fridge, the frozen food in the freezer, and everything else is just sitting on the counter. They didn't want to rummage around anymore than necessary and invade your privacy. At least they tried not to as much as possible."

"Who *are* you people? Why are you so nice to me? You don't even know me."

"Let's just say I had a good feeling about you when I saw you laying there helpless on the ground. I knew that we'd definitely be doing a good deed tonight."

Bella reached out her hand and took ahold of mine.

"I think I may just cry. You're too much."

"Okay, now don't cry. If you cry then I'll cry and we'll look like a couple of babies."

"You, the big strong firefighter cry? You don't seem like the type to cry easily."

"Why do you say that?" I asked, somewhat taken aback. I know that I'm sort of tomboyish looking overall, but I didn't think I looked rough.

"I don't mean the way you look. I think you're pretty. I meant you're just so calm and assured. Helping me tonight you were always completely analytical and methodical. You just seem like you have a very strong character. I promise you, I didn't mean any disrespect. Truly."

"Oh, forget it. I know you didn't," I said. I was still holding her hand; she hadn't let go. I looked down at her and smiled. I reached out with my free hand and brushed her hair back to the sides of her head. Then she let go of my hand. How I wished she didn't. If I could only tell her how good it felt.

"How are you feeling now?"

"Tired. Really tired."

"Just wait until Sunday. You're going to be sore tomorrow and achy, but the second day after is always the worst day."

Maggie came with the release papers for Bella along with a written prescription for painkillers. Bella signed the papers and then I helped her get her coat on. They brought her a wheelchair which already had a donut cushion in it.

"Oh, ha, ha, it is to laugh," Bella quipped, quoting Daffy Duck.

"Oh, lookit. A funny little rubber pillow," I retorted.

"I haven't figured out yet whether you're an angel that's been sent down from Heaven to help me in my hour of need or if instead you might be Satan sent from Hell to make my life miserable."

"I'm sorry. I'm just trying to keep the mood light. Come on, let's try sitting down and see how it feels."

Bella slowly sat down. And stopped abruptly as soon as her ass hit the seat.

"That hurts like *hell!*"

"At least you'll have the cushion for the ride home." I got Bella into my SUV and shut her door. As I climbed into the driver's seat, I paused before shutting the door.

"You still haven't said. Do you want me to camp out on your couch tonight? I gladly will. It's not a problem at all. I just don't want you to think I'm making you agree to something you don't want to do."

"Actually, I can't think of anything more wonderful than having you stay with me tonight. If you're sure you don't mind...."

"Are you kidding me? The chance to wait hand and foot on the cutest girl from Houston now living in Minnesota? What could be better?" I offered in return, staring straight ahead at the road, trying not to give anything away.

"You're delightful Kathleen. I mean it. I think I'd rather have you take care of me for a day than have my own mother fly up. At least you won't pester me to death. I don't think you will, will you? You know how mothers can be."

"Actually, I don't know much about having a mother. Mine died when I was two."

"Oh, my God, I'm so sorry!"

"Don't worry, you didn't have any way to know. And I don't have any direct memories of her. Just what Pops has told me about her. I actually have a step-mom, but she didn't come along until I was fourteen. She keeps trying to act like she's my mother and I keep telling her it's okay, just be herself and stop trying to fill a gap that isn't there. She's nice enough but Pops could have done so much better. Sometimes I think she just wants his pension. He's only got two years left until he can retire. My folks had me when they were pretty old."

"What does your father do?" asked Bella.

"He's a Detective Sergeant for the St. Paul Police Department. He's not rich or anything, but he owns the mortgage on his house outright and both he and Martha drive relatively new cars."

"Martha, that's your step-mom?"

"Yup."

"Uh… I know that you're a local firefighter and know all the streets better than me, the new girl in town… But I don't think this is the way to my apartment."

"It isn't. This is the way to the twenty-four-hour pharmacy. You're really going to need those pills come morning."

"Oh, I'd forgotten. Thank you so much. I mean it Kathleen."

"I get it. You're grateful. How about you just wait until you kick me out and give me one great big thank you," I grinned at her.

"Okay. I'll try. No promises."

"Good. One of my rules in life. Never make a promise you can't keep. I hate that more than just about anything. That and lies. Two big no-nos. My ex did both the same night. Sort of messed up my head for a long time. But enough about that. Let's talk about something more fun."

We chatted about Bella's move from Houston to Minnesota, her job a bit, my job a bit, this, that, the other… Finally, we were at her apartment. Thank goodness, she had an elevator. I parked in front of the building, helped her get out and into the vestibule, then parked my truck. I returned to the building and helped get her upstairs and into her apartment.

"Wow, this really is a nice place," I said as I looked around and turned on lights.

"Thank you. The company is actually paying for this place for a year as part of my signing bonus. It's on a long-term lease with a block of ten apartments. A couple of them are used for people like me that are transfers or new people. A couple of them are held mostly empty for high-end guests or execs from our offices in other countries. Some are used just from one to three months for whatever reason. There's another guy here that also graduated last fall from Villanova who works for accounting."

"Who do you work for? And what do you do?" I asked Bella.

"Pfister-Blankenship. And I'm a group manager for one of the divisions."

While we were talking I removed the boot that she was still wearing, her gloves, and her coat. I put them at the end of the couch. I put her purse on the end of the counter in the kitchen. I got Bella situated on the couch where she could be at least somewhat comfortable.

"You just graduated and you're already the manager? That's impressive."

"Well I did three unpaid internships to begin with. And I was on a combined program. I did five and a half years of study. I don't actually have a Bachelor's degree. I just have a Master's. And between the fourth and fifth years I took off a year to do a paid internship. So, I've got both extensive education and experience."

"You're lying to me. I'm calling you on this one," I said grinning at her.

"What? I'm telling you the truth. I swear it."

"Did you start college when you were fourteen? Because you only look like you're about twenty or twenty-one now!"

"Actually, I started when I was seventeen. I skipped a year in grade school and then because my birthday fell in the summer I was always younger than everybody else in school."

"How old are you now?"

"Almost twenty-four."

"I bet if you tried you could get into movies for half price, you look so young."

Bella laughed at that one.

"Believe it or not, I do get that a lot."

"Here," I said standing up in front of Bella and reaching out my arm. "Give me your arm and let me get you into your bedroom, I'll get your pajamas out for you, and then you can sit on your bed and change. I'll come in here and catch some z's."

Bella put her arm up and wrapped it around my neck and let me pull her up. She limped only on her left leg and let me sort of carry her into her bedroom. I have to say, I've helped a lot of civilians in my six years with the fire department, especially during my practicum for EMT 1. And being in the close proximity to a woman had never created a firestorm inside me like Bella did. Maybe this was an indication that I was at long last over Melanie?

Whatever it was, whenever I was touching Bella, lightning bolts shot through me. I really had to focus. Bella had her pajamas under her pillow. They were really cute flannel PJ's, that were sky blue with clouds printed on them. With any luck, I would get to see her in them sometime.

"These aren't going to work. You'll never get your cast through them."

"I'll wear the tops. Look in the closet toward the back on the shelf. I've got some shorts stacked up there. Any pair."

"Where are extra blankets hanging out?" I asked her as I handed her the shorts.

"Between the bathroom and the second bedroom. I'm really sorry I don't have a guest bed yet. I'm planning on getting one I just haven't had the chance.'

"Don't worry, I'll be fine. I like camping and I'm sure that the couch will be softer than the ground up in the North Woods in a tent."

"I suppose so."

I scratched the top of her head and bade her goodnight and headed for the living room.

"Hey, Kathleen?"

I stopped in my tracks and returned to the bedroom.

"Do you think you could help me get into the bathroom? I still need to brush my teeth and go to the bathroom."

"No problem. Upsie-daisies," I said as I helped her up. I got her into the bathroom and standing in front of the sink, then backed out and pulled the door shut.

I could hear the water in the sink, then it went quiet. I heard the sound of her peeing and had to absolutely force myself not to draw images in my mind's eye.

"Kathleen? I, uh, can't get back up. I think I could use your help one more time tonight."

I opened the door and walked over to the toilet. I tried my best. I really, truly, honestly tried my best. But I failed my task. My head was tilted down but my eyes were aimed up. I looked directly above the cloth of her shorts, exactly where I shouldn't have, directly at the core of her womanhood. I was instantly damp. I just hoped she didn't notice. She just couldn't get that initial shove up to get to the standing position.

Once I had her standing, she pulled up her bottoms. I wanted so badly to take them back off. For the first time, as she was leaning into me, I noticed the smell of her hair. I really liked the aroma of her shampoo or conditioner or whatever it was. I helped her back into her bedroom and this time I actually got her covers pulled back, got her onto the bed, got her rotated into it, and scooted her over without her thinking twice about it. Then I pulled her covers up over her chest.

One last time I reached down and moved the stray strands of hair off her face. Just as I was turning to go, she spoke to me.

"Hey, Kathleen?"

"Yeah?"

"Lean down, would you?"

I turned directly to her and bent over. Not into her face but with plenty of space between us. She reached up with both hands and ran them through my hair. I thought my heart would melt on the spot.

"What was that for?"

"I told you at the hospital that I thought you had really pretty hair. I love the way that even when the wind blows it like outside tonight, you just walk inside and it's immediately back into place. I like the color of it. I just think you have the nicest hair. And I wanted to feel it. I'm sorry. I didn't mean to upset you," she said as she pulled her hands back.

"Trust me, you're not bothering me at all. It's just been over two years since anybody's done that. It actually felt really nice. Thank you," I said reaching for the lamp. I switched it off. "Goodnight, Bella. Sweet dreams."

"I know you said to wait until I kicked you out, but thank you again, Kathleen. You're wonderful."

I smiled to myself as I walked into the bathroom to brush my own teeth. I didn't find an extra toothbrush so I just used my finger. Then I went to the bathroom and went back into the hall to find a blanket or two. She just had one, but it wasn't particularly chilly inside, so that would be fine. I took off my hiking boots by the door and took off my outer shirt and my khakis and laid them over the opposite end of the couch. I lay down on the couch in my tank and underwear and covered up, using a couple of couch cushions for pillows. Sleep came within seconds.

CHAPTER TWO

I heard Bella moving around before she even had the chance to call out to me. I rushed into the kitchen, poured a glass of orange juice from the fridge and grabbed two of the painkillers out of the pill bottle on the counter top. I went into her bedroom and held out the pills and the glass of juice.

"Here, take these. You're going to need these, I'm sure."

Bella just stared at me for a minute. I was standing there in my tank and my underwear. I hadn't thought about it, I'd just jumped up and set about the job at hand. Then she pushed herself upright and held out her hands for the pills and juice. She downed the pills, then kept gulping the juice down.

"I just realized I hadn't had anything to eat since lunch yesterday. I'm famished."

"I haven't either. I was going to fix something for us after I got up. I was just going to get dressed first. Sorry, I should have put my clothes on."

"Don't be silly. You have a great body. I'd kill to have your body. And it's not like we're out on the street in full view."

"Now you just sound like you're hitting on me," I said laughing.

"You think I'm hitting on you?"

"I don't know. Are you?"

Bella didn't answer. She motioned for me to come closer to her. I moved over close enough so that my leg was directly against the side of the bed. She reached up and rubbed her hand up and down my thigh for a couple of strokes.

"I'm sorry, I just had to see what that felt like. You have killer muscles in your legs. I didn't mean to touch you."

"You don't bother me at all," I said smiling at her. "How about we get you into the bathroom real quick before breakfast?"

"Okay."

She let me help her up and we walked into the bathroom. She wasn't walking any better at all. I suspected she wouldn't for two or three days. I told her to go ahead and brush her teeth. We weren't going anywhere today and she didn't need to get up again after she ate just to do that. I chatted with her while she brushed. Then I sat on the counter top and faced the shower while she went to the bathroom. Again, she was able to get down, but not back up. As I helped her up I think she noticed me stealing a glance at her pelvic area. Whether she actually did or not she smiled when I happened to glance in that direction. I helped her get back to bed. When I put her back into bed I put her on the side opposite the bedside table. I picked up the empty juice glass.

"What do you have in the kitchen to eat? Eggs, maybe?"

"Sure. I even had some before I broke the dozen last night," she laughed.

"Yeah, Mike said there was a little mess. They rinsed the other things off real quick though, before putting them up. I'll be done in a few."

I went into the kitchen without getting dressed. If she liked looking at my body, then who was I to interfere? Besides, it was more comfortable than being fully dressed. If I were at home I wouldn't have been dressed yet. I found eggs, salsa, onions, mushrooms, and bell peppers. I put some margarine in a saucepan and started heating it. I chopped a bell pepper in small pieces and dropped it in the pan. Then I cross cut the end of an onion and sliced it over the pan. I added the mushrooms and covered the pan. I let it cook for about ten minutes to make the veggies nice and soft.

Then I poured some salsa into the pan and mixed it up. I broke six eggs into the pan and stirred them into the mix, then added salt and pepper. I was putting things back up and noticed a small bag of grated cheese. I stirred the eggs until they were almost done and then added some cheese stirring one last time. I looked in the cabinets until I found two plates and put them on the counter. I turned the heat off and piled the eggs on the plates and poured some orange juice for myself and refilled Bella's glass.

I took the glasses into the bedroom and put them on the bedside table. Then I returned to the kitchen and found a couple of forks and picked up the plates and went back into the bedroom, still wearing only my underwear and my tank top. I sat down on the side of the bed by the table and handed Bella one of the plates.

"Oh, this looks delicious!"

"Well, before you pass judgment, taste it."

Bella did exactly that.

"Oh my God! Oh my God! When can you move in?"

"My feelings are hurt. I thought you wanted me for my body. You just either don't know how or don't want to cook," I said making a pouty face.

"Right now, I know four things. One: my foot and my ass hurt like shit. Two: I hate being beat up and not being able to function on my own. Three: and notice that these four things are in order of importance, I love your body. And four: you're a *great* cook."

We both ate for a couple of minutes without talking at all. When we'd both eaten about half our food, I decided to ask her.

"Is it normal for you to like the way another woman's body looks?"

"I like amazing bodies whether they're men or women. What do you mean?"

"You seem to express... Well... An above average... Shall we say... Curiosity? Is that the right word? Maybe attraction. An above average attraction to my physique," I answered.

"I don't know. I just think you're beautiful. Is that so bad?"

"Not at all. "

I returned to my breakfast. Then after a couple of more bites I handed her the juice glass. She drank some of it and handed it back. I sat it down on the table and drank some of my juice.

"You're really going to make me work for this, aren't you?" I asked Bella.

"I have no idea what you mean," she said absolutely deadpan.

"Are you straight or gay?"

"Why do you ask?"

"Because I'm definitely gay and since last night I can't keep my mind focused on anything but you. I don't want to sour what could be a wonderful, yet accidental friendship over this though. And even if you were gay you wouldn't necessarily be attracted to me. Maybe you're sending signals. Or maybe you're not and I'm just falsely hopeful. Too bad you're not a redhead. I've always had this fantasy about making out with Lucille Ball...."

"Gee thanks... First you say you want me, then my being a brunette isn't good enough! Well... Hmmm... How to answer that one...?"

"Maybe just a straight up answer."

"Straight answer. That's a good one," she giggled.

"Sorry, I didn't even think about it when I said it," I said chuckling.

Bella ate the rest of her eggs without saying a thing. Then she put the plate on the bed beside her and reached her hand out for her glass. I gave her the glass and then picked mine up and finished it off. After Bella had emptied her glass she handed it back to me and I sat it on the table. I put my plate on the bed and put her plate on mine with the forks on top. I just stared at Bella, and she just stared back.

"I'm as gay as they come. And you're definitely my type."

"You're evil, little girl."

"Hey, I can't help it that I'm so short."

"It doesn't have anything to do with your physical stature. It has to do with the fact that you're sitting there all innocent like, similar to a jack in the box. You keep cranking and keep cranking and keep cranking to the pretty music... Then suddenly the top pops open and the puppet jumps up, scaring the bejesus out of you."

That sent Bella into a maniacal laugh that she couldn't stop but which caused her a lot of pain. The harder she tried to stop laughing, the more it hurt, and the harder she laughed. I got up from the bed, picked up the plates, put the glasses on them, and went into the kitchen to do the dishes.

"Kathleen... Kathleen? Please come back. Oh, Kathleen, I'm sorry. Kathleen?" she called out to me.

I slowly and deliberately rinsed all the dishes off and put them in the dishwasher and wiped off the counter tops. Then I walked back into the bedroom. Bella had a moderately worried look on her face.

"I'm sorry, Kathleen. I am. I didn't mean to upset you. You've done so much to help me...."

I put my finger to my lips to tell her to shush. Then I pulled the covers back and slid into the bed and up against Bella. I was very careful not to push against her too hard or hit her foot since I was on that side of the bed. I ran my hand up under the bottom of her pajama top just a few inches and gently rubbed her tummy. I continued rubbing her for almost twenty minutes.

Then she pulled one of the pillows out from behind her and slid down on the bed. She pushed the pillow behind my head making me rise up and let her push it under me. After I had my head down on the pillow she scooted over closer to me and pushed her face right into mine.

"You've been so good to me. You truly have a heart of gold. Tell me, how often do you go around rescuing damsels in distress?"

"You're my first."

"I find that hard to believe."

"Why? You think I'm easy?"

"No, I can't think of why somebody with so obviously as huge a heart as yours, doesn't share it with more people. That's all."

"Well, just over two years ago, in fact on Halloween night, I had my heart broken. Into little bitty pieces. I was at a costume party. There was a lot of alcohol I suppose. I went to find a place to get away from everybody to just sit for half an hour and chill by myself. The room I went into had a couple of people making out in it. One of them was Melanie, my ex. And the other person... Well let's just say that it wasn't me. Like I said yesterday, there are two things I can't stand. Lying and breaking promises. She promised to be faithful to me and she lied to me when she said she was going to go outside for a little fresh air."

"I'm so sorry. I don't know anything about her, but she must have been stupid. To give you up for anyone else...."

Bella leaned into me and softly brushed her lips against mine. In response, I pushed back against her and she slid her hand up against the side of my face. After several minutes of gently kissing each other, Bella was the first to speak.

"I don't know what the future has in store for us, but I will make you this promise: I will see only you as long as we're together, whether it's just this weekend or if it's a lifetime. And if ever there comes a time that I don't want us to be an item, I'll tell you that I need to move on. I'll say it to your face, and before I break my first promise. Okay?"

In response, I put my arm underneath her head and wrapped my arm around her waist and pulled her into me while I kissed her lips, her face, her nose, her neck, her eyelids, her forehead, her chin... Then started back at the beginning and worked my way back around again.

Bella reached over and grabbed my butt and partially pulled me onto her. We melted into each other for the rest of the morning. Somewhere in the midst of our weaving and swaying back and forth with each other all of our clothes ended up on the floor and the covers had come completely off because it was simply too hot. Suddenly we both got a chill and I scrambled to get the covers back over us and we snuggled up to each other.

Bella's hand ran through my hair over and over. Slowly at first. Then she shook it all over and made a mess of it. After that I swished my head once each way and it all fell back into place.

"I hate you. You're so perfect."

"Far from it. You'll find out quickly enough. Like I said yesterday when you get ready to kick me out...."

"And what if I don't want to kick you out?"

"Then maybe I'll stay for a little while."

"You don't have to go, what is it you called it, 'back on shift'? You don't have to back on shift until Sunday, right?"

"How do you remember this? You were in total pain and stoned out of your gourd!"

"I don't know. I just do. And I remember first noticing your hair when you handed me the coffee in the ER. And felt your strong, but gentle hands when we were holding hands. That's when I first fell for you. Right then and there. But I didn't know for sure whether you were receptive. Or maybe if even you were gay but had a girlfriend already. So, I decided to let it play out. But when you came in this morning practically naked, I couldn't help it. I wasn't too invested yet so I decided that if I was rejected it wouldn't be that much of a letdown."

"You're pretty cocky for a young girl, you know?"

"Young girl? I told you that I'm twenty-three. How old are you? No, let me guess. I'd say you've been with the Fire Department from five to seven years. I bet you've always known you were going to be a firefighter, and you have to be twenty-one for that. Maybe a year to get hired on. That would make you maybe twenty-eight?"

"Damn. That's why they made you a manager. I got hired on five weeks after my twenty-first birthday. I've been there for six years. I'm twenty-seven. You have me pegged."

"But that was just measuring the situation. Analytical analysis. It's not always accurate. You can always end up biasing your conclusion due to bad data or incorrect assumptions. But you only look like you're about twenty-three or four."

"That's sweet of you."

"It's just what I see in front of me. Say, would you do me a huge favor?"

"If I can. What?"

"Scratch my right ankle. It's killing me."

I laughed. The one thing I couldn't do for her right now was scratch her ankle.

"And it's only going to get worse. I broke my arm when I was twelve. It was hard-casted for six weeks. I guarantee to this day I remember the itch. And the smell when the cast came off. Jesus!" I told her.

"How did you break it?"

"Let's say that I developed at an early age. Tim Brewster, one of the kids at my school, grabbed my boobs while we were playing dodge ball. That made me jump on him and hit him until his face was pretty much swollen shut and his left shoulder was disjointed. Somehow in the tousle I managed to break my radius. Probably against his head. It took the entire class to pull me off him. It took them a *long* time."

"Somehow, I can picture it. A gentle giant. Kind of like having a Great Dane. Massively powerful dogs of calm demeanor. A kid throws a ball over the fence and goes to retrieve it. The dog wants to play with the kid. But let an intruder, maybe a burglar, jump the same fence, and the dog becomes an army of one."

"That's a pretty good analogy, I think. But I've only struck somebody in anger twice in my life. I don't get that mad usually. I just find a way around the obstacle. Or the irritation."

"What was the other time you struck someone in anger?"

"The second time a snot-nosed brat in High School called me a dyke."

"Ouch. I remember that. I didn't exactly hit him. Or in my case, her. But I did dump my lunch tray over her head."

"I think that would still count," I laughed.

"I remember it as if it were yesterday. I'd heard people talking about me already. It wasn't the first time I'd heard it. But the girl, Patsy was her name, was at the table behind me. I don't know what they were talking about at her table. I had just sat down and I heard her raise her voice really loud and say, 'well at least I'm not a dyke like Bella*donna*'. I slowly got up, picked up my tray, turned around, dumped it over her head, then poured my milk over her. I drew an in-school suspension for five days. My only black mark in my entire academic career."

"I knew a Patsy. Mine was different. Way different. We were the last two getting dressed after swim class. There's so much water, so many rivers and lakes here in Minnesota that every kid graduating from school has to pass a basic swim test. She walked up to me and asked if I would do something for her. I said sure. She leaned up and gave me a quick kiss. She said it was different. Softer. But she still liked boys. I assured her that it was okay for her to like boys. She told me thanks a lot though; she said she enjoyed it."

"That was pretty random."

"We were relatively good friends already. And the next day in homeroom she sat next to me and thanked me again. I said any time. She said 'really?' But she never asked again. I would have. And without trying to turn her, just offering to satisfy her curiosity."

"There it is again. Your heart of gold."

"You're full of crap, Bella."

"Maybe but it doesn't stop me from being completely smitten by you."

"Are you? Are you completely smitten by me?"

"I've known I was gay since I was about seven or eight years old. I mean, really knew. And I've fallen in lust over and over again over the years. There have been women that with one look could push the air out of my lungs. But no one before you has ever made me fall in love at first sight."

"Whoa! Love at first sight? Are you listening to yourself? Don't you maybe want to wean off the codeine before you say things like that."

"No, it's pretty much how I feel. I don't expect you to feel the same way and I'm sorry if I've scared you away by being so intense, but you said you appreciated honesty. Or at least implied it with your two rules."

"Bella, sweet Bella. It's not that. You've made me feel things I didn't think I'd ever feel again. And you did it within a matter of about an hour. So, if that isn't love at first sight, I'm not sure what is. I just wasn't expecting this. It's more than I would have hoped for in a million years. And yeah, it scares me."

With both confessions being given I leaned over and kissed her on the forehead while brushing her cheek with the back of my curled fingers. She took my fingers into her hand, and brought them to her mouth and kissed them. I was floating off the ground and the room was spinning. I moved my lips down the side of her head until they were resting against her ear. I whispered as softly as I could.

"Bella. I love you. I love you so much."

She reached her hand around my head and pulled it tightly into the side of hers and with her other hand she wrapped it around my back rubbing it up and down against my bare skin. Her hands were so soft and smooth.

"I love you too. I love you too."

We fell asleep like that and didn't wake up for almost two hours.

"Hey, you," Bella said as my eyes fluttered open.

"Hey, yourself. How long have you been awake?" I asked.

"Only about five minutes. I need to go to the bathroom. Would you help me?"

"Of course. Why wouldn't I?"

"If I don't get dressed, you won't have to try and sneak a peek," Bella snickered.

"I guess I got caught, huh?"

"Both times. Even half out of it I'm pretty observant."

"Well, I guess I'll have to always remember that! I could get in serious trouble."

"Well don't worry, I don't mind if you look around when you're out, just don't touch. As they say, you can read the menu just don't order anything."

"That's not what I meant, but it's a good rule," I laughed.

I helped her into the bathroom, but this time I stood right in front of her while she peed.

"You didn't even look."

"I was looking into your eyes. Sorry."

"That's so sweet. Just so you know, I've had lovers before and I've broken up with them and cried over them. But I've never been head over heels in love, and I've never had my heart broken because of that fact. I hope you don't break my heart. If you do, do it relatively quickly, please?"

"I don't plan on doing it at all."

"I'd like to think that's true."

"Okay, you made two promises to me. I promise you two things myself. The first is that the same two promises that you made to me, I reciprocate and make to you. The second is that I will never intentionally break your heart and that I will do everything in my power to do whatever it takes to avoid breaking your heart."

Bella reached around my legs with her arms and hugged me tightly into her. I reached down and stroked her hair with both hands. We stayed like that for several minutes before I reached out an arm for her to take ahold of and lift herself up.

"Jesus. You've got some serious biceps. How often do you work out, anyway? And for how long?"

"Depends on my shifts. From three to five days a week. From as little as twice a day for fifteen minutes to a little over an hour and a half in a day. Usually no more than two forty-five-minute sessions in a day."

"I keep promising myself that I'll start exercising but never do."

"Get a treadmill for the apartment, and you can walk on it while you watch TV for a half hour three times a week. It'll probably be boring for you. But it's doable. And I'll set you up with some small free weights. Fifteen minutes twice a week. That's all. Not much time involved. I guarantee that you'll feel like you have a thousand percent more energy."

"We'll see. I have to get healed first."

"True. True. Okay, so after getting an inventory of your pitiful pantry this morning, I've decided that I'm going to get dressed, go to my place, get some clothes, and pick up some vitals so I can cook for us. I'll cook plenty of food and put it in containers that you can just heat up so you can eat some decent food with little effort."

"Oh, baby, no, that's too much."

"I'm not asking your permission. I'm just letting you know what I'm going to do. Oh, that reminds me. One sec...."

I got her phone out of her purse and took it back into the bedroom.

"What's your number?"

I put her number in my phone and all three numbers for me in her phone -- my cell number, the Station number, which is Engine and Ladder Company 7, and Pops' house.

"Where's your charger? It's about dead."

"It's there beside the bed. It may have fallen down. It does a lot."

I fished up the cord and plugged it in. Then I put my bra and underwear and tank top on in the bedroom. I went into the living room and got dressed the rest of the way and put on my boots. I went back into the bedroom.

"I'll be back in about two hours. It'll be about time for lunch by then. I'm going to stop and get some killer hamburgers from a little pub around the corner from Pops' place after checking in on him and Martha. I see them pretty much once a week or so. I was going to see them on my off time so I'll drop in on them and tell them what's going on. I'll already have my clothes and some groceries."

"Clothes, huh? Planning on just moving in? No questions asked?"

"I'm just going to help you for a few days. If you don't mind."

"I couldn't think of anything grander. So, you're just going to tell your folks just like that about me?"

"Like you, I'm pretty much straight forward. Is it a problem for you at your office?"

"Actually, no. They made it very clear during orientation and everything that we have insurance available for spouse or domestic partner. I'm completely out. No secrets here."

"Cool. That uncomplicates the living daylights out of everything. I'll see you in a bit. Call me if you need anything. I mean *anything*."

"Okay. I will. Drive safely. Remember, there's ice out there!"

"Oh, you're such a comedian. Since you're not going anywhere and it's hard for you to get up to the door, I'm going to take your keys with me so I can deadbolt the door behind me, okay?"

"Okay, baby. Bye."

Damn. I'd have hit the remote starter to get the SUV going, but the vehicle was too far from the apartment window to start. Oh well. I'd just sit and wait a few minutes. I see so many people sit down, start the car, and throw it in gear. I don't. I let it warm up. That's why I've only had three cars in my life. I've gotten over two hundred twenty-five thousand miles on my first two. I've got less than two hundred on my current one and I'm thinking I'll probably get a new one next fall, if everything goes to plan.

I hit my house first. It's a small house and it's got a mortgage with twenty-eight years left to go, but it's my house. I got clothes and groceries. I put out food for Tinkerbell and filled up her water dish. She purred her little furry butt off so I stopped and scratched her for a few minutes, then picked her up in my lap, kissing the top of her fuzzy head. I apologized for ignoring her but told her that I was on a short mission. On impulse, I got out my phone and sent a text to Bella. Three simple letters: I L Y.

Next stop was Pops' house. I didn't see his car in the driveway. Crap. I didn't like being there with just Martha. She always tried too damned hard. Always had, always would. I got out anyway, walked up onto the porch, and rang the bell. Thank goodness at that exact moment Pops drove up in the driveway. He honked his horn at me. He got out and came up on the porch. He was giving me a giant bear hug just as Martha was opening the door.

"Well, if it isn't my two-favorite people in the world!" Pops bellowed in that deep baritone voice of his.

We all went inside and shut the door. I told everybody to go in the kitchen and sit down. I knew that Martha kept a fresh coffee pot going non-stop so I got out three cups and poured for everybody without saying anything.

"Well, this must be pretty serious, Kitten, if you're this quiet. Is it a good serious or a bad serious?"

I waited until I was seated at the table with them.

"Well, I ran across somebody in the parking lot yesterday night who had fallen on the ice. Stupid girl from Texas that didn't know how to walk on ice. Just like she got off the boat yesterday. Anyway, she couldn't get up. Messed up her ankle real bad. Couldn't drive if she had been able to get up. Also turns out she broke her tailbone. I gave her a ride in my wheels to the ER.

"I figured it was probably busier than crap with all the weather-related injuries. And it was. Anyway, since I know pretty much everybody that works there I got her right in. You should see her Pops. She's the most gorgeous woman I think I've ever seen in my life. She has dark brown hair and brilliant emerald eyes. And skin like a porcelain doll. Clear and smooth and perfect... Ugh! Words just don't convey what I see...."

"So, I'm guessing that this is a good serious thing, then?" said Pops with a grin.

"Well naturally I couldn't let her go home alone without being able to take care of herself."

"Naturally. It wouldn't be decent of you."

"And naturally I told her I'd bunk out on her couch and stay just one night to get her eased into it. She just moved here from Houston last month and doesn't have any family or even any friends yet to help her."

"Naturally. So, you didn't end up bunking on her couch then, huh?"

"Oh, no Pops. I bunked on her couch okay."

"Be careful then, Kitten. I know you've had a long time to get over Melanie, but I don't want you to get your hopes up and then things not work out for you."

"Well, it's a little beyond that already. I went in first thing this morning to give her some juice and her painkillers. I didn't think about it and hadn't put my shirt and trousers back on yet. She told me I had beautiful legs. And she ran her hand up and down one of them. We danced around it for a while. She really made me work for it while we were eating breakfast. Finally, I just came out with it and told her I was gay and asked her if she was too."

"And?"

"She said she was as gay as they come and yes she was coming onto me, and had already fallen for me when she could see me in the bright lights of the ER. She said that for her; it was love at first sight."

"I would say this is a very good sign at the very least."

"Oh, I would say a very good sign," avowed Martha. She was neither here nor there about me being gay. As usual she was just a world-class wallflower.

"Actually, Pops, I think it was for me too. Last night. She was asleep on the bed in the ER and I was holding her hand and I kept having to tell myself that it wasn't a possibility, to push it out of my mind, but I couldn't help myself."

"So, you've got a new girlfriend?" asked Pops.

"Well, much more than that. We were intimate today. Let's just say that we're very compatible. And not only is she totally out herself, but her office is cool about it too. They even offer domestic partner insurance like the City does, and they have HR rules offering her protection and all of that."

"Okay, I'm happy for you but the details of your love life could actually be left out if you don't mind."

"Yeah, Pops. I was honestly just trying to help someone who looked like she needed help. It just happened. At the ER I called Mike Capcheczi to get somebody to help him drive her car and groceries to her apartment for her and bring her keys back."

"Mike? He's a great guy. You can always count on him. Me and his old man go way back. His sister was always a whore but Mike's alright."

"Kevin!" Martha shouted at Pops.

"Well, it's true."

"You know as well as I do that if you don't have something nice to say about somebody, don't say anything at all," she iterated.

"She's got a point, Pops. It's one of your rules, you know?"

"Okay, she acts like a whore but with the demeanor of a lamb, is that better?"

I kicked him under the table in not so subtle a manor and he yelled at me in pain. Good, he deserved it.

"Well, I'd like to stay and have lunch with you old folks today but I've got kitchen duties at thirteen hundred hours. I gotta shove off."

"Bye Kitten. See you next week sometime. Be careful on the job."

"You too. Wear your vest."

"Will do."

Besides being in some very bad neighborhoods doing his work, Pops has put away a lot of really bad characters over his career and it wouldn't be anything for one of them to get out and hunt him down, or even still be in stir and get somebody on the outside to do it for them. I went down to the pub and got lunch. For a minute, I bandied about the idea of taking home some fried walleye, but it wouldn't do well being out in the cold for too long. It would be better to wait until I could take Bella somewhere and eat it hot.

I made it back just about the time I said I would, just before one o'clock. I grabbed the groceries and clothes and lunch and headed up to the apartment. I set everything down so that I could get the key out and unlock the door. I opened the door and called out to Bella.

"Lucy, I'm ho'."

Then I got everything inside. I wondered how I got all that up in one load. But I got everything either in the kitchen or on the coffee table, and went into the bedroom. Bella looked so beautiful there asleep. I slowly put my hands on both sides of her and leaned down and kissed her softly on the lips. Without even opening her eyes she let out a soft moan of contentment.

"I missed you."

"How could you? You were asleep."

"It is what it is. I love you so much I missed you in my sleep."

"Well it's official. I broke the news to Pops and Martha."

"How'd they take it?"

"Martha like every else. Mindlessly. The only reaction she had was when Pops made a snide comment about the sister of the guy that drove your car home. She told him not to speak ill of people."

"Well, sounds like she's not all bad."

"I never said she was bad, she's just not somebody I'd know if it weren't for being married to Pops. I think she was just a lonely divorcee who wanted to be a housewife again and Pops was a widower, who after many years, wanted to have a housewife around to keep the house and maybe a couple of times a week do the nasty and they both got what they wanted."

"Please don't ever do that with me and my parents."

"What do you mean?"

"Create images in my brain that can never be erased no matter how long I live."

I laughed at her.

"But Pops got a huge grin on his face. He's known how hard a time I've had. He's told me many times that Melanie doing what she did and breaking us up was in many ways the same as what happened to him when Mom died."

"So, Pops giving us the St. Paul Police Official Seal of Approval makes us girlfriends, huh?"

"So it seems. That and the fact that I love you. Bella, are we girlfriends?"

"I'd certainly like to think so. If somebody off the street asked me what you were to me, that's what I'd tell them. What about you?"

"I wouldn't even hesitate. So, you were asleep. Did you even wake up when you got my text?"

"What text?"

She picked her phone with a quizzical look on her face, which quickly turned to a smile.

"Aww, how sweet. I love you too, sweetie," she said rising up with her arms out for me to come give her a kiss.

I did. Over and over.

"Okay, do you need to go to the bathroom before we eat lunch?"

"Nope. I'm good. Can we go in the living room? I could probably sit on the couch okay."

"Sure. Let's get you dressed first. You want your jammies back on or do you want clothes?"

"Clothes. Bra and underwear top drawer, tee shirt in second drawer, sweatpants in the bottom drawer," she said pointing to the dresser.

I got out everything we needed and got her dressed relatively pain free. There was plenty of room getting her sweatpants over her cast. If she wasn't wearing a skirt last night they would have had to cut her pants off and it would have ruined them. After we got her dressed I got her into the living room and on the couch. I went into the kitchen and heated the burgers and fries up. The fries were the old-fashioned kind that you put a whole potato in the cutter and it comes out in quarter inch squares the length of the potato.

"Wow, these are great. I've never had a burger like this before. And these are from a pub?"

"Yeah, a little mom and pop place. Look at the size of them. They're only seven fifty a piece. With fries and pickles. Amazing isn't it, considering how huge they are. They're right at a half pound of beef."

Bella nodded her head while she was chewing. She was sitting at one end of the couch sideways and I was sitting on the other end. She reached over at me and rubbed her good foot up and down my inside of my calf. I blew her a kiss. She closed her eyes and blew one back. Silly little girl stuff, maybe, but hell, I was in love. Madly so. And I realized at that very moment that I'd never been in love before. Not like this. I was in a relationship that ripped me apart when it ended because it trod on my entire system of values. But this… This was true love.

After we finished eating we watched *King Solomon's Mine* on TCM Channel on TV. Afterwards, we talked about the movies and music that we liked, and it turned out that we were about a ninety percent overlap in taste. That was a serious bonus. We spent the rest of the afternoon chatting and watching television and just lying around, having a great time with each other.

"Would you please get me another dose of codeine and Coke?"

"Okay, if you're from Texas, Oklahoma, all the way over to Colorado, you say a Coke whenever you mean a carbonated beverage. In New England, you ask for a beverage. On the west coast, you ask for a soda. But if you're going to be a true Minnesotan, or from our area all the way over to Michigan, you're going to have to start asking for a pop."

"You're too funny. Okay, would you please bring me my pills and a *pop*? Pretty please?"

"Don't beg. It's not becoming."

Bella giggled at me.

"You know, from now on when people ask me why I work out so much, instead of telling them it's so I can drag fire hoses around, I can tell them it's so I can impress my girlfriend."

"Well, let me tell you, your muscles I didn't get to see until today. Before that you were fully clothed and covered up. I just thought that you were beautiful and your blue eyes and blonde hair just lit up the room. Your eyes are almost a blue-black. Even though I was in so much pain, and even through the medication, I noticed."

"Be careful. It's easy to be acting on a case of transference. It could come from a doctor, a lawyer, a policeman, even a firefighter, that's come to your rescue. You can develop false feelings for that person."

"Oh, honey, my feelings for you are one hundred percent real. Remember the lines from *Top Gun*? Meg Ryan says, 'You know, I've known Pete for a lot of years now, and one thing's for certain, hearts are breakin' wide open all over the world tonight.' Kelly McGillis returns, 'Why?' Meg answers, 'Because unless you are a fool, that boy is off the market, he is 100 percent prime time in love with you.'"

I got up from my end of the couch and knelt down on the floor in front of Bella. I wrapped my arms around her and held her close.

"Sweetie, that's exactly how I feel about you. I couldn't have said it any better."

Bella put one arm over my shoulder and onto my back pulling me in tighter, and with her other hand she softly combed her fingers through my hair.

CHAPTER THREE

    I fixed a chef salad for dinner out of some chicken breasts that I'd already cooked at my house. It made it easy; I just cut things up and threw them into a bowl. I put the dishes on the table with the bowl of salad between them and made some iced tea. I pretty much loved iced tea, but any more than maybe four cups of hot tea inside a year was pushing it for me. I grabbed Bella's crutches and walked over to the couch.
    "Come on, ya big baby! Time to face the music. Don't worry, I'll be right with you. Nothing can happen."
    I put my arm loosely in front of her left arm and across her back, not supporting her but to be able to in a second if she needed me. She walked very gingerly across the living room floor to the dining area and sat in the chair. I'd already brought her cushion over.
    "This hurts. Really badly."
    "Well, you're going to have to start doing it. Just look at it as the first phase in physical therapy. You've done physical therapy before, haven't you? "

"Actually, no. I've never gotten an injury that required it. And besides if I don't need you to help me around you'll leave me all alone..." she said making a sad face.

"I somehow don't think that's going to happen. At least I hope not. Say, I have to ask you a serious question. Totally serious."

"That sounds rather ominous."

"No, it's just about Tinkerbelle. You don't have a problem with her, do you?"

"Why in the world would I have a problem with your kitty-kitty?"

"Some people just aren't cat people. They don't care for them. Or they're terribly allergic. And she's fourteen years old. I've had her more than half my life and she's getting old too. I don't want to lose her and I don't want to lose you."

Bella smiled at me and reached her hand across the table and held mine in hers.

"I have a cat back in Houston. His name is Ivan. As in 'Ivan the Terrible'. It used to be Winston, but he turned out to be a total terror. He bullies the other cats in the neighborhood and the occasional dog."

I was relieved to hear that.

"What kind of cat is he?"

"A Chocolate Seal Point Siamese. He's not a pure bred. He's got a bulkier body, so he's probably been crossed at some point with Birman. Say, when's my next dose of medicine due? I don't have my watch on."

I glanced at my arm.

"In about two hours. Think you can hold on?"

"Can I have a couple of glasses of wine in the meanwhile," Bella laughed.

"I don't stink so, twirp," I winked at her.

"We used to say that in Junior High. I haven't heard that phrase in years."

"So, you know about my family. What about yours? Parents, brothers, sisters?"

"My Daddy's name is Steven. He's the Assistant Medical Director in charge of Research for a hospital in Houston. He's an MD but he's always worked in hospitals, never small offices. Mama's name is Della, and she sells high-end real estate. I have a brother two years older than me that is a resident in med school, taking after my dad. His name is Bryce. And I have a sister, Nancy, that's a year younger than me who's married to a guy that is richer than the dickens, has a three-year-old daughter and is four months pregnant. That's what she'll do for the rest of her life.

"That's cool. We were strictly blue collar all the way. And I wouldn't have it any other way. Not one minute of it. Even growing up I noticed something at a very early age. Other kids around us had a little more than me, even though they were from a blue-collar neighborhood too, but nobody had the love and closeness that me and Pops had. Nobody. But just out of curiosity, how did your brother and sister get such lame names and yours is wonderful? The Deadly Nightshade."

"How did you know that?" Bella asked.

"Watching Public Broadcasting Corporation on the weekends with Pops when he wasn't on duty."

"Dad went to a medical convention down in Biloxi, Mississippi while mom was pregnant with me. It was a hot day, but the evening breeze blew in off the water. Instead of staying at a hotel, they were at another doctor's house, as their guests, in next-door Ocean Springs. After they ate dinner, they went out for a stroll in this really old neighborhood they were in, possibly even Antebellum, and they saw these beautiful purple flowers. They asked the hosts what they were called, and upon hearing the answer, Mama shouted out, 'Belladonna! That's her name!' As for my brother and sister? No idea. Maybe they were just in a plain boring place during the entire other two pregnancies."

"That's actually a cool story. So, who was your first date?" I asked Bella.

"What?"

"What was her name?"

"I'm not sure if you could call it a date or not. A girl named Alecia Higgenbothom. We were in the auditorium for an assembly in seventh grade. We were watching a movie playing on the back wall, which was just painted white so that they could project onto it, and she slowly moved her hand over onto my thigh. I was frozen with fear. But I didn't stop her. It was right at the beginning of school at the first of September and hot. We got to wear shorts to school. Mine were just terrycloth, and within five minutes she had two fingers under the leg band and on my clit. She just rubbed up and down over and over for almost half an hour. I must have had three or four orgasms. I barely knew what an orgasm was then. You might call that my moment of validation."

"Wow. Nobody else noticed?"

"I don't know. My eyes were closed the whole time. How about you?"

"Tara. Tara Coleman. She was pretty rough-cut. And she wasn't very nice to me. I ran into her years later and we talked over lunch. She told me that she was so over the top because she was totally insecure at the time. She's still relatively stone cold but she's really nice and friendly."

"You want to follow me into the bedroom?"

"Let me clean up in here first. It'll only take a minute."

I wrapped plastic over the salad bowl. I rinsed out the glasses and dishes and put them into the dishwasher. This time I added soap and started it. After wiping down and washing the cutting board, I nodded sideways with my head toward the door. Bella leaned way over to the left to straighten out her right leg, then put it directly in front of her and used both hands to push up with and get her left leg under her.

"Tada! I did it. All by myself."

"Can I still help you go to the bathroom?"

"Of course, silly," she said and apparently, she was headed there first anyway. Instead of just pulling her sweat pants down part way she stepped out of them. Then she took her underwear off. Staring right into my eyes, she pulled off her top, then reached behind and unclasped her bra and let it fall to the floor before sitting down on the toilet. I reached down and picked up her clothes and neatly folded them into a stack waiting for her. I did still have to help her up, though, unlike the couch. She leaned up against the counter and started brushing her teeth. I took my clothes off and folded them as I went and laid them on the edge of the bathtub in a pile.

When I got up from the toilet, I pushed her a little to one side as she was toweling her face off. I squeezed out some toothpaste on my finger.

"I totally forgot to get my toothbrush when I went home today."

"Oh, for goodness sake! You've had your tongue in my mouth half of the day. Just share mine!" she chided.

I took her brush and gathered the paste from my finger and brushed my teeth. I stacked both sets of clothes on top of each other and we went into the bedroom.

"Pajamas or bare skin?" I asked Bella.

"I want bare skin, but it's a little chilly. I don't really want to turn up the heat because then the apartment gets too hot."

"Wait one," I said.

I went into the living room and retrieved the blanket I'd covered up with last night and spread it out on top of the other covers.

"How about this? Bare skin and not too cool."

"Perfect. I know it's early, but would you come to bed with me?" Bella asked me.

"Let me go get your medicine first. It's time."

"Oh, thank you sweet Jesus!"

I laughed. I'd been in the same situation many times before with injuries, believe me. And I'm sure there would be many more in the future. I had goose bumps from walking around the apartment nude and was ready to jump under the covers right then. Bella already had the television turned on and had pulled up an old John Wayne Western. That was fine by me. Gay or straight, all women love The Duke!

We were both shivering against each other at first.

"Make me warm. I got chilled," said Bella.

I nonchalantly put one arm behind her neck. Then with that hand I began to rub her breast on that side. With my near hand, I started stroking her pubic hair.

"Okay, that will certainly warm me up."

"You told me to. It's not my fault. Want me to stop?"

"No way. I like that. You're very slow and gentle. It's wonderful. I haven't had a girlfriend in about a year, so there's been no need, but if you want, I can shave."

"Actually, I like it just the way it is. You just might have noticed that mine is trimmed but I never shave. If you want to, go ahead, but I think you're pretty just like you are."

"Huh. Most girls liked it when I shaved…" she trailed off.

"Most? Damn, girl, how many have there been?" I laughed.

"Believe me, it sounds way worse than it is. I had more girlfriends in high school than all the ones together since. It's been few and far between."

I kept my ministrations up for some period of time. Eventually she moved her hand up to play with her free breast and began to knead and squeeze it as I did with her other one. My hand on her pelvis had not stopped. She had long since stopped talking and kept licking her lips as they kept drying out. Suddenly she made a guttural noise and her back arched completely off the bed. I didn't stop. She kept coming up off the bed over and over. Finally, she spoke one word.

"S-s-s-stop...."

I stopped all movement but didn't remove my hands. She put her hands over mine and squeezed.

"That was the most intense orgasm I've had in my life. Ever! Oh my God. I can't breathe. No, I don't think I'm going to be kicking you to the curb anytime soon."

"So, it's not my cooking after all?"

"Oh, baby, you can cook alright. And I don't mean in the kitchen. Give me a few minutes and I'll return the favor."

"You don't have to. There will be plenty of other days. Why don't you take a nap?"

"Okay."

Bella rolled over where she could get comfortable on her side and took my arm and wrapped it around her and drifted quickly off to sleep. Soon thereafter, I followed her off into the twilight of dreams. When I woke up a couple of hours later, I thought I was being shaken. Then I realized I wasn't being shaken. I felt a hand on my butt, caressing it all over and another hand reached around and running its fingers up and down my pelvic region. I caught fire immediately. I reached up and grabbed my breasts and squeezed them and played with them.

It didn't take me long. I was still pretty worked up about bestowing pleasure on my wonderful partner earlier. After I finished, I turned to face her and took her hands into mine, gazing into her emerald eyes.

"You know you didn't have to do that."

"I wanted to. I enjoyed myself."

"Well, I did too."

"Obviously," she said.

I think I'd finally found what I had been searching for all those years. We talked for a couple of hours and the next thing I knew, it was Sunday morning and the light was shining through the curtain. It was hideously bright. Bella's bedroom windows faced east. It was just too much to take. I tried to roll over and just shut my eyes, but it was no use. I was fully awake. I looked down at my wrist. Holy cow, after nine already. I never slept that late on my day off unless there was a heavy consumption of alcohol involved. I slipped out of the bed and into a robe I brought over. I went the bathroom and brushed my teeth.

I wasn't in the mood to cook this morning, so I made toast with butter and jam and coffee. Bella didn't have a bed tray so I just put all the toast on one plate and balanced the cups. I took it into the bedroom, then went back for a glass of OJ and Bella's pain pills.

"Bella. Bella, sweetie. Oh, Beeellllaaaaa…."

"Yeah, yeah. I'm here. Don't shout."

I laughed at her and tickled her tummy.

"Wake up sleepy head. Time for breakfast and medicine."

"You didn't have to cook breakfast again this morning."

"I didn't. I just fixed toast. I assume you like toast and jam because it's your jam. Here, take your medicine first," I said holding out juice and pills.

"Oh my God! You were supposed to be on shift today! You're going to be in so much trouble!"

"No, when I was at my house yesterday I called in and took the day off. I won't have to go back until Wednesday now. We work twenty-four hours then we're off for forty-eight."

"I wish you'd have said something about it. You almost gave me a heart attack."

Bella pushed herself up and then took the juice from me and swallowed the pills. She gave the glass back to me and I set it on the table.

"Here, take some toast. The coffee's probably still too hot," I said, holding up the plate to her.

Bella took a piece of toast and started munching on it. I noticed a stray strand of her hair in the corner of her mouth and reached up and pulled it out, and then brushed the rest out of her face on both sides and put it behind her ears.

"Thanks."

"Don't talk with food in your mouth."

"Naah! See food?" she asked opening her mouth and showing me her half-eaten bite of toast.

That made me laugh so hard that I choked on the bite I'd just put in my mouth and managed to blow it all over the sheet. We both started laughing so hard that we couldn't eat. Then so hard we couldn't breathe. Finally, we calmed down.

"Well, I guess I'm washing sheets today."

"I'm sorry, I'm not sure what made me do that. It's probably because you sounded exactly like my mother and it just made me do something goofy."

"Don't worry. I wasn't really getting on you. I was just joking around. I didn't mean to come across as scolding you."

"Oh, you didn't. Like I said, it just got weird in my head for some reason."

"Okay, so I have to wash the sheets today. I'm guessing coming up on the weekend you already had laundry piling up. I'll gather that up too and get everything clean for you. Where's your laundry room?"

"That door in the kitchen on the right-hand side of the fridge? If you open it you find a stacked set of the tiniest washer/dryer combination known to man. You can only do about four or five pieces of clothing at a time in it at best. But that way you can drop something in it almost every day and keep up with it. Beats having to go to a laundry room though."

"I like having my laundry in my basement at my house. The only thing I don't like about my house is my narrow driveway and single car garage. But everything else is fine for me. It's just me and Tinkerbelle so it's plenty big enough."

"You never know, though. Maybe someday somebody else could end up living with you. Would it still be big enough?"

"It's small but it's got two bedrooms and a study that could be a third if you hung a curtain up on it. It's got vinyl siding and a new roof about five years ago. Pipes are all copper. Modern wiring. Central heat and air. Why do you ask?" I queried with a grin.

"No big deal. Just wondered how territorial you are."

"I'm an open book. I have nothing to hide. When you get better and can get around a little, I'll take you over and you can see it for yourself and see if it measures up to your standards."

"My standards are more likely to be met by the owner, not the house itself," she returned with a smile.

We finally finished the toast and coffee and I took all the dishes into the kitchen and loaded them into the dishwasher. When I got back to the bedroom, Bella was already standing up and was walking to the bathroom. I went with her and we talked the whole time. When it was time to get up from the toilet, she tried pushing up with the crutches and failed to make it up. She tried twice more, and on the third try she made it.

"Bravo! The first step toward a good recovery. I'm not harping on you sweetie, but if you'd been on my simple, completely *not* overdoing it exercise program before your fall you'd already have been able to push up. I'm just saying, this is one reason you need it."

"I know. Like I already told you, I've been meaning to do it for the last three years and just haven't made the time to do it."

"Come on. Put on your sweat pants and grab a shirt. I'll get you a towel and we'll go into the kitchen and I'll wash your hair in the sink," I said picking up the shampoo and conditioner from the shower, and then a towel from the hallway cabinet.

Bella got dressed by herself and then made it into the kitchen. I got her over to the sink, put a chair sideways so she could put her knees on it and not have to worry about her foot.

"I never in a million years would have thought to do this. You're brilliant."

"No, I'm just a firefighter. Besides, didn't your mother ever wash your hair in the sink? Even Pops did it for me when I broke my arm and couldn't get in the shower for about three weeks," I began while adjusting the water to the right temperature.

"Tell me when it feels right to you."

Bella felt the water and gave me a thumb up when it was warm enough for her.

I began by getting her hair good and wet and then rubbing in some shampoo. While I was washing her hair, I began to fill in a couple of gaps about myself I just never got around to telling her.

"Like I said before, I was hired by the department when I was twenty-one. But I'd already started working on my degree since my senior year in High School. I got my Bachelor of Science from Oklahoma State University's School of Fire Protection online. I did it in three years working as a night dispatcher for the St. Paul P.D. Most of my electives are in Geography and History."

"Crap, you were a cop, too?"

"No, just a radio dispatcher in a dark room in front of a bunch of computer screens, telephone lines, radios, and a headset. Anyway, after I'd been with the department for a year I also started taking classes through Hennepin County Technical College to get my EMT certificate. I did my first rotation two and a half years ago. I was gone from my Station House for four months to do a practicum. I'm not a Paramedic yet, but I am an EMT 1. Having seen a few people banged up in accidents, especially from slips, trips, and falls, as we say, was how I could tell that you were messed up."

I had thoroughly rinsed her hair by now and was beginning to apply the conditioner.

"And that's also why I've actually manhandled more people that the average firefighter will over the course of a career. It wasn't until I got you into the light that my heart started going pitty-pat," I giggled.

I turned off the water and wrung her hair out a few times. Then I took the second towel and, getting her to sit straight up, started to dry her hair off.

"There. All done."

Bella reached out to me. I thought she was trying to steady herself so I instinctively grabbed her on both sides of her waist quickly.

"No. Put your arm back up."

"What?"

"I want your arms back up and out to the side."

I did as I was told. Bella reached out and tried to wrap her hands around my biceps. I'm not exactly bulked out like a body builder or anything like that. But I'm not a skinny person to start with and I do work out a lot. A whole lot.

"You have beautiful muscles. I wish I could get an artist to sculpt you into a marble statue."

"Don't be stupid."

"I'm not. Don't be modest. You are so beautiful."

"I'm so average. I realize that I'm a touch on the androgynous side."

"How can you say that? Oh, if only you could see in yourself what I see in you."

"Now you, on the other hand… You're a goddess. You practically had my underwear wet in the ER. No joke. You had me both emotionally and physically at the same time. And in two seconds flat."

Bella reached out and put her arms around me and squeezed me tightly.

"Have I told you lately how much I absolutely love you?" she said leaning in and kissing me.

"Yes, but don't stop. I can take it as much as you want to say it."

"I have a couple of emergency numbers for work. I should probably try to contact somebody to let them know what's happened. I suspect Monday I'll be online most of the day in meetings. Thank goodness for web sharing. That way I can meet with my department's people in Hong Kong, London, Switzerland, and Brasilia all at the same time. And the coolest thing? *They all have to be up at my hours!* That'll give you plenty of time to go to the gym and do whatever else you need to do."

"That sounds good."

We lay around the apartment most of the day. That evening I cooked several meals and put them all in containers. I cooked chicken paella, beef fajitas, a hamburger/cheese casserole, and put a pot of stew on. Bella wasn't able to get in touch with anybody from her office, but then I don't think she really tried very hard. I think she really wanted a little more time without being engaged in the process. We went to bed early. Bella asked me if I wanted to make love to her. I told her no. She gave me a pouty face.

"If you don't mind, instead I'd rather just have some rabid, full-on, nasty-dance sex. If that's alright with you."

"Or that. That's sounds pretty good too."

All bets were off. We made so much friction I'm surprised the paint didn't peel off the walls.

CHAPTER FOUR

"Well, your phones charged. Keep it with you for the next couple of days. That way if you need me you can get to it easily. If you have a fall or something, don't dick around. Call 9-1-1 first, and then call me if you can. If you can't, let whoever shows up know you're with me and they'll call me. Okay?"

"Okay. I'm going to really miss you today."

"Me too, mi amapole."

"Amapole?"

"It's Spanish for poppy."

"Yo se. Estudiaba por cuatros años los clases españoles en la escuela secundaria." (I know, I studied Spanish clases for four years in high school.)

"Pienso, lo que realmente era suerte que nos trajo juntos." (I think it was really luck that brought us together.)

We both laughed out loud. For a long time.

"Yes, truly fate. We were meant to be together," I said.

"I love you. See you tonight for dinner? About what time?"

"I'll be back before dinner. I don't want to get stuck in commuter traffic. I'll plan on being here about three or three-thirty. That'll give me time to play with Tinkerbelle, go work out, go to the station and talk the guys, go to the grocery store... Maybe even enough time to go to the nursing home."

"What do you do at the nursing home? Do you know somebody there?"

"No, it's the home where my grandpa was, and I just still go by and volunteer periodically. Like now when I have some down time. Say, I never asked or looked. Are you wireless here or cabled in?"

"WIFI. The whole building is covered, included with the rent."

"Cool. I'll bring my laptop over."

"Okay. See you later. I love you."

"Love you too, sweetie. Talk to you tonight. Bye."

"Oh, wait, one last thing," Bella yelled out at me.

"What?"

"Top right-hand drawer of the desk over there. There's a paper clip and staple and pushpin tray? Has the second key to the apartment. Go ahead and take that."

"That'll make it easier and let you keep your keys with you."

"No, that's not it. I've given you the key to my heart. It comes with a key to my apartment as well."

I got the key out of the drawer and put it on my key ring. Then I walked over and gave her one last kiss. I headed out the door. Damn, I should have come down ten minutes ago and started my SUV with the remote-control starter. At home, I can just walk to the front of the house and click the button and it's a go. Oh well, it was only, ah, minus fifteen according to the gauge in my truck. Brrr. Even for a girl born and bred in the far north, this was a chilly morning. It was still only about seven-fifteen. There would be plenty of traffic to battle.

I got to the station house just before eight. A couple of the guys were still asleep, but most were up and moving around. One of the trucks had been out to a house fire in the early morning hours for about three hours and had just gotten back, been cleaned, and parked inside. The men were tired and hungry.

"Hey, you guys want me to rustle you up some hot grub while you get changed and get ready for a nap?"

"That sounds great, Kath. About a half dozen of your fantastic scrambled eggs?" answered Fred.

"And some bacon maybe?" chimed in Dave.

"No problems, no worries. It'll be ready when you get out of the shower and changed," I said.

I had just put the food out on one of the tables when Fred and Dave came walking in. Right behind them was Greek. His first name was actually Ambrocio, but for whatever reason he didn't like it and wanted everybody to just call him Greek. He was the biggest and toughest member of our Station. Huge. A step behind him was Stew.

"Hey, I only count two plates. What about us?" asked Greek, pointing his thumb at himself and Stew.

"You snooze, you lose. Besides, you didn't do any work. You were just sleeping," I replied.

"Yeah, but I was dreaming I was on a fire. That should count for something," blurted out Stew.

Everybody laughed.

"Best I can do is a fresh pot of coffee ready for you. The rest you'll have to do for yourself, ya big goof."

"Okay, okay. We'll manage."

I was sipping my cup of coffee, having already eaten with Bella. I suddenly noticed that the whole group was staring at me.

"What? Do I have something on me?"

"Yeah. Eyeliner and lip gloss," said Greek.

"So?"

"You got laid!" exclaimed Dave.

"Don't be a pig."

"You did. You got laid," said Greek.

Everybody pointed a finger at me and started taunting me.

"Let's just say that I met a girl this weekend. And we... Uh... Well, I have a girlfriend. We're going steady."

"Told you so!" said Greek.

"It's not like that. I know it happened really quickly, but this is serious guys. Let me show you something."

I pulled my keys out, holding up Bella's apartment key.

"No shit? You already have the key to her apartment? You aren't kidding -- this is serious. Are you sure this isn't some sort of overreaction to Melanie? I mean, you were hurt pretty bad and were down a long time. We all saw it, even if we didn't talk to you much about it. We just don't want to see you get hurt."

"Who is she?" asked Stew.

"Well, Mike's been to her apartment, along with whoever was with him Friday night."

"That was me! I took thirty minutes out of here and went with him!" yelled Greek. "You picked up a street urchin and took her in. How frickin' sweet."

Everybody thought that was enormously funny.

"Actually, I didn't take her in. I sort of made her take me in so I could take care of her for a couple of days. She just moved here. She has no friends or family to help her. I played it straight and normal just like I should Friday night. Saturday, I wasn't sure, but I thought she was hitting on me. I kept trying to get it out of her if she actually was or if I was just getting signals that weren't really signals but wishful thinking on my part. She made me squirm. Finally, she gave it up that she was as gay as a three-dollar bill, I was definitely her type, and she wasn't involved. The trifecta!"

"Well good for you. Maybe you'll finally quit moping around this place and do a full day's work."

"Bullshit. I work as hard as anybody else here and you know it. I pull my weight!"

"I was just kidding you. We could tell you came out of your funk from your ex about a year ago. It just took you a long time to be happy again. But nothing like you are today. This could be a seriously good thing for you."

"That's what I'm trying to tell you guys. She's the one. I can already tell."

"When can we meet her?"

"When she can walk on her own."

"Oh, yeah. There is that."

"Well, I'd love to stay and chat, but you guys are just plain boring and I'm going to the gym. I haven't been in a couple of days."

"Go on, tough guy. Go pump some iron."

"You're lucky I don't pump you."

"Is that an invitation?"

"You know I'm not into boys. Even little ones like you."

"Okay, when HR Hell calls from City Hall, leave me out of this convo, okay girls and boys?" begged Stew, his arms up in an 'I surrender' pose, laughing, walking away.

I turned around and gave everybody a wave on the way out. I worked with the best bunch of guys in the world, no matter how it sounded sometimes when we bantered back and forth. I was off to the gym.

Being at the gym felt great. It was always a good way to focus my brain, to clear out my troubles. It was almost a Zen thing for me, a form of meditation. I decided today needed to be a heavy workout day. I grabbed my gym bag out of the truck and went inside. The workout clothes were a little chilly, having been in the truck overnight for a couple of days. But the chill only lasted for a second or two.

I started with a good long jog on the treadmill. I put in thirty minutes before I even started into the machines. I did slightly lighter weights that I usually did, but I made four full rounds of the machines. That took me almost an hour and fifteen minutes. I was definitely burning today. I decided enough was enough, but being with Bella I wouldn't be coming back for a second session today.

I headed for my house. I spent a good two hours on the laptop, goofing around, and reading email. I even sent one to Pops that he'd get at work just to say hi and that I loved him. I actually said 'you and Martha,' even though I didn't mean it. And I think he knows that I don't really mean it. But he's hopeful and that's what he'd like to believe, so we let it go at that. Tinkerbelle sat beside me the whole time, purring her heart out. I love my little kitty. Well, not so little. She's actually a huge cat. And not fat, either, just a huge cat weighing about eighteen pounds.

I picked up an extra toothbrush to leave at Bella's, and some toiletries that I had forgotten about when I came by during the weekend. My cell phone chirped showing me I had a text message. It was from Bella.

'Not taking any time off. Just working from home. They're going to courier me docs that they can't send electronically. Not having to take even one day of sick time. Sorry, babe, but it's going to mean long hours. I can always stop and eat dinner with you though. And we'll be able to squeeze in a nooner, I'm sure. I L Y'

I couldn't help but grin. I mean a big, wide grin.

I went over the grocery store next, to get some stock for Bella's fridge. Man, it had looked more like a bachelor's fridge than a woman's fridge. Next stop was the liquor store for some wine and some beer. I took a wild guess at something Bella would like. If she didn't, I'd just take it over to Pops' and we'd drink it when I was there. Of course, I was hoping it would be pretty soon when Bella and I would be able to get out and go over together for lunch on the weekend. My last stop was a flower shop. I got three dozen daisies in a vase. It made a big, bright bouquet to lift up the mood of the apartment, I thought.

I'd gotten everything done and it was still only two o'clock. I had my laptop so I could get online, but I'd already been on for a couple of hours and was pretty much caught up with work. I decided to visit the nursing home.

"Kathleen, so good to see you. Cold enough for you out there?" asked Ethel, a worker at the nursing home. She was almost old enough to be one of the residents here.

"It's pretty cold out there all right. Worst time of year to fight a fire. You have a blast furnace in your face and then the water you spray immediately turns to ice."

"You here to read for a while?"

"Sure am."

"Mrs. Coulton has been asking about you lately. Would you mind terribly going down to her room today and reading to her for a little while? I'm sure she'd be so happy."

"No problem."

I went down to Mrs. Coulton's room that she shared with Mrs. Grzybowski.

"Hi, Mary. Hi, Eileen. I've come to read a little bit more in our book, if you want."

Both ladies were ecstatic. I took the book from the top of the dresser that we had been reading, *The Great Gatsby*, and read them three complete chapters, which took just about an hour. It was time for me to go. I bade them both goodbye for the day and promised to come back soon and read more. I hit the streets and made my way back to Bella's.

I made two trips up to the hallway right outside the apartment with things I'd picked up during the day. Then I opened the door and scooted everything inside. Bella was using a USB headset through her laptop and was talking to people. Either she already had software on it or they had remoted in and installed it. I tried to be as quiet as possible as I put away the items I'd brought. The wine and beer went in the fridge along with the cold items from the grocery store. I put up the dry goods from the grocery store in the pantry. I put my toothbrush and toiletries in the bathroom. I put my gym bag along the wall in the empty second bedroom. I put the flowers out on the island counter in the kitchen. Then I unlaced my hiking boots, set them by the door, and walked up behind Bella.

I collected Bella's hair in the back and pulled it all over to one side, then quietly leaned over and kissed the back of her neck. She took her right hand and reached back and rubbed my cheek. I left her alone to work. I went over to the couch and lay down, putting on my mp3 player, and took a nap. I woke up about two hours later and Bella was still going strong. I wasn't that hungry so I decided I'd just wait until she finished up to go about that task, especially since we had another week's worth of food already prepared. I pulled out my tablet and started streaming a movie.

About fifteen minutes after the movie was done, Bella turned around in her chair.

"Hey, civil servant."

"Hey what, corporate executive?"

"Sorry I took so long to end the day. But I'll warn you now that many go that way. Not quite as long as tonight though, I'll admit."

"Do I have to remind you that I do twenty-four hour shifts at the station and then get forty-eight hours off? What's the difference in that?"

"I just wanted you to know what you're in for. Oh, what pretty flowers. Thank you. That was sweet of you."

"I thought you might enjoy them. I don't know what your favorites are, but those just said, 'buy me', so I did."

"Come here and give me some loving. Some of that good loving that you can find on sale at the five and dime."

"Kathy Mattea! I love that song. It makes me cry."

By now I was standing next to Bella and she had her arms around me. I don't know what sparked it in me -- I actually have a good voice and was even in Chorus in Junior High and High School, but I don't sing in front of other people. No Karaoke. No impromptu singing out loud. But something possessed me and I sang the entire song to Bella. She joined in at the start of the chorus and sang the rest with me. She had a wonderful voice too and was able to do something I can't do: sing harmony. When I was done I hugged and kissed her several times.

"I don't really like to go out dancing much, but when we've got you healed up we'll need to do that. You like to dance?"

"Rock, pop, club, country, DJ... Pretty much anything but hip-hop. I'm so totally *not* a racist by any form of measure; I just don't like the music. It's not very... Musical."

"Pretty much the same for me. Except you have to throw in Spanish musicians and flamenco guitar. And Celtic harp. And definitely Mike Oldfield and Bruce Cockburn. Not that you can dance to the last four. I'm just saying, it's the music that I like. By the way... You have a marvelous voice."

"So do you. You surprised me. I didn't figure that many people up here would like country music"

"Oh, it's huge up here. But most of them don't think of Kathy really as country. They think of her more as country/pop. And most people have never heard of her."

"I suppose you're right. I used to go over to Austin for the weekend almost once a month for several years after I got my driver's license. I've seen Kathy Mattea twice. You wouldn't believe the different music you can find there. Country, Rock, Classical, Blues, Gospel, Pop, you name it, it's there. That's where I saw The Barber of Seville my first time."

"How many times have you seen it?"

"Three. My first time in Austin when I was seventeen. Once in San Francisco. And the last time in Chicago."

"Well, you certainly are well travelled. All of my travels have been to surrounding states to go hiking and camping. And once I went to Missouri down in the Ozarks to attend my cousin's graduation from Basic Military Training School in the Army. Ft. Leonard Wood. She's in Supply for one of the units of the 34th Infantry Division, Red Bulls."

"Why does that not surprise me? Is everybody in your family in government service?"

"Pretty much."

"What's her name and what does she do for her regular job?"

"Penny, and she works the flight line at the MSP International Airport. Fuel trucks and plane movement and things like that."

"Your family has a list of strong women."

"She's actually totally straight. Married, three kids. Doesn't even particular like me being gay, but leaves me alone about it and doesn't stir up any family trouble. But I'm telling you if you walked down the street and saw her, you'd say to yourself 'Damn, she's gay!' I guarantee it."

"Can I sit on the couch and put my foot up over your legs?"

"Sure you can. Want some help?"

"I do, but I should probably do it myself to build up strength."

I sat down in the middle of the couch. Bella limped her way over and sat on the end cushion, then swung her legs up so she was sitting sideways. I started rubbing her calf above the cast.

"Does that hurt?"

"A little bit. My ankle is totally throbbing right now. And the itch... Argh. It's driving me nuts."

"It'll be over before you know it."

"Not soon enough."

"You should be glad that it will be mostly healed before the worst of the snow and ice comes. You might be able to get into a walking cast in about three or four weeks. Then you'll have a lot more mobility. Which reminds me, I forgot to go by the drugstore. I'll go out after dinner and get your refill."

"And what's out there now isn't the worst of it? Imaging how badly I would have crashed and burned if I'd done it in the worst of it."

"It was probably worse right now because it's not enough snow cover, just some ice."

"I hate to make you go out in the cold again just for my pills. Oh my God! I just remembered... How could I have been so stupid?"

"What?"

"There's a heated garage under the building. Give me my keys and get the control out of my car so that when you come back you can park inside. Space 48. How could I have forgotten that?"

"Cool."

"What's for dinner? You want some of the stew that's been cooking?"

"Sure. Let me go dish it up."

I set out bowls and silverware at the table along with glasses. I opened two beer bottles and set them down as well. I got Bella's cushion, put it on one of the chairs then called her in to eat while I dished up the stew. I grabbed one of the sleeves of saltines that I'd just gotten at the grocery store, opened it, and set them in the middle of the table. She was managing pretty well with her crutches by now. That was a good sign. I only had one more day with her.

"This is pretty good. Really. The meat is really tender and there's a bit of spiciness to it."

"Well, the meat is actually thick cut sirloin so it's much better than stew meat or roast. And the spiciness comes from the crab boil. I use a little bit of Zatarain's liquid seafood seasoning. The sesame oil infuses the meat with the spices. A touch of Cajun."

"We'll definitely have to have this again on a cold Saturday night sitting around the house."

"I caught three things from that. You imply that we're going to be in an ongoing relationship, which is a very, very good thing. You also said house, so it could mean that you either just refer to this place as your house or you may have been speaking about my house, which again, would be a very, very good thing. Lastly, you told me that you loved me more than anything else in the world. With the exception of maybe your family back in Houston."

"I never said anything about loving you."

"It was implied," I grinned to her.

Her hand came across the table and grabbed mine.

"I know it's early, but I do truly think that wherever you are is where home is for me. From now on."

"I may just hold you to that."

"I'm hoping you do."

"Not only do I love you Bella, but you are one of the most beautiful women I've ever seen in my life. Ever. I love your dark hair against your green eyes."

"Can I make a confession to you? Until I met you I always preferred black hair and chocolate eyes. Ojos de cacao. But you... You've completely redefined what I look for in a woman. And you have the most perfect body. You totally turn me on. I mean, I thought you were cute in the ER, but when you came into the bedroom Saturday I thought I would have an orgasm on the spot."

"Stop. Now you're just embarrassing me."

"Okay. For now. But I don't promise to stop forever. I'll keep saying it over and over. Just like I'll keep saying that I love you over and over. Because I do," she said quickly followed by the three motions for 'I love you' used in American Sign Language.

I responded by just putting my hand over my heart and patting my chest a few times.

CHAPTER FIVE

Tuesday morning, I left early again headed for the gym. I stayed for over an hour again. I jogged on the treadmill for about forty-five minutes. Then I did one rotation on the machines. I'd do free weights tonight at home. Then I headed for the house.

First things first, according to Tinkerbelle. She wanted attention. Lots of it. I apologized over and over to her and told her that soon this silly situation would be different. Even though she had plenty of water and food in her dispensers I cleaned both and refilled them. Then I cleaned the sink out. I don't know why, I hadn't used it. Probably out of habit. I made sure I packed my Station bag with a couple of uniforms. We have a washer and dryer at the Station if we need it, but I like to take extra changes of clothes just to have them.

I got out my EMT II study guide and read through it for almost two hours. I'd read it completely through about a dozen times by now. But when I got my rotation doing my practicum for the department, I wanted to fit in like I was a seasoned veteran. That's just the way I do things. I always try to be perfect. If that's true, why had I always made such bad choices in my love life? But now it was different. It might just be perfect. Time would tell.

I put the book down on the table and went to the kitchen. I had some deli ham, sliced a quarter inch thick, in the fridge. I took some out and cut it up, along with some cherry tomatoes, mushrooms, and red leaf lettuce. I added some cottage cheese, and crushed pineapple and topped it off with a healthy (or maybe unhealthy) squirt of salad dressing. I sat down and ate my salad, watching television and letting my mind go pretty numb for a brief rest. Tomorrow I was on shift. Some days are totally boring and you can't find enough to do, and some days you work a full twenty-four hours without a break. That's part of the game.

I got up and washed my dishes and cleaned up the kitchen again. I looked at the date on my watch. Almost the first of December. I hoped that Bella wasn't planning on going home for the holidays. I know she was here for Thanksgiving, but Christmas and New Year's might be a different thing altogether. I would have liked her to be around her family, but I would do nothing but sit at home feeling sorry for myself, counting the seconds until she returned to Minnesota. I picked out some free weights, both five pounders and twenty-five pounders and took them with me as I left the house.

The Blood Center had sent me an email last week letting me know I was eligible again to donate. I had meant to do it during the weekend, but things sort of didn't go as planned. So I scratched Tinks on the head and told her to be a good girl and drove to do that. They were a little backed up, so it took almost two hours before I could get in and out. I was way ahead of commuter traffic still, so I drove back to Bella's.

This time I parked underground. I went upstairs and went inside as quietly as possible. This time Bella was on the laptop but wasn't talking on the phone. I walked up behind her and wrapped my arms around hers and kissed her on the top of her head. Bella raised her arms up to hug me back.

"I missed you."

"How much?" I asked.

"This much," she said holding her hands out at arm's length like kids do.

"And how much do you love me?"

"This much," she said holding out her hands again.

"I'm glad. You make me so happy I feel like I've died and gone to Heaven."

"Oh, don't die on me. I want you right here with me."

"Okay, lover. If you say so."

"I say so."

"Bella? How did we find each other? I mean what were the chances? I think for the first time in my life I might believe in fate."

"Me too. Me too."

"Well, I'll let you get back to work. I'm going to take your car keys and go run your motor for about twenty minutes."

"What for?"

"You Texas girls. You don't know much about cars, batteries, and cold weather, do you?" I laughed.

"Take the keys and go. Leave me alone. I'm working."

"Yes Ma'am."

I went out and started the car, programmed my favorite radio station into the second FM band so I wouldn't mess up Bella's stations, and just let the car run until the heater was blowing good and hot and defrosted all the windows. I went back up to the apartment and put Bella's keys up, took out my mp3 player, and lay down on the couch and shut my eyes. I didn't go to sleep but did get really relaxed.

About half an hour later I sensed something in front of my face. It was Bella. As soon as my eyes opened, she swooped down on me for a kiss. Nothing gentle about it either. Passionate. Greedy. Forceful. I responded in kind. About ten minutes later she stopped.

"Back to work now?"

"Yup. Have to. But I had to have my 'coffee break'."

"I love you, sweetie."

"I love you too."

Then, as quickly as she came, she left. Immediately I heard the keystrokes on the laptop. I put my earphones back in and started the music again. Only this time, I fell asleep. I probably was asleep for about an hour and a half when I felt somebody tugging at me.

"What the...?"

I looked down and Bella was taking off my belt and undoing my pants.

"What are you doing?"

"Getting you undressed so I can have sex with you."

"Well, that's one way of going about it."

I rose up so that it would make it easier for her to take my jeans off. Then I rose up the upper half of my body and she pulled my tee shirt over my head, stripping my sports bra off with it. She then stood back up and unbuttoned her shirt. It seemed odd to me that she was wearing a dress shirt and sweat pants. After she took off her shirt and bra, she took off her sweat pants and underwear.

"Dress shirt?"

"Video conference today."

"Ah."

"Here. We forgot these," she said taking off my underwear.

Just as she was starting to lie down on the couch, the crutches, which she had leaned up against the coffee table, fell and hit me in the head.

"Oh, baby, I'm so sorry. Are you all right? Baby?"

I put my finger to her lips quieting her.

"I'm perfectly fine. Now, didn't you have something you were going to do to me?"

"You bet your sweet ass. And I'm still going to do it."

"Are you done with work for the day?"

"I told my Administrative Assistant that the pain was just too much and I was done for the day."

"You have an Admin?"

"Would you shut up and let me molest you?"

"Okay."

And I did. And she did. I'd never known such total bliss in my life.

❦ ❦ ❦

After dinner I gave Bella a quick five-minute crash course on how to use the five pound weights. I had her doing seven exercises for only ten reps each. Very light to start, not taking much time at all.

"But I don't even feel anything. Are you sure this is starting right? Maybe a little heavier?"

"No, start exactly here. And only do the ten reps at a time. No more. Not even if you think you have it in you. It's better if you do them in the morning. That way in the evening, if you feel like it, you can do it again. That's the best way."

"Okay, you're the boss."

"You know, even though I somehow still feel that I forced myself on you, I don't feel like the boss. You're the smart one."

"Are you kidding me? You've been in the police department and know all their procedures. You're a firefighter and know all their procedures. You're an EMT 1 and know all their procedures. You've got a degree in a technology field. You're a complete expert on physical exercise. Don't give me that shit. You're a shining star, Kathleen. You're *my* shining star."

"That's very sweet of you to say anyway. So, let me go lie down for a little bit. I'd hate to get an alarm first thing into shift and be sapped."

"Okay. I'll come with you. I promise I'll keep my hands off you."

"No, don't do that. Just don't move them around," I laughed.

"Aye, aye, Captain," she said giving me an exaggerated salute.

I stretched out on the bed with Bella and we held each other, looking into each other's eyes.

"I wrote a telephone number down on a piece of yellow paper on your desk. That's Mike Capcheczi's number. He's one of two guys that brought your car home and put up your groceries. I've already told him that you'll call him if you ever need anything. He or his wife Estefanía will come running."

"This Mike. He must be pretty special."

"He's like my big brother. He was my mentor as a Newbie. He minimized the jokes and the hazing too. Which was great moral support. He lost a son in Iraq the first year of the war. He was the crew chief on a Blackhawk helicopter that was shot down. He has five sons and all of them joined the service. One in the Air Force, one in the Marine Corps, and the other two are in the Army. And of course, Jameson, who was killed in action."

"That's so sad. Now you've made me unhappy."

"Next summer when we go over for a barbeque, he'll show you his memorial room. Besides having the coffin flag for Jameson, he's got a flag and decoration case for all of the boys. Each of them has an insignia showing their branch of service, their grade, and a copy of their medals and ribbons. Another case has Mike's. He was in the Navy just like his father was. But they only did their four and out."

"Another family that just can't seem to get enough of public service. It sort of makes me feel ashamed of growing up in the lap of luxury."

"Don't be silly. It's not for everybody. And it's not a choice, I don't think. It's something that's in your genetic makeup at birth. I mean, we still need people to be doctors and run businesses, don't we?"

"Don't you want to sleep for a little while before you have to get up?"

"No. I want to talk to you. I want to spend some quiet time with you. I love you, sweetie."

Bella took my hands and put them together and drew them up to her mouth and kissed them all over. After she did that she put my hands against her cheek and snuggled in closer to me and closed her eyes. She was the one who needed the nap. My watch went off at eleven o'clock, which woke her up.

"Hi, baby," Bella said to me.

"Hi."

"If you have to go out to a fire this week, please be careful. Be safe. Come home to me in one piece."

"That's the plan. We try our best."

"Have you ever been hurt?"

"I've gotten several sprains. I've gotten overwhelmed by smoke inhalation a few times. But I've never gotten seriously injured. The worst that ever happened was when I fell through the roof on a house fire and cut my leg. They had to work for ten minutes to cut me out of that one. Have you noticed the scar on my left calf?"

"Yes, but I wasn't going to ask."

"Well, later this week, I'll take off all my clothes in broad daylight, show you all the scars I have and tell how I got every one of them."

"That'll be fun," she said, her voice dripping in sarcasm.

"Okay, make sure you keep your phone charged and with you. I've got to shove off. If you need anything, and I mean anything, call me. Any time of day. If you can't get ahold of me, call the station house. Remember, I'm Engine company 7. Our Station is Engine 7, Ladder 7, and District Chief 3. If they can't get word to me, call Pops. I already told him you had his number and I put your number in his phone."

"Give me a kiss."

I did.

I pulled into the Station half an hour before shift and picked up my duffel and went inside. All of the A shift people were already awake and changing the laundry from their bunks. B shift, my shift, would do the same thing at the end of our shift, and so would C shift.

Greek was the first one to greet me.

"Kathleen Pope! How's your new girlfriend?"

Some of the guys from B shift hadn't heard yet.

"You've got a new girlfriend? Does this mean you won't be moping around anymore?"

"Bite my ass, John."

"Well, that's a good thing, isn't it?"

"You might say that. For me anyway. And apparently to her."

"Don't worry Kath, anything she needs while you're here, just have her call me. Either me or Estefanía will be happy to go around," said Mike.

"You're the best Mike. Wait until you meet her. You saw her car and you saw her place but you never got to see her. She's hot. I'm telling you. Very hot."

"I'd expect nothing less from you. Or should I say for you. Whatever."

The two lieutenants from the opposite shifts were in the main office talking about items for handing off control of the station. I like the Lieutenants for all three shifts. They are all regular guys, not caught up with hierarchy. And it was nothing to see one of them grabbing equipment when necessary. Mostly they ran Command Post on scene and did paperwork back at the Station.

I grabbed my bag and put it in my locker, then got out my tablet and lay down on my bunk. Lights out was twelve-thirty. There was always somebody that wasn't sleepy so they used the day room to study, read, play cards, go online, BS, whatever, until they got tired enough to sleep. Then everybody was up at seven-thirty a.m.

Sure as shit I'd been asleep for about two hours and the alarm sounded at the station. Carl, our Lieutenant, immediately woke up and ran to the computer in his office and looked at the alarm specifics while talking on the radio to dispatch. Within moments he stuck his head into the bunk bay and snapped on the lights.

"Alright boys and girls, everybody up. Full team. Four alarm. Warehouse fire. It's going to be a long-damned day."

Everybody scrambled up and into their bunker gear, sometimes called turnout gear. It was already nested at the end of everybody's bed so you just step into it, pull everything up and go. Within five minutes we had all our apparatus fired up and the bay doors open. (What everybody grew up calling a fire truck is officially called an apparatus.)

Carl led the way in his Suburban with the District Chief, who happened to be bunking overnight simply as an in-service check, and we went in our little train. It took about ten minutes to get over to the fire. Two out of the other three companies were already either moving into place or already pulling hoses.

The Command Post was already set up on the street between the first two trucks to get in place. Orders were being barked out and fingers being pointed every which way. There were also about six squad cars from the police department around the building and more coming, blocking off access on the streets. It was bitterly cold and everybody already knew that the sooner we got this behemoth under control the sooner we could go home.

A fire on the hottest day of summer is hard to work with. But a winter fire is worse. The air around you can be down to thirty below and the fire in your face can be five hundred degrees if it's burning wood and paper, and up to fifteen hundred degrees if chemicals are involved. And wherever the water goes, it freezes almost instantly so you increase the chance for slips, trips, and falls. You can build up a foot of ice within an hour and still have to work the area.

Fortunately for us, though this building was full, it was all furniture. No chemicals. Plenty of tinder to burn though. We had a Ladder truck with a bucket already extended up with two firefighters breaking out the windows around the top of building so they could start spraying in. While they were doing that, I was assigned to attach the reducers to the four-inch hoses that were already attached to a couple of pumps for both my engine and one of the engines from another station. The guy next to me was dragging the smaller hoses off the hose truck toward me. I held the large hose up, and he twisted the smaller three hoses on, using reducers, and working as a team of two. There were two other teams doing exactly what we were doing as the fourth company pulled up to the opposite side of the building.

We were basically working three sides of the building. The front is usually considered the A Side. The left side is the B Side, the right side the C side, and lastly the back is considered as D Side. From the front of the building there were two companies that had breached the front of the building through some large plate glass windows that were broken out. It was a wicked fire. At nine or nine-thirty, two of the companies were recalled, one company was covering hot spots in the back of the building, and our company was covering hotspots in the front of the building. It took another hour before we started packing up our equipment. That took an hour in and of itself.

It was noon before we pulled back up at the station, after refueling each apparatus on the way home. The order of business was laid out specifically. Above everything else, it was important to refill all of the air tanks. You never know if you're going to be called out again within minutes. The second order of business was to go inside the equipment bay. Beside where the trucks go, we had two showers side by side, nozzles hanging from the ceiling with pull handles to run them, similar to the showers for chemical spills that are in laboratories and factories. Two by two, we ran through the showers and washed each other down, getting our boots and bunker coats and helmets cleaned. When I first started, a couple of the guys had been embarrassed to use the brush on my chest and my butt, but I was now just another one of the guys.

The next order of business was to wash the trucks and clean and inspect the hoses. All of that took us out to about two o'clock. Way past time to eat. Two people had already pulled off cleanup duties and gone into the kitchen and started cooking lunch. When we were done we had a huge pot of chili and hotdogs ready to eat. There's nothing like a hot chili-cheese dog to warm you up after a morning like this. Or two or three. Okay, four each, minimum.

Then we started the boring half of the routine. Every day the entire building was cleaned just like in the military. Everything. Floors, counters, cabinets, bathrooms, offices, tables, the equipment bay where all the trucks are stored. Plus, all the hand equipment. About half past three I called Bella.

"Kathleen! I was watching the news at noon and there was this big fire! Were you called out on that?"

"Sure was. It was frickin' cold out there!"

"Oh, baby, are you okay? You didn't get hurt or anything, did you?"

"Hon, you're going to have to stop this. I go out on average once or twice a week. You're going to have to learn that it's seldom that anybody gets seriously injured and fatalities are extremely rare."

"Oh, I know, but I couldn't help thinking about you."

"I'm glad you were thinking about me. But I don't want you worrying about me. That won't do anything but give you an ulcer. If we're going to stay together, you'll have to find a way to control your fears. And I definitely want us to stay together."

"Understood," she said as she exhaled a long sigh.
"I do want us to stay together."
"So do I. I'll work on it."
"Bella? I want us to stay together forever."
"Forever?"
"That's what I said. What about you?"
"That would be wonderful. I love you so much."
"I love you too, sweetie. I'll call you tonight when I get a chance and you're done with work. Okay?"
"Okay. Bye-bye."
As I put my phone back in my pocket, the guys around me all started up with woo's and whistles.
"Somebody's got a girrrlfrieeeend," said Oliver.
"Yes, as a matter of fact, I do."
I couldn't keep from smiling. I tried but I couldn't. I could feel a burn start on my face. I was turning red as a beet. I turned my back to everybody and took a couple of deep breaths. I even fanned my face, but it wasn't working.
"Look at that! She's on cloud nine!" said John.
"Why don't you all leave me alone? It's not like none of you have ever had a girlfriend."
"True, but we do the same thing to any of the single guys who get a girlfriend. The only thing is that over the years, everybody's gotten married. You're the only single person on both shifts."
"Not true. Simon from Shift C is single."
"Oh, I forgot about that. Damn. I can't believe that when I was young I used to think nothing of driving drunk. I did it every single weekend. There weren't as many people on the roads back then and the attitudes were different. Such a waste. Charlene was such a sweet girl. And that rat bastard that hit her didn't get a single scratch. And only had to do probation and AA for a year. That totally sucks," said John.
"Yes, it does," I agreed.
I was holding a pop. We had just finished eating and everybody was drinking either coffee or tea or a pop and had something in their hands.
"To the memory of Charlene," I toasted in the air.
"To Charlene," said everybody else in unison as they toasted as well.

Nobody said a word for the next half hour. Everybody was very somber and in a grumbly mood. In a way, I wished I hadn't said anything. But the thing about firefighters is that we're all a great big family, and what happens to one of us happens to all of us.

Since we had a really late lunch, that night the Lieutenant bought us pizza. That was pretty cool. Didn't happen too often, but it does happen. Every once in a while, we get sandwiches too. After I ate, I went in and lay down on my bunk.

"Hi. I was waiting for you to call."

"Hi. I want you to do something for me."

"Anything. What do you want?"

"Take a picture of yourself with your phone and send it to me. Make it a good one too. I want to make it where when it rings, you've got your own ring tone and you picture comes up."

"Okay. I will as soon as we finish talking."

"I love my job. More than just about anything in the world. Except now I feel like I'm trapped in this stupid Station. I'm tempted to grab a radio and take a personal trip out and come see you."

"You can do that?"

"Oh sure. We do it all the time. But you don't want to abuse the privilege. And it's only my first day on shift since we met. Since we fell in love."

"I like the sound of that."

"What time did you finish work today?"

"Since you weren't here, I decided to get as much done as I could and worked until about seven. I just got finished eating. I'm so glad you cooked all that food and had it in the fridge. It saved me a lot of work in the kitchen on this bum foot. God, it itches. It doesn't hurt quite as badly, but it itches like the dickens. "

"Have you checked your email lately?"

"Yes, I have. I got one from my mom. She and dad hate the fact that I could have taken the job offer in Houston and came up here. She's nagging me in that way that only a mother can do."

"That all you get?"

"Just junk email. Unsolicited stuff, you know... Like a photo of a bunch of yellow roses from you. Thank you. That was thoughtful of you."

"I sent it right before we ate dinner."

"Well, they're very pretty and I appreciate it a lot."

"I'll see you tonight when I get home, okay?"

"Okay. Just be careful...."

"Bella, for goodness sakes, stop it! We always try to be as safe as possible. We train for this. Even after our basic school, every three months we have additional school. And we have safety briefings every month. Sometimes more! So, stop it!"

"I'll try. I'll send you a picture in a few minutes, okay?"

"Okay. I love you sweetie."

"I love you too."

"Sweet dreams my angel."

"Night-night."

About fifteen minutes later I got a text message on my phone. 'Check your email.' I did and there were about ten photos of Bella. In the living room. In the kitchen. At her desk. From the bedroom. Even one with her peeking out from the shower with just her face and the phone showing. I wonder how she did that walking on crutches. But I chose the one from the kitchen, and made it her profile picture. I stored the rest in a new folder under her name. Then I picked up my tablet and went in search of John.

"Hey, John, wanna see something special?"

"Sure. What do you have?"

"Jesus H. Christ! She's fantastic looking. Hey guys, come in here. Look at this. Unbelievable."

Everybody came in and looked at the photos of Bella.

"This is the chick from the parking lot? Damn! I don't blame you for picking her up," said Oliver.

"I'm telling you, I didn't even get a look at her until I got her to the ER."

"What grocery store were you at? I think I want to start shopping there, too. Maybe I'll find somebody like that."

"You're married."

"So what, so is my wife. She can come along if she wants."

"You're a perv."

"That's affirmative."

I went into the bunkroom and lay down early. I had my tablet in my hand and just kept touching Bella's face in all the photos. Then I took the tablet and hugged it into my chest and closed my eyes. Oh, my dear sweet Bella. Bella, Bella, Bella. The girl with the strange name. My girl. All mine.

I had just about drifted off to sleep even with the lights on when my phone rang.

"I love seeing your picture when the phone rings. And I changed your ringtone to Oasis."

"Which song?"

"Falling."

"You're such a bitch. Is this something you'll ever let me live down?"

"Highly doubtful. Watcha want?" I asked.

"I just wanted to tell you that I have my orthopedist appointment on Friday to get my second cast. At two-thirty. Anyway, that's all I had, just wanted to call you before too late."

"Okay. Love you. Goodnight."

"Love you too. Sweet dreams."

There were no calls out from our Station for the rest of the night, so at midnight I hit the starter on my SUV. I was out the door at fifteen after, and was home in another twenty minutes because there was virtually no traffic. I parked in the underground lot again. I tried to be quiet down the hallways since other people were probably all asleep being during the week. I put my key in the lock and twisted it, then opened the door and walked in. I took my boots off by the door and put my bag down in the second bedroom with my coat and hat on top of it.

I walked into the bedroom and the light was still on. Bella was lying on one side and her eyes were closed. Even in my stocking feet her eyes fluttered open.

"Kathleen? Can I tell you something?"

"Sure. What?"

"You look totally cute in uniform. It's always been one of my weaknesses. Cops. Firefighters. Soldiers. Sailors. You name it. Especially cute girls like you."

"Well, I'm glad you like it because I'll be in a uniform until I retire. You didn't have to wait up for me, you know. Are you going to do that every single shift change?"

"You bet I am. I can't wait to see my baby."

"I'm glad you did. I already took a shower earlier this evening at the station, and I just want to get out of my uniform and into bed."

"What are you going to do when you get to bed?"

"That depends on you…."

"I want a removable cast. I hate this one."

"Come on, sour puss, let's go to sleep."

Even though Bella had to get up early, we made no effort to go to sleep right away.

CHAPTER SIX

    Bella's alarm clock going off was still something strange to me. I didn't own one. I always just used the alarm on my watch. And oh, was it early. Fortunately, she didn't have to drive to work right now so I just got up with her and cooked some blueberry pancakes for us. I was surprised that Bella knew of blueberry pancakes but had somehow managed to escape eating them her whole life. Not once had she ever tasted one. And they were so hard to make: instant pancake mix, water, and blueberries. Tada!
    "So, is it a Texas thing or a Rich Kid thing?"
    "What do you mean," Bella asked.
    "Never having these before."
    "I've had plenty of chances, but I usually preferred chocolate chip waffles. I guess I better get a waffle maker and we can have waffles. Even blueberry waffles. If it's anything like blueberry pancakes. These are delicious."
    "You better hurry. You have to be online in fifteen minutes. Say, do you think you can do a little more walking around the apartment

with your crutches to get used to being more mobile? Maybe do some walking in the hallway to have a long straight shot?"

"I guess so. Why? You think I'm progressing too slowly?"

"No, it's not that. I got a call from Pops last night. Today's the fifth. A week from next Wednesday night on the eighteenth is the annual Policemen's dinner. He mentioned that I might want to be there this year. I certainly haven't made every one of them but I've been to plenty. They always have it at a swanky hotel and there's around three hundred or so people there. Brass from every department in the city. Mayor. Directors. All that. He sort of wants me there for whatever reason. Maybe Martha can't go this year. He didn't say. But he also went out of his way to say that if wasn't possible because of my commitment to you, he'd understand. And when he says he understands, he really does."

"Truthfully? I'm not sure if I'm ready, but I'm willing to work really hard at it. I'd love to go with you and I'd really, *really*, love to get out of the apartment for an evening. And if I can't make it, you'll go without me. I'm a big girl. I understand. After all I broke my parents' hearts and left the state. One evening I can certainly manage. I managed last night when you were gone. Although I missed you tremendously."

"Okay. We'll work on it and I'll put in two RSVP's. Chicken, fish, or beef?"

"I would think chicken."

"Good choice. Their fish is dry, their beef isn't enough food, but the chicken isn't too bad."

Bella placed her hands up on my shoulders, looking into my eyes.

"It's a date, then. Right? It'll be our first night out as a couple. We've sort of gone about this backwards..." She winked at me.

"That sounds wonderful. Now finish your breakfast and get to work."

I did the dishes and made the bed. I usually don't make the bed at home. I just throw the covers back up to the top and let it go at that. But I thought I'd be nice and make the bed here. I straightened up a little and then took a shower.

I got dressed in some warm clothes, tiptoed over to Bella, and kissed her lightly on the top of the head. I laid her phone down on her desk within her reach. She ran her hand down along the bottom of my leg behind her. Then I went down to the garage and started up my SUV for the day's activities.

I went to the gym first. This morning I only did about forty-five minutes because I was going to come back in the afternoon and do some more. Since I was only doing a short time, I really pushed myself hard. I set the treadmill to ten miles an hour and a twenty-degree incline for twenty minutes. That, in and of itself, almost killed me. Then I did free weights for the rest of the time. I was burning.

I was tempted to shower at the gym, but I just threw on an old tracksuit that I kept in my bag and went home to jump in the shower there. Tinkerbelle was ecstatic I was home. I kept getting cold drafts in the shower since I left the bathroom door open for her so she could get up on the sink to be with me. She likes doing that which is not a problem in the summer but a little chilly in the winter.

After I got dried and dressed, I went through the house gathering towels, uniforms, socks, and everything else that was already in the hamper. Tinks followed me everywhere. She wasn't used to me being gone for so long. Pops offered to come over and check in but with her food and water dispensers, I told him it would be foolish, that she'd be fine. There was so much laundry that washing and drying everything took over three hours. I spent most of my time watching television, but also read my study guide a little bit.

After all the clothes were finished and either folded and put up or hung up in the closet, I packed a couple of more things in my bag to take back to Bella's and picked my blue evening gown out of the closet to take to the cleaners. I hadn't worn it in a long time, probably four years or more, and even though it was clean, it was covered in dust and cat hair. I'd need that next week. I didn't plan on taking it over to Bella's. I was going to dress at my house and pick her up. After all, it was our first date. Even if we didn't do things in the right order, I wanted our date to be a true date!

I went to the organic market and picked up some fresh vegetables and fruits. Way overpriced, and probably not any better for you than the crap you buy at any other store, but it all looked good and tasted even better. While I was there I got a couple of more bottles of wine. Now that Bella and I had talked for a while, I learned more what she liked and didn't like to drink. Among other things, she hated Scotch. Apparently one summer she got three-sheets-to-the-wind, falling down, pissed drunk and vomited over and over drinking some really cheap

Scotch. Since then, she can't stand even McAllen double oak that goes for over seventy dollars a bottle.

I had time left still so I went over to the nursing home. Twice in one week. They'd think I was a regular. I read to the same old dears that I had earlier in the week. It was as if I hadn't even put the book down. I got through two more chapters before it was time for me to go. I promised them that I'd be back again, but probably not quite so soon.

I walked through the door with my bag and the groceries and wine about a quarter to four. Once again, Bella was on the headset telephone in a conference of some sort. I didn't understand any of the jargon she used at all but from the conversation there were a ton of people in the conference. She kept using different names every five seconds it seemed.

After putting everything in its place, I went into the kitchen and tried as quietly as possible to get out a large skillet. I poured some olive oil into the pan, and got out carrots, celery, onions, and mushrooms. Even though Bella had an electric can opener, to keep things quiet, I used a hand opener and opened a can of tomato puree and a can of tomato sauce, pouring them into the pan. I added a heaping tablespoon of sugar to the mix, along with a little garlic salt and some white pepper.

I walked over to Bella's desk and picked up a small pad of paper. I wrote down, 'Let me know when it's safe to make some noise.' She nodded her head at me, and held up all ten fingers letting me know it would be soon. I went back to the kitchen and cut the ends off the celery and carrots getting them ready for the food processor, and peeled the onion and cut it into wedges. I pulled a beer out of the fridge and twisted the top off. I just leaned back against the counter, looking at my beautiful Bella, drinking beer, waiting....

Finally, Bella turned around and looked into the kitchen.

"Hi. How was your day?"

"Not too bad. Let me get these through the food processor, and I'll talk to you."

I ran the veggies through food processor until they were finely pureed, and then put them in a dish with a little water to soften them quickly in the microwave. Then I took them out, turning the saucepan up to a medium heat. I stirred the mix several times and then covered the pan and went over to the desk. I leaned down to Bella and kissed her hard, with passion.

"Goodness, did somebody miss me today?"

"You know I did. I just hope you missed me half as much as I missed you."

"To tell you the truth, the job keeps me fairly distracted with so much to do. But let's just say that you keep seeping into my thoughts anyway. You're a major distraction, Ms. Pope."

"So, you want me to leave?"

"Don't even joke about that. I mean it. Never. Okay?"

"Okay, Okay. I promise," I said, holding up my hands.

"That's better. It took too long to find you. I don't want to lose you. I knew that if I looked long and hard I might find somebody, but never anybody as good for me as you."

"Sweetie, the same holds true for me, believe me."

"What are you making for dinner?"

"Spaghetti. But I'm making it with chicken instead of ground meat. And it's probably different than you've ever had it. It's from a recipe that I got from the grandmother of one of the guys at Engine company 24. He said if his grandmother ever knew he was giving out the recipe she'd roll over in her grave," I laughed.

"Well everything else you've cooked has been delicious. I don't see how this would be any different. By the way, during the day today, I walked all the way down to both ends of the hallway and back. I'm beginning to be pretty mobile. I don't think next Wednesday is going to be a problem."

"Yeah, about that. See, here's the thing...."

I could see a puzzled and somewhat concerned look on her face. But it didn't last long when I told her what I had in mind.

"This is going to be our first 'date'. So, I'm going to spend the day at my house. Then I'm going to come over here and pick you up to take you to the banquet room at the hotel. Like it's supposed to be done. Is that okay with you?"

"Perfectly. That would be divine. What do you want me to wear?"

"Well, it'll have to be a skirt or a dress. The first part because of your cast, and the second because it's somewhat formal. Sorry I forgot to tell you that part."

"So, you're going in pants then, I take it? You're going to be the butch on our team?" she laughed at me.

"No, nothing like that. You'll just have to see."

"Wait here a minute..." Bella said as she grabbed her crutches and made her way into the bedroom.

She was actually getting around quickly and with a lot of agility. She reached toward the back of the closet and took out a knee length red dress with an applique of holly in green and silver at the top of the neckline.

"It's very Christmassy. Is it formal enough?"

"It'll be perfect. Just right for the holidays."

"So? What *are* you going to wear?"

"You'll just have to see. It's a date, right? Don't I have the right to surprise you?"

"I suppose," Bella said, in an exaggerated pout with her arms crossed against her chest.

"You never know. You might actually like what I'm going to be wearing."

"What? A tuxedo?" she asked with a grin.

I went into the kitchen to start cooking the chicken with some seasoned olive oil and ghee that I'd brought from my house. Bella came over and stood behind me after about fifteen minutes, leaning her crutches up against the island. She wrapped her arms around my body from behind and squeezed me tightly.

"It smells simply wonderful."

"Wait until you taste it."

I grabbed the bottle of white wine and uncorked it. I removed the lid to the skillet and poured about a cup and a half into the sauce and mixed it again, covering it up again when I was done. I already had the oven on, so I took out a cookie sheet and lined it with foil. I put a loaf of bread on the pan that I'd cut into slices. I had taken a small saucepan and put some ghee in it, with some garlic I'd just put through the press. I used a brush to make sure all the faces of the bread were coated with the manna of the Italian gods and wrapped the foil up around the bread, placing it in the oven.

I took the chicken off the stove and put it on the cutting board. I dropped a pound of pasta into a pot of water to get that boiling. I took the chicken breasts and used two forks back to back, shredded the meat down into small irregular pieces and bits, then put them all in the sauce. I mixed it one last time and covered it. I took the bread out of the oven and, leaving it covered, I set it on the island. The pasta was ready so I poured it into a colander and left it sitting in the sink.

"Normally, I'd make the pasta fresh. I'm just being lazy tonight if you don't mind."

"Aren't you going to rinse it off? We always rinsed in cold water to get the starch off and then with hot water to get it hot again."

"Or you could just let it sit there hot."

"God, you're going to make me so fat."

"Most of the time I eat more healthily than this. I promise you when I'm through trying to impress you I'll make healthy food and keep the rich stuff for one or twice a week."

"Oh, baby, you don't have to impress me. There isn't one single thing that you could do that would impress me more than you already do. Give me a kiss."

I turned around setting the pan down and gave her a giant hug and a kiss.

"I love you, Bella. I've loved you since the day I was born, I just didn't know it yet."

Bella giggled at me.

"That's the funniest way I've ever heard that put. And I love it. I love you too, my darling, wonderful girlfriend."

We sat down to eat and I watched Bella start taking it in. I poured us both a glass of white wine. Not common for pasta but I did it because of the chicken base.

"I'd kill to be able to go to a restaurant in Houston and get this food served to me. I'm not kidding you one bit. And there are a *lot* of good restaurants in Houston."

"I'm glad you like it. Let's hope I can keep this string of wins going, huh? Speaking of wins, you aren't a big Astros fan, are you?"

"Of course, dumbass. Why wouldn't I be?"

"Because from today forward you're a Minnesota Twins fan, good year or bad year. Got it?"

Bella showed me the back of her right hand. Slowly, ever so slowly, her pointer, ring, and pinkie fingers and thumb began curling inwardly, leaving me the international sign of 'you're number one'."

"I suppose I'm now a Vikings fan instead of a Texans fan too, huh? It's going to take somebody bigger and tougher than you to cure me of my homeys."

I just shook my head. Indoctrination was definitely needed if this was going to work! Maybe a full-on intervention! We finished dinner and I cleaned the table and the kitchen. We took our wine glasses into the living room and watched television.

"Aren't we just like an old married couple?" asked Bella.

"Is that a threat?"

"No. Just pondering life's possibilities."

"Christ, woman, you move faster than anybody I've ever known."

"I know a guy who went out on his first date with a girl. He didn't even really know her, he knew her roommate. But he somehow asked her out. Their first date was Wednesday, March twenty-ninth, nineteen seventy-eight. One week later to the day he asked her to marry him, on April fifth of the same year. They've now been married for thirty-four years. Three kids all in their twenties. Not bad, huh?"

"That's amazing. It's amazing that they knew that fast and it's amazing that they've lasted, both."

"Anytime you're ready, my love, let me know."

I eyed Bella carefully. Was she asking me to marry her?

"There are many reasons I moved to Minnesota, you know. Not just the job. Let's just say that my acceptance within my own house is limited. It's more of a 'if we don't talk about it, it doesn't exist' kind of thing. Don't ask, don't tell. And in public? Give me a break. I mean the community is pretty large since the city has almost three million people, but being out is still a hardship."

I reached out and took her hand in mine and we quietly watched the television. Every once in a while one or the other of us would glance over at the other, smiling. Our hands never separated. Finally, it was time for bed.

"Can you go to sleep with the television on? If not, I can grab my tablet or my mp3 player. I just can't always go sleep so early because of my shifts," I asked Bella.

"Television on is fine. I'm watching a movie a lot of times and I end up drifting off. Does that mean you don't want to make love to me tonight?"

"No. I'm talking about after," I grinned.

Bella picked up her crutches and went into the bedroom while I rinsed the wine glasses, put them in the dishwasher with all the other dishes, and started it up. When I got to the bedroom, a candle was lit on the table, and she was on top of the covers with no clothes on.

"Come here. It's too cold not to either have some clothes on or be under the covers."

I did something I rarely did. I started stripping off my clothes letting each piece drop on the floor in a trail as I moved toward the bed. I didn't pick anything up, I didn't fold anything, I didn't put anything on a chair or the dresser. I climbed into the bed and showed Bella how much I loved her without saying a word. Her eyes shut and she communicated solely with her lips and fingers for what seemed like an eternity. Finally, she lay next to me, motionless with the exception of her rapid breathing, gradually decreasing, until she was completely still. Her eyes remained closed and she was asleep.

"Come on, sweetie. Let's get you under the covers so that you won't get too cold."

Bella's eyes flickered open and she said three words. The last three she would say for the night.

"I love you."

CHAPTER SEVEN

On Saturday, we had a small house fire that took less than an hour to control. It was late in the evening, in the kitchen. It probably started from the stove catching something on fire. We didn't even drag hoses. We did the whole suppression by extinguishers. Very messy but a lot cheaper to clean and repair than the damage from massive amounts of water. It was an easy shift.

On my shift the day before the Policemen's dinner, we were at the station the entire day. No calls whatsoever. We have to take out the apparatus for short drives to keep the engines and drive trains in working order, and days when we have no calls, we typically either take them out of the bays to run the motors in the drive, or we drive them through the neighborhoods for a few miles. Today Lieutenant Reed poked his head in the day room and told Oliver, who is the prime driver for Engine 7, to take her for a road trip. Everybody on the crew is trained on the apparatus, but there is still a primary and a secondary driver for each truck. I've driven some, but usually I'm a back-seater.

I wasn't paying attention at first to where we were going. Then a big grin came over my face that I couldn't stop. John looked over at me and was smiling. He poked Chris in the front right seat, who looked back and me, and he smiled too.

"Hey, Oliver. She just figured it out. I wondered how long it would take her," said Chris.

Everybody laughed at me. I blushed, I'm sure. My face was hot. Within a few minutes we pulled up in front of Bella's apartment building. Parked at the curb, John turned on all the lights and honked the air horn four or five times. I grabbed a radio and sprinted into the building. I skipped the elevator and sprinted up the stairwell and ran down the hallway. I banged on the door to the apartment like nobody's business.

"Just a minute, I'm coming!" I heard from inside.

Finally, the door opened to the surprised look on Bella's face.

"Hello, Ma'am. We were told somebody called in a residential fire?" I shouted at her.

"Wait just a second," Bella said.

She turned around on her crutches and made her way back to the desk. She picked up the headset for the phone.

"I'm going to have to call you back. There's an emergency here with the fire department knocking on my door. I'll call you when I can."

I ran over to her and got right in her face.

"Hey, lover. I'm told that somebody was on fire. Is it you?"

"You're terrible."

"I didn't get you in any trouble, did I?"

"No, nothing like that. They're just wondering what's going on, probably. You look so cute in your uniform. Dressed up in your firefighter's coat and boots and hat, you're simply adorable. I could just eat you up."

"It's not a firefighter's coat, it's a bunker coat. And it's not a hat, it's a helmet. They are boots though. The pants and bib are called turnout pants. We also have a turnout jacket over them and under the bunker coat when it's unreasonably cold. And this is my radio, also called a handy talkie by some. Or a two-way. And I really do have to get back downstairs. We have to run the apparatus around the streets a few miles when we don't have a call. And there hasn't been a call for three days. So today instead of just running the motors at the Station we're taking a 'road trip'."

"Apparatus?" asked Bella.

"It's what we call all of the vehicles. You civilians probably know them as fire trucks," I giggled.

"I'm glad you came by. It's just what I needed."

"I love you."

"I love you too, Kathleen. I'm going to miss you so much tonight. Are you sure you won't spend the night then go to your place tomorrow?"

"I'm sure. I'll be here at six thirty to pick you up. Be ready, and don't keep me waiting. I'm going to wait long enough for all the traffic to clear out but still want to be there on time."

"I'm a big girl. And we've had every night together. I'll be okay. But don't be surprised if you don't get a call from me at the station house."

"I'm counting on it. I love you. Bye."

I kissed Bella and hugged her and as quickly as I'd shown up I sprinted back down the hall, took the stairs to save time, and sprinted out to the truck. John turned off the lights and we started moving back to the station. Total time out, twenty-five minutes.

As soon as we had the truck back in the bay and the door closed, Lieutenant Reed yelled through the Station.

"Pope!"

I went running into his office.

"Yes sir?"

"Did you enjoy yourself?"

"How so, sir?"

"Give me a break. Whose idea do you think it was to do a drive by anyway?" he laughed.

"Thanks, Lieu. That was actually pretty nice of you."

"Don't let it get around. I don't want to get the reputation of being an old softy! Take off and find something to do."

"Aye, aye."

I got a call around ten-thirty from Bella. We talked for almost an hour. I was so lonesome for Bella that it made me hurt inside. I was pretty sure that she was feeling the same way. I told her finally that it was lights out and I had to go lie down. In truth, I could have stayed in the day room, but if I hadn't hung up the phone I would have crawled in my truck and driven to her apartment. Finally, midnight rolled around and I started my truck to warm it up. Even so I had to do just a little scraping on the windows, since I wasn't willing to wait even fifteen extra minutes to let the windows defrost.

I think Tinkerbelle nearly had a stroke to find a stranger in the house. I'd been going over every two out of three days for two to four hours, but she was used to spending much more time than that glued to me. I went into the kitchen and made a sandwich and grabbed a pop and took them into the living room. Tinks and I watched a movie until very late and then crawled up to bed. I put on some shorts and a tank, eased between the sheets, and tucked her under my chin and my arm. She purred and purred and purred. I fell asleep with her motor gently falling off.

On Wednesday, I didn't wake up until almost ten o'clock. I started the truck remotely, got dressed in some nice warm clothes, and ate some toast with butter and black currant preserves. All the stores would already be open, so that wouldn't be a problem. I drove to the one that had been used by Pops for years to buy jewelry for both mom and me. And now Martha. It was a small, locally-owned shop run by an elderly gentleman and his wife. They had a couple of other people working in the store as well. Old Man Edgars, the owner, was a jeweler, and he had a younger guy that was also a jeweler. Everybody else just sold items, although some of the girls strung pearls.

I waved at Mrs. Edgars.

"My, oh my! Kathleen! I haven't seen you in here for years! How is your father doing, bless his heart?"

"He's great. He's doing just fine."

"You know, that new wife of his can't hold a match to your mother, Kathleen. I know that you probably don't know much about her because you were so young, but I knew your grandparents. They were oh, so proud of her. She was a magical woman. She could do anything. Wonderful woman. But enough about that. Listen to me prattle on... What can I help you with today?"

"Well, to tell you the truth, I'm looking for an engagement ring. Nothing too fancy. Just a solitaire on a single white gold band."

"Who's the lucky bride? A friend of yours? Or are you shopping for yourself, maybe... Did you land a good looking young fella?"

"Well, the lucky bride, if the proposal is accepted, is a Miss Belladonna Ward, from Houston, Texas."

"And who's the lucky groom?"

"There won't be one. I'll be the other bride."

"You mean you're... I never knew that about you! Well I'm so happy for you. I hope everything goes well and I hope she says yes. When did you meet her?"

"About two and a half weeks ago."

"No!"

"True story. Life is moving like a freight train and I'm holding on tight for the ride."

"Well let's look in this case over here maybe to start with. Let me know if anything you see catches your eye."

"That one right there. But the diamond isn't big enough.'

"Don't worry about that we can change the diamond. We may already have one ready to go in the back anyway in stock, and if we don't we'll reset it."

"I'd have to have it today."

"How about twenty minutes? Is that quick enough for you? I'll be right back."

Mrs. Edgars disappeared for a few minutes.

"Nope, not what we want. So now, let's look at these. You can get two types of diamonds -- those that are graded and guaranteed by the Gemological Society, or you can get the same exact thing for about forty percent less, sometimes more. Non-certified stones don't come with the x-ray diffraction graphs for insurance purposes, but we have our own machine and can make one in thirty seconds. So here is a three eighth's carat stone. And here is a half-carat stone. And here is a forty-point stone, half way between the two. Let me get one more stone to show you what I was talking about."

She disappeared into the back again for a couple of minutes.

"Now then, here's the half carat stone. And here's a three-quarter carat stone. And this one, the square one, is called a Princess cut, and is a full carat. You'll notice that these three are just as sparkly, if you look with this magnifying loop you'll see the flaws in the stones are all about the same, but the price for the three smaller diamonds is the same range as the price on the three larger stones, because the larger ones aren't GIA certified. For anybody else walking in that door I'd push them on the need to be certified. But to your family, I'm telling you the truth," she said laughing.

I pointed to the one-carat diamond and asked her how much it cost set in the ring. Right about two thousand dollars.

"Mount it before I change my mind. I'm going to ask her tonight at the Policemen's dinner."

"I'll go get it done right now. Probably take fifteen to twenty minutes."

I browsed through cases looking at all the nice play pretties. If I ever got a ring it would have to be a plain band or I wouldn't be able to wear it. And even plain bands are actually discouraged, although some of the firefighters refuse to take them off. I know a couple of guys who wear a ball chain around their necks and hang the ring from the chain while on shift. Mrs. Edgars walked up to me within just a few minutes with the ring in a ring box, ready to go.

"Do you have a blue box instead of a black one?"

"Well sure we do dear. Let me get you one."

She reached under the counter and swapped the boxes, putting the ring in the blue box. She put the box in a small bag for me and we chatted for a few minutes before I took off. I was starting to sweat. Was I totally crazy? Was this for real? Was I being goaded into this? Then I thought of Bella's sweet, beautiful smile and all my trepidation went away. I drove with determination in my demeanor. I headed home after stopping by the cleaners. Tuxedo? Bwahaha... I think not!

I had a nice leisurely lunch with Tinkerbelle, watching a movie. Then I cleaned out her dispensers and generally dusted in the house and tidied up a bit, although there really wasn't much to do. I decided to run the vacuum cleaner just to pick up the dust that had settled over the last three weeks or so. Finally, I got a little too nervous and started getting ready early. I took a shower and shaved my legs. I blew dry my hair. I moisturized my entire body. Not that it needed it really, but it was a nervous thing. I put my underwear, my tights and my open-toed, three-inch heels on the bed. Me, in heels! I put on my underwear and went into the bathroom. The one that Bella had never seen. I knew when she finally did she'd be amazed. Girl stuff. Makeup, hair products, nail polish, things like that. Only for special occasions. And tonight was definitely a special occasion.

I sat on the toilet with the lid closed just as a chair to start putting on fingernail polish. And of course, in came Tinkerbelle. I put her out of the bathroom and shut the door so she didn't get hair everywhere, much to her chagrin and a hail of meows. I went back to the task at hand of putting a crimson polish on my hands. Then I put a dark, smoky blue eye shadow, then some mascara with a little eyeliner. I touched it all off with a touch of blush and with matching crimson lipstick. Actually, I guess I do clean up relatively well.

I pulled on my tights, heavy pantyhose with a lace pattern woven in. Finally, I took the plastic off the dress and brought it down over my neck and onto my body. The hemline stopped halfway between my knees and ankles. I reached behind and zipped it up. There was a sash built in across the middle and I reached behind and closed the two snaps on it. I looked, once again, in the mirror giving it my nominal approval. Then I put on my shoes. I got a purse out of my closet. I think just seeing me carrying a purse instead of a billfold or a gym bag would be more of a shock to Bella than anything else.

I gave Tinks a few scratches and grabbed my wool dress coat and left before I ended up with hair all over me. Tinks doesn't shed very much, but just when you want no hair is the day she sheds a lot. I wasn't taking a chance.

I drove around a while. I went to a department store close to Bella's, and walked the aisles for over an hour and a half, and I *hate* shopping for the sake of shopping. Finally, the appointed hour rolled around. I got back in the SUV and headed to Bella's. Her ring was in my purse, and I was *not* just toying with the idea of giving it to her tonight; I was *definitely* going to give it to her tonight! Finally, I pulled up to the apartment and stopped in front of the main door. I put my St. P.F.D. card on the dashboard in the window and went inside. I stopped in front of her door holding the yellow roses in my hands with my purse strap over my arm covered by my coat. That way she would get the full effect of the dress and the shoes and the makeup all at once. Good, bad, or indifferent, we'd see what Bella thought of me as a girl and not a semi butch firefighter.

I used my key to get in downstairs, but upstairs I knocked on the door.

"Just a minute. Let me get my purse and I'll be right there."

A few moments later both our eyes lit up like Christmas trees when we saw each other.

As beautiful as I thought Bella was, that was nothing compared to tonight. And the Christmas dress was perfect on her. She was wearing a leather backpack style bag to make it easier to carry when she was walking on her crutches. But I think the biggest surprise was Bella's reaction to me. Not what she was expecting. I think she really thought I was going to show up in a suit or a tux or something.

"Oh, my baby, you are so, so beautiful! Never doubt me again when I tell you how beautiful you are. Never. You hear me?" Bella said as she leaned in and kissed me.

"Including my fat hips and thighs?" I asked.

"Oh, puh-lease!"

I dashed in quickly and put the flowers in water after she cradled them to her face and drunk in their aroma deeply.

"You know, the meaning isn't lost on me, Kaths! Your Yellow Rose of Texas! You're just too sweet!"

"We better get going if we're going to be there on time."

"Okay. Let's do this."

We went downstairs where the truck was idling right in front of the door, making it easy for Bella to get in.

"Oh, crap, your donut pillow. Let me go get it real quick."

"Kathleen, I may take crutches to the ball, but Cinderella ain't taking no stinking cushion. Got it?"

"Yes Ma'am."

At the hotel, I pulled right up to the front and helped Bella out. I gave the valet the keys and had her park it. We moved at a nice slow pace to get back to the banquet room. We looked up our assigned seats and headed for them. About half way there I noticed that Pops and Martha were already seated. About three quarters of the attendees were already in place. Pops was wearing his formal black police department uniform with service ribbons. He looked so handsome to me. Martha was wearing an evening gown. How unlike her. She actually looked pretty decent for a change, instead of looking like a Minnesota version of Edith Bunker.

Pops did a double take. Martha on the other hand did about a triple take. Both stood up.

"Kevin Pope, Martha Pope, Belladonna Ward. Bella, Pops and Martha."

"Well it's certainly good to finally meet you. Kathleen talks of nothing anymore but you. You're very good for my little girl's morale. Welcome to Minnesota. You're from Oklahoma, right?"

"Actually, I'm from Tex..." she started before noticing he had the biggest grin on his face, and figuring out he was just cranking her up.

"Gotcha!!"

"Yeah, you got me, you got me big time. Now I know where Kathleen gets it."

"Everybody let's sit down. Let me have your crutches, Bella, and I'll put them up under the table. Kathleen, you look so beautiful tonight. I'm glad you didn't wear your dress department uniform. You remind me so much of your mother," said Pops.

It apparently didn't bother Martha when Pops talked about my mother. He talked about her quite a bit, and she either truly didn't mind or shrugged it off, but she remained emotionless. Everybody sat down and took a sip of water.

"So, Pops, what's going on with this year's dinner? What's so special we needed to be here for this one in particular? You getting a recognition or something?"

"Or something. You'll see. Just be patient."

"You know that patience never was one of my strong suits."

"Oh, believe me Kitten, I know all too well."

"Well, Kathleen, is there anything new going on to speak of?" asked Martha as the food began arriving to the tables.

I figured this was as good a time as any, although I had planned on doing it well into dinner instead of at the very beginning.

"Only this…" I said as I pulled the ring box out of my purse and set it on the table in front of Bella. Her eyes opened as wide as saucers and she got very still. She reached out with her left hand and held onto the bottom of the box. She moved the fingers from her right hand to the top of the box but made no move to open it.

"Maybe I should wait until desert to open this. What do you think, Kath?"

"I think maybe you should open the stupid box or you're going to drive me crazy. After all it was your idea."

"It was not!"

"You practically begged me to ask you. Let's just say that you planted the seeds of the idea by telling me a story of a friend of yours. That was a true story, wasn't it?" I asked.

"Very true. I wouldn't lie to you. Oh, what the hell, I'll just have a little peek."

She opened the top of the ring box and almost fell out of her chair.

"Kathleen! I don't know what to say! It's so…so…beautiful!"

She held the box up to me.

"I've already seen it."

"No, you idiot, you're supposed to put it on my finger!" Bella practically yelled at me.

She certainly did turn a few heads with our little outburst.

"So that means your answer would be yes, you would marry me. Forever and a day?"

"Like they say in court, three consecutive life sentences plus forty years."

I put the ring on her finger and we hugged each other for the longest time. Finally, we sat back up straight.

"Say, Bella, are you aware that the Chief of Police for Minneapolis is married to one of her Sergeants? They've been together twenty-five years," I asked.

"Yessir, those people over in Minneapolis are a bunch of progressive left coasters!" laughed Pops.

Martha laughed but I doubt she knew what her own real opinion was.

"So, let's see that thing," said Pops taking Bella's hand and looking at the ring.

"It's so awfully pretty, isn't it?" said Martha.

"I'd say it's right at one carat, too," said Pops.

"Is that right, Kathleen?" asked Bella.

"Ninety-eight and one-half points. As close as you can come to a carat without actually going over."

"And I was just blown away initially because you are so stunningly beautiful tonight. Not that I don't think you are any other day though."

"Are you talking about my fat thighs again, chick? 'Cause I can lay on a lick on you you'll feel well on to next week."

"Pops, please tell your daughter she's being foolish and that any woman, or any man for that matter, would consider herself or himself lucky to have her. She's a full package. And those are few and far between these days," said Bella, her eyes a sparkle.

"Well, Bella, I will agree with you, but the way I see it, Kathleen has found a full package as well."

Bella blushed at that. I mean seriously blushed. Bright red from the tip of her chin to her temples and back to her ears, fully matching her dress.

"Okay, here we go, the awards and recognitions…" Martha said, shushing everybody.

The gentlemen on the dais were the Chief of Police for the City of St. Paul and the Mayor. There was an administrator from City Hall with him, along with the Chief of the Fire Department, as a courtesy. And several other VIP's from around the city.

The Chief of Police recognized four officers for outstanding community service. Then two officers for completing their Master's degrees in Law Enforcement. There were three officers given commendations for life saving. Then they got to the one that apparently was the reason Pops had wanted me there so badly.

"It is my special honor and privilege this year to announce a special award for overall contribution to the function of the St. Paul Police Department. He works within his own department as a Detective Sergeant, but is a liaison with the Fire Department on special occasions. He also coordinates parks and recreation events with safety planning. He coordinates interdepartmental efforts between local departments within Ramsey County, as well as act on behalf of our city with other agencies including other city, county, state, federal, and even up to international level with Interpol... And lastly, he has the single highest arrest and conviction record in the history of our dear city. I am proud tonight to throw out the old Detective Sergeant Kevin Pope and usher in the new Detective Lieutenant Kevin Pope. My hope is that when your golden ring comes up in two years, you seriously consider that you've got lots of good years left and stay in the game. Ladies and gentlemen, I give you Lieutenant Kevin Lynn Pope!"

I was blown away. None of had us any inkling it was coming. Obviously, Pops did or he wouldn't have insisted we try and be there tonight. Oh, it was grand. Both Bella and I let him know it, too.

"Pops?" asked Bella when he'd come back down from the platform with his plaque.

"Yes dear. What is it?"

"My family won't be here for Christmas. I won't be able to go home. And I know that I'll get attention from Kathleen. But I'd really like to have the four of us get together for Christmas dinner at your house if that would be okay with you."

"I'd love to have you over but it depends on Kathleen's schedule. No, actually, it doesn't. You're welcome whether she is on shift or not. After all, you're family now!"

"I'm not. I work the twenty-sixth."

"Good, then it's settled."

Bella turned to me.

"Look what I have," and held her arm out but her hand down so it would be obvious that she was wearing a ring, much like many women do when they first get a new ring.

"Admit it, you were planting seeds of thoughts, weren't you?"

"Well, actually… yes… I hope you didn't buy me the ring because you think I was pressuring you. I mean, you have to admit this is wicked crazy fast."

"The purchase I made was based on alternate research and decision making. You can relax."

Bella smiled and looped her arm through mine. Before too long, everybody was done with speeches and awards. Our table was already finished with dinner, so we headed out. I got the SUV from the valet and got Bella loaded in.

"Where are we going?"

"La maison du Kathleen. Votre première visite."

"Your house, right? I thought all you spoke was Spanish. When did you learn French?"

"The same four years. I took both languages each year. Spanish I and French I, Spanish II and French II, etc. Took them simultaneously."

"Kathleen?"

"Yes, hon?"

"I have to tell you. When you showed up at my door dressed up, you took my breath away. I mean, I guess with the things you do, you sort of have to be somewhat tomboyish. But as good looking as I already thought you were, I never expected in a million years that you were that damned beautiful. You made my heart light as a feather."

"In other words, the way I see you every waking minute of every waking day…" I replied.

"Oh, stop it. Let's get inside where it's warmer and let me meet Tinkerbelle that I've heard so much about.

I opened the door and reached in to flip on the lights. Tinkerbelle came running, but stopped when she got to us and she saw us coming through the front door. Not just me. This was new to Tinkerbelle. She normally doesn't get visitors. She had to do a careful reconnoiter to find out if this new human passed muster.

Bella handed me her crutches and bent down to pick up Tinks. Tinks didn't growl, scratch, or even try to get away.

"I guess that means I'm approved, right?"

"Pretty much. Let me get some more lights on."

I handed Bella back her crutches and moved through the house to turn on all the lights so she could get a good look at everything. She walked slowly through the downstairs, taking it all in. The living room with fireplace, the dining room and kitchen, and toward the back of the house there was an office, which was a room with no separating wall, just open to the hallway. Right by that there was the back door, and curling around to the left was the staircase going to the basement for storage, heater, hot water tank, water softener, and the washer and dryer. Bella just looked from the top of the stairs. Nothing too interesting there, just the location of where things were. She turned around and made her way to the staircase going up.

"Go up behind me in case I fall. You can catch me."

"I'm on it."

She resumed her ascent of the stairs. To the right was the master bedroom and to the left was the second bedroom and the main bathroom. She looked into the second bedroom first. There was a little bit of stuff in boxes for storage, which somehow had never gotten moved to the basement, but it did have a full-size bed for guests. She got to the bathroom and flipped the light switch up. She looked around for a couple of minutes and noticed a long counter with double sinks.

"Very nice. Very nice. And new stone tile, too. Very pretty."

Then she reversed directions and entered the master bedroom. She looked at the dual walk in closets with a nod. There were two dressers, one a four-drawer, low unit and a six-drawer, tall one, both made of cherry and finished in a dark natural stain. They matched the headboard and footboard to the king-sized bed. There were also two bedside tables that matched the other furniture.

She made her way over to the bed and sat down on the side. She put the crutches on the floor beside the bed and lay down. Bella looked up at me with a soft smile and patted the other side of the bed indicating she wanted me to lie down with her. I did as she wished. I slowly moved toward the center of the bed and closer to Bella.

Bella reached up to my cheek with the palm of her hand and stroked it lightly.

"I love you."

"I love you too."

"So. This is our bed, huh? Which side do you normally sleep on?"

"Generally, all over it. I don't have a preferred side. You can pick."

"Where I am now, on the side away from the door, I think. But I can change for you, if you want."

"I'm fine. Just so long as you're here."

"I know the weather will be totally crappy probably, but I could move in January. That'll give me a little more time to build up my strength before I have to tackle both sets of stairs."

"You don't have to move that quickly if you don't want to. I know this place isn't nearly as nice or as modern as yours."

"I won't kid you. I grew up in a house that was thirty-six hundred square feet. And had a huge yard. But the house and the whole neighborhood were sterile. They had no character. I love it here. And I'll love being with you. And you won't have to maintain two places. And I'll be here every night for Tinkerbelle. Unless you don't want me to move in so quickly."

"Don't be silly. You do remember that I asked you to marry me tonight and you said yes, don't you?"

"Your dad and Martha took it pretty well. So, I'm guessing they're really okay with you? With us?"

"Oh, yeah. One hundred percent. How about your family?"

"Let's just say that I doubt any of them will be here for the wedding. No matter what."

"That's too bad."

"All I want is a small little gathering of a few people and a homemade sheet cake. A Justice of the Peace is as good as anything for me."

"Are you spiritual?"

"Yes, but that doesn't mean I agree with the misguided teachings of the church I grew up in."

"I get that. Pretty much the same for me. I grew up Catholic, but I don't know that the Church and I agree on a lot of things anymore. So, if I don't agree with it, I basically don't believe in it. So I guess I'm an ex-Catholic now. I believe in God but not the Church."

I snuggled up tightly to Bella. Somewhere in the mix, Tinkerbelle had come in, jumped on the bed, and climbed up on top of the pillows.

"Test number two. You have to be able to sleep with the cat."

"I don't mind. She's cute and cuddly."

"Have you ever had a one-night stand?"

"Never, believe it or not. And if you include the fact that I didn't come onto you until the Saturday morning, I still didn't put out on the first date, so to speak."

"Well now, come on, that was a slightly different set of circumstances."

"Okay. If you want to be snarky about it, I've only put out on the first date once. That was with you."

"You have on subsequent dates slept overnight with a woman and worn the same set of clothes home the next morning, though, haven't you?"

"Wait, wait, wait… What about you? Have you ever had a one-night stand?"

"Several after my big disaster. But every one of them was a mistake. Now back to you, have you slept over and gone home in the same clothes?"

"Yes. As a matter of fact, I have," answered Bella.

"Well you're going to do it tonight. Or I can even give you some sweats to wear home tomorrow. But for tonight, we sleep in our bed."

"I like the sound of that. Our bed."

I picked up Bella's hand and looked at the ring on her finger.

"It looks so much prettier on your hand that it did in the box."

I brought her hand up to my face and kissed her ring.

"I like that. Do it again."

So, I did. I kissed it again. Then Bella wrapped her arms around me and held me tightly. After about fifteen minutes of this, she leaned down and undid the straps on her left shoe and let it hit the floor. She stood up on the floor on her side of the bed with her bad leg bent and her knee supporting her against the bed. She reached behind her and unzipped her dress, staring into my eyes with her emerald beacons. She dropped her dress to the floor. Her underwear was also red, matching her dress. She removed this as well and now was wearing nothing but a red silk ribbon as a headband, which she left in place. Then she pulled the covers back and slid underneath. She held her hand out to me.

I took her hand in mine and brought it to my face and kissed her palm and rubbed her hand all over my face and neck. I placed it on my right breast with my hand over it and squeezed. I let go of it and took off my shoes. I unzipped my dress and let it fall to the floor as well. Unlike Bella's red, I was wearing black underneath. I took everything off, then crept over to the wall switch and turned off the light. I used my hand held out to follow the outline of the bed until I got back to the side. I turned on the light.

"Would you rather have it out?" I asked Bella.

"No, my love. I want to see you like you're made up tonight. I normally don't get to. Kathleen, you are so beautiful to me."

I didn't argue with her this particular night. After all, I had made up just to make an impression on her. Thankfully it did its job quite well. I pulled back the edge of the covers, slid underneath, and snuggled up to Bella to fight off the freeze. My house was always a little drafty and cooler than Bella's apartment. I barely got moved over before Bella's hands started playing my body like a Steinway piano. She sent me over the edge. And over. And over. I reciprocated gladly. Finally, we fell asleep in each other's arms. When I woke up at about four in the morning having to go to the bathroom, Tinks was snuggled on the pillows at our heads. I guess it was official.

CHAPTER EIGHT

I don't have a clock in my bedroom at all. My alarm is on my arm. Even dressed up, I can't take my watch off. It may make me look dorky but it's just the way life is. It's a military issue watch in subdued olive drab. It has multiple alarms, a lap timer, the time, day of the week, and date. I realized this while I was in the bathroom. Crap. I didn't want to turn on the stupid light. But I gave in and set my alarm for six-thirty. I turned the light off and made my way back to bed. The covers were already pulled back for me and Bella had her arm up waiting for me to hold her.

As I slid up against her, I whispered softly in her ear.

"You phone is downstairs in your purse. So is mine. What are you going to do to wake up on time for work tomorrow?"

"Ugh. Would you mind terribly going and getting my purse? Just in the interest of time."

"Yes, I would. Considering that while I was in the bathroom peeing I set my watch to go off for you. See? I'll always try and take care of you, sweetie."

"I don't deserve you."

"Wait for a while on that one. Wait until after the weather has warmed up and I drag you out into the wilderness, up in the hills, along North Shore of Superior, and into Canada... Then we'll see how you feel."

"Houston was so flat and treeless. Austin was beautiful rolling hills, but a desert. Still beautiful, but I'm looking forward to exploring up here."

"And do you own your car?"

"No, it's a lease."

"That's going to change. You're getting at least all-wheel drive if not four-wheel drive. You can still get that in a sedan if you don't want a bigger car."

"What's the difference? All wheels *is* four, isn't it?"

I laughed at her for that one. How would she know?

"All-wheel only kicks in when it's needed. When four-wheel is selected they all four work all the time. You don't need something big. Just something like an SUV. You can even stick with a Lexus like you have now and get AWD."

"Oh, no. That thing has been my pride and joy, but it's way too expensive and if I'd saved the difference in that and a regular car payment I could have bought a normal car and owned it outright instead of having to give the keys back. I'll never lease again."

"I hate this. Now I'm awake. I do that. One of the side effects of shift work."

"Let me see if I can't work off a little of that tension you seem to have stored up and maybe you'll be able to drop off to sleep again. Hmm? What do you think about that?"

Suddenly there were hands running up and down my body. And they weren't mine. And they felt absolutely wonderful. I'd only had half dozen serious girlfriends my whole life. And Melanie lasted for two years. But I'd never experienced this before. I know it had only been a couple of brief weeks, but I still felt electricity every time Bella touched me.

"Bell?"

"Mmm... Yeah?"

"Promise me you'll never stop doing that to me."

"Oh, now you want three promises, not just two. And is this..." she said rubbing her hand up my side, "what you want me to promise to never stop doing?"

"No. Making me *feel* like I do when you touch me. In bed or out."

"I...absolutely...promise," she said between kisses.

Unfortunately, by the time we finished bringing each other to heaven it was almost time to get up. Nonetheless we dropped off to sleep immediately.

When my watch did go off I went and grabbed a pair of sweats out of the dresser for both Bella and me. I laid one pair on the bed. I went to the bathroom and did my morning routine. When I came back into the bedroom Bella had put her underwear back on and was slipping into the sweat bottoms.

"What the hell is it with you people?" she asked.

"What in the world are you talking about?"

"Are all of your sweats navy colored and have fire department symbols on them? "

I laughed my ass off.

"For the most part. I even have some that I've traded other people that I've met in training across the state and at national conferences. I do have a set of black ones with green Army logos. It's a big deal. That and trading sleeve patches. When you come down to the Station sometime you'll see our board of traded patches. Pops has the same deal going on at his office. It's really big. Do they fit you?"

"Just fine."

"I was wondering. I was afraid that they'd fall off your ass if they fit me."

"First off, I told you to stop talking like that. I meant it then and I mean it now. Stop it. Secondly, they do have a draw string, you know?"

"Oh, yeah. I forgot about that. I always just tie it off once and forget about it."

"Let me get into the bathroom," she said pulling the top over her head and picking up her crutches.

"There's an extra toothbrush behind the left mirror in the cabinet."

"Okay. Thanks."

"Leave it down in the glass. It's yours now, sweetie."

While Bella was in the bathroom, I picked up our dresses and shoes. I put her shoe on top of the dresser and mine up in the closet. I folded the dresses neatly to take to the cleaners today. Even though Tinkerbelle is a fairly short-haired cat, she was shedding right now like a damned snowstorm. Maybe a little extra stress since her owner had missed a lot of time for a couple of weeks. In the interest of time, we drove through a fast food restaurant for a couple of breakfast sandwiches and some juice.

Bella spoke first after we finished the sandwiches.

"I forgot to tell you. They're sending a car for me later this morning. We have some visitors coming in that they want me to meet. My manager asked me if I could handle only a couple of hours. And he assured me that if at any time I couldn't handle it, he'd have me driven either home or to the ER. I told him I could probably do that without too much trouble."

"Okay. Just be careful, sweetie."

"May I ask you a question?"

"Sure."

"I know that you had a really bad breakup that lasted a long time. But were you in love with Melanie?"

"I thought I was then. But after being with you, I can honestly say I never was. It was the relationship I was in love with. And that's all it was. A relationship. You and I have sort of skipped right over that part," I said laughingly.

"I guess we have," said Bella taking my hand in hers. "I'm going to tell my parents today. Might as well get it over with."

"You know them better than me. Just let me know if you need any help with anything."

We pulled up at the apartment and I parked underground. We walked over to the elevator and went upstairs. I noticed that Bella was practically a pro on the crutches now. She'd do just fine at work I figured. Once inside, she immediately washed her face and then put on fresh makeup. She picked out an indigo blue sweater and a grey wool plaid skirt. She had a pair of black boots to go with the outfit, but could only wear the left one.

"You know, if you had a pair of grey or black tights or panty hose, I bet I could carefully get them over the cast. They're usually stretchy enough. It might look a little better since you're an executive and all."

"Top dresser drawer, at the back, on the right."

I got a pair out and managed to get them on her without a run. Amazing.

"Thanks. That looks a lot better. I felt absolutely hideous."

"You're anything but hideous. You're so beautiful. I think you're the most beautiful lesbian I've ever met in my life. You're really 'Hollywood' material.'"

"Shut up."

"Well it's true."

"No surgeries, no Botox, nothing like that for me. Ever."

"That's not what I meant and you know it."

"I do. I just don't like people making such a fuss over me. I mean, I'm good in business because I studied hard and I worked for it. Plus, I had the intelligence my parents passed along to me. But my looks? I use makeup, I buy nice clothes, but I look like God made me. I didn't do anything to deserve it. I just happened to luck into it. That's all."

"However it happened, I'm glad it did."

"Are you now?"

I didn't answer her. I just kissed her. She got up and went into the living room and over to the desk. She put on the headset and dialed into her AA.

"Good morning, Courtney. How are you today? Yes, I'll be coming sometime this morning… I think about ten or so. They're sending a driver around for me… Yup, still on crutches," she laughed.

At that point, her head was in the game. Fully. No distractions. I admired her for that. In her own way, she was doing in her world what I did in my world when I was working a fire or an ambulance. We weren't so different after all. She just worked with her head alone, and I worked with my head and my back and my hands.

I took a shower, then I got dressed, grabbed my gym bag, and went to give Bella a kiss on the top of her head. She reached around and grabbed my leg, stopping me from leaving.

"Okay. I'll see you in about two hours. Bye now," she said to the person on the other end of the call.

Bella stood up and turned to face me.

"And where do you think you're going without a proper kiss, my fiancée?"

"You're really eating that up, aren't you?"

"I told you that I came to Minnesota for more than one reason. How did I know it was going to be so magical and happen my first time up to bat?"

I put my bag down and took Bella's face in my palms and gently kissed her over and over. I heard her sigh. And that made my heart sing.

"Bell?"

"Yes?"

"At first you were afraid you were pressuring me. Now I'm afraid I'm pressuring you. When do you maybe want to get married? Wait until late spring or the start of summer so we can be outside and comfortable? Wait a couple of years and just live together first to make sure?"

"I have another suggestion."

"What's that?" I asked.

"I could take a half day off next week. Tell the office it's a doctor's visit. We could get married. If Pops could get off for a couple of hours, he and Martha could be our witnesses. Then when the weather is warm, maybe the end of May or the first of June, we could have a reception. What would you think about that option, lover?"

"I personally like door number two."

I leaned in and kissed her again and hung on for several minutes.

"I'm going to take off now and get some things ready at the house. At *our* house. With *our* cat. And *our* washer and dryer. And *our* bed," I smiled.

Bella didn't say anything in return, she just smiled. I turned to go and our hands separated. I felt my heart sink when they did, even though I knew that within a few hours we'd be back together.

The car from Bella's office came for her right after ten o'clock. She was actually in the building for a little over three hours. Finally, she told them that her foot was hurting and she had neglected to bring her pain medication (which was a lie) with her and needed to return home. She made many apologies, and everyone assured her that she need not worry, that it was perfectly okay and that even working from home she was performing far and above the last two people that held her position.

When Bella got home she went into the bedroom and took a nap. She didn't even bother changing clothes. I found her there snoring gently. I giggled quietly to myself. How funny, I thought. I quietly climbed into bed next to her, and got as close to her as I thought I could without waking her up.

"Hi, baby. I'm glad you're home."

"I was trying not to wake you up."

"I heard the keys in the lock. I hear things even when I'm asleep."

"Then I'll warn you now, our house creaks. It might take some getting used to. Speaking of which, I made a list today of everything we'll have to change. Names, create a joint bank account that we can take a portion of both our accounts and have entered with auto deposit we can use for the mortgage and utilities, things like that. I mean, you're the business head, maybe you know better than I do, but I just had some free time and I was thinking about it and put it in a quick database."

"You used a database? Which one?"

"Office Libre. It's open licensed and completely compatible with Microsoft's suite of products."

"I'm familiar with Libre. It used to be Open Office. It's just so rare that anybody knows about it. Everybody thinks that they absolutely have to have Microsoft's product. That and the fact that everybody uses text documents or spreadsheets to do the stuff you did today. I'm proud of you. It shows initiative."

"I just figured I'd make a database since that way we could put dates in it if we needed to. And even when it comes time for the reception I can just add a child table and enter guest names."

"Now *that's* what I'm talking about! I think you would have been good in business school."

"But I would have been bored to tears. I like working with my body."

"I like working with your body, too."

"You dirty girl!" I said to Bella.

"So, I called my parents today. I was lucky to get ahold of Daddy during a weekday. He's usually booked in one meeting after another. I left a message and he called back in less than a half hour. I wanted to give him first shot at it because he's the least objectionable to my lifestyle. Let's just say that not only does he think that it's bad enough having a girlfriend, getting married is simply not an available choice to be made, and even if it were, we're rushing into things. I told him we don't have any set date. I sort of lied. Not any set date, but a set week," she said as she fluttered her eyelids at me.

"Oh, you're a wicked little girl. You should be punished. You need to be spanked!"

"Do you think so? And will you spank me, Teacher?"

I laughed and she laughed and we laughed. And when we were done, we both laughed some more.

"So, then I called my Mama. Unfortunately, she wasn't showing a home, so she answered. I asked her if she and Daddy could take off for about three or four days. She wanted to know what for? Was it to come up here for Christmas? Because it was too close to booking and the price of tickets would be high and they didn't know if their schedules would both allow it and... blah, blah, blah...I said, 'No Mom, I want you to come to my wedding'."

"What was her response?" I asked on the edge of my seat.

"She asked if I'd finally come to my senses and found a nice young man now that I was working for a proper company. I told her that I'd known since I was in first grade I was a lesbian and that I told both her and Daddy when I was in the third grade, she should have learned the ship for change had sailed a long, long time ago. I told her that I'd met somebody just a little older than I was and that she was wonderful and we're engaged. There was nothing but silence."

I waited for Bella to go on, but she just sat there saying nothing.

"Don't leave me hanging. What did she say?"

"I told her that we were of course getting married here because it's illegal in Texas. And we don't want a civil union, we want a wedding. She still hadn't said a word. I finally told her, 'Mom, say the words. We've done this before. Say the words. 'You're a lesbian.'' She didn't say anything. I told her this was her last chance to say the words. She said nothing. So, I hung up on her. I want to get some wedding announcements rather than invitations letting people know we've gotten married and send them to everybody I know. Good, bad, or indifferent. What do you think?"

"I think it sounds like a plan, sweetie. Well, so much for the downer news. Dad's free next Tuesday. It'll be Christmas Eve, if you want to do that. City Hall will be open and he said he can ask the Mayor to perform the ceremony, or he has enough pull to get a County Court judge to give us ten minutes in his chambers for a very private, very exclusive ceremony. What would you think about that? Wanna get married on Christmas Eve?"

"I couldn't think of a more romantic day of the year than that. Let's do it! Oh, and one more thing. It's short notice, but they didn't think I'd be ambulatory soon enough. There's a huge office party in the top floor of our building which is used for banquets, bar and bat mitzvahs, weddings, things like that. Apparently, it's a pretty big deal. My supervisor is Mike McNally. His supervisor is Niall Reynolds. Niall laid into him for not telling me about the party to let me make my own decision of whether or not to attend. He said that I might have even wanted to come in a wheel chair if I wanted to. Called him an ass. Mike squirmed."

"Do you want to wear the same dresses we wore to Pop's thingy? I took them into the cleaners today. I can pick them up first thing Saturday morning."

"Sounds good to me. I doubt anybody from one crowd would run into the other. Oh, I'm sorry, that sounded really snobby, didn't it? I didn't mean it that way. I meant that the people from my building wouldn't know which end of a screwdriver to hold much less do anything of use with it."

I laughed at Bella.

"I didn't take offense to it. And no, I doubt anybody at all from either side would rub elbows with the other."

"You sure you want to go? We don't have to, you know. It's not like it's a mandatory meeting."

"Listen, you and I both know that the people at the top pay attention to who is and who isn't there. It's all about loyalty. And you need to earn any and all loyalty points you can along the way. Being this close to Christmas it wouldn't be any big deal if somebody was already on a road trip home over the river and through the woods to see Grandma. So, they won't notice who's gone. But they will notice who's there. And they will notice somebody that's there on crutches making an effort. And besides, you'll be able to show off your new ring."

"Don't think that wasn't a big part of whether I wanted to put up with this boring thing or not," Bella smiled at me.

"If you want to go, we'll go, and if you don't, we won't. But I also wanted to talk to you about something else. Does the company care if you're living here? I mean if you happened to have somewhere else to live will they get bent out of shape since they have a year's lease and you've moved out?"

"Oh, God no. Like I said, we have ten units regardless of who's in them. And this is furnished. Even the sheets, blankets, and towels belong to the unit. Just like leasing a flat in London. Dishes. Television. The only things that are mine are my laptop, my CD's and DVD's, and my clothes. That's it."

"That's going to make this easy. Sunday I'm getting a couple of guys to help me and we're going to get everything out of here and get you moved home. If you're ready."

Bella snaked her arm through mine. She looked into my eyes; those bright green eyes of hers pierced the air like beacons. Like the eyes of a tiger.

"I can't wait. It couldn't be soon enough for me... so... You're putting the house in my name, too, huh? Pretty gutsy move on your part, isn't it?"

"I live for danger. But, why wouldn't I? We'll be married. What's mine is yours."

"And what's mine is yours. You know, I probably make a little bit more money than you. I hope that's not going to be a problem."

"I told you, one joint account where we both put in money for joint upkeep. We can still keep our separate accounts," I said.

"I have a better idea. How about we create a joint account, and put both checks in there. Then we use automatic deposit to put only a small amount into separate accounts for you and me. Our mad money, if you will. I don't want to keep all my money from you. You just tell me before you spend money out of the main account, if you can. If it's an emergency, then so be it, just tell me after you do it. And I'll do my best to tell you I want to spend on something before I do it."

"Actually, I was willing to give up my private account altogether. But your idea seems to be a pretty good one."

"What's your salary, Kathleen?"

"Thirty-nine thousand, seven hundred, roughly. Although after overtime last year I pulled down just over fifty-one thousand. The only way I got this house was that Pops made the down payment for me and it was a foreclosure auction. I expect that within five years I'll be making about fifty-three or fifty-five base pay, in that range."

"I make one hundred twenty-six thousand a year. Be prepared to be supported in a lifestyle in which you'd like to become accustomed."

"Shit. I'm cleaning the garage out and you're going to park inside," I laughed.

"Not bad for a 'lil' ol' girl from Houston', huh?"

"Not at all. So, when you lease a flat in London you get it furnished?"

"Not necessarily. You can get unfurnished or furnished. But if it comes furnished it comes with everything. I mean everything."

"How'd you find out about this? One of your friends lease a flat in London?"

"Nope. Me. One of my unpaid internships meant I didn't get a salary per se. I got a free place to live, a stipend for food and I got my public transportation cards paid for. Mama and Daddy still had to shell out a butt load of money for four months. But they wanted me to have experience in another country. And it paid off big time."

"What do you want for dinner tonight? If it's going to take a long time to fix, I better get started."

"How about pizza and a beer?"

"Now you're talking a Minnesota Seven Course Meal: a six pack and a pizza!"

"That's what we call a Redneck's seven course meal in Houston. Too funny."

"Let me help get you out of those clothes and get them hung up first. You look beat."

"I am."

I helped Bella get undressed and into some of her own sweats which were grey with 'Rice' written down the front of one leg in blue gothic lettering. After she was comfy she stayed on the bed, rolled onto her side, and closed her eyes for a nap. I went into the living room and ordered the pizza. Then I called Pops. He said he'd make a call or two and get one of the judges to do the ceremony. He said that, to him, a judge carried a lot more prestige than an elected official, unless you were into playing the games of the socialites or the politicos anyway.

"Pops?"

"Yeah, Kitten?"

"Thank you."

"For what?"

"For supporting me all these years. For raising me. For giving me just a small part of your character."

"You know I never did it because it was my job, don't you? I did it because you were, and are, my favorite person in the whole world, along with your mother, God rest her soul. Martha is my wife, and I love her very much, but she's never taken your mother's place and she knows that. Hell, she knew it coming in. I so much as told her so. So you're not the same as most people. But then most people aren't firefighter material like you. Or police officer material like me. And you could have been either. You don't ever have to worry about me.

I've got your back, and you've got mine. We're forever partners, right?"

"I got it, Pops. I love you."

"Me too, Kitten. I'll let you know when I get us a courtroom. Do something for me, though, would you?"

"What's that?"

"I know you've never gotten along that well with Martha. But know that she's not trying to take your mother's place, and accept her for who she is. Try. For me, please?"

"I don't dislike Martha...."

"But you don't like her either. All I'm asking is that you try. Both Martha and I deserve the same chance that you and Bella are getting, don't we?"

"You're absolutely right. I guess I've never seen it with that perspective. I'll be nicer to her. Really, I will. Bye Pops."

"Bye Kath."

My phone rang and the delivery person called to say she was in front of the building. I went downstairs and let her in. She gave me the receipt to sign since I'd charged it to my bankcard, and I gave her a nice tip and thanked her. I went back upstairs and put the pizza on the counter. I walked into the bedroom and saw Bella still sleeping. I lay down on the bed next to her.

"Sweetie, I thought you heard everything."

"I do. Pizza's here. Just give me a second to pull myself together."

"While you're doing that, we need to consider a couple of things. We're on a time line. I know a photo shop where they do your portraits and use one of the really high-end color ink-jet printers on photographic paper with fade resistant ink. Anyway, you get all of your prints within an hour of taking the pictures. How about we throw on a couple of sweaters and go get our picture taken? You can just leave on your sweats bottoms, since they won't show anything below your waist anyway. We could go after dinner. Are you up for it?"

"Sure. That sounds like fun. Count me in."

"And what about dresses for the wedding. We're going to be hard pressed to find white dresses without going to a bridal shop this time of year. I hadn't thought about that when we just jumped on the plan. Or do you want to wear something else?"

"I have a heather grey dress that I would like to wear. Very neutral. It would go well with a necklace and earrings. But I have a request of you and your father."

"You do, huh? And what would that be?"

"I want you both to wear your dress uniforms."

"Somehow I knew that's what you were going to ask. I knew it. Are you're sure that's what you want?"

"Yes. I told you I'm a sucker for uniforms. And I'll have somebody take a couple of pictures of us. You'll be immortalized."

"I'll think about it."

"Please? Please, please, please, please? Pretty please?"

"Okay. I've thought about it. I'll do it."

"Thank you, baby. I love you."

"I love you too. Now come and eat so we can go get our pictures done tonight.

We moved into the dining room and drank a couple of beers each and ate some pizza. I put the leftovers into plastic storage bags and put them in the fridge.

"I wish you didn't have to go to work tonight."

"It doesn't change. I mean, I can take days off but the shifts don't change. And remember that every day that I take off is twenty-four hours."

"I know. It'll be better when I have Tinkerbelle with me."

"So, you like Tinks, huh? She sure took a shine to you. Don't worry. We'll have you moved into the house by the end of the weekend no matter what. You'll be just fine on the stairs. You're walking really strongly right now. And the stairs will be a great workout for your legs. And by the way, I'm really glad you've been keeping up with the free weights. I have a ton of them in my basement. Sorry, in *the* basement. I'll move you from five to eight pounds in about another week. You never want to just keep going higher and higher. What you'll eventually do is keep using relatively light weights, but move to a butt load of repetitions. That way you get great tone and strength but don't bulk up."

"You mean don't start looking like you?"

"Now you're just being catty."

"Meee-ow. What of it?"

Bella reached over with a napkin and wiped the corner of my mouth and smiled at me. She melted my heart constantly when she just looked at me and smiled without saying anything. We sat around chatting for about fifteen minutes and then got our coats and made for the garage. We got to the photography studio and it was packed. I forgot everybody would be getting Christmas pictures. I had borrowed a cable knit sweater from Bella and she wore a multi-colored turtle necked sweater. We didn't have on the usual Christmassy looking clothes that everybody else did.

After about thirty minutes of standing on her crutches a man finally stood up and offered her his chair. She thanked him and sat down. It took another hour and fifteen minutes to get into the studio itself. We got several different shots. Together looking straight ahead, Bella's head leaning over on my shoulder, the two of us kissing facing each other (a perfectly innocent kiss), Bella sitting down and me behind her standing up, but leaning down where my head was just above hers with my arms wrapped around her, me sitting down, and Bella sitting on my lap, with her arms around my neck.

After we got all the images taken, we went to one of the two printing stations. All of the images came up on the screen. We picked out which ones we wanted and what size and how many, right on the touch screen monitor. The rest was, as they say, "automagically done." It took about twenty minutes to print out everything. We paid for the photos and went home.

"Just so you know, in the fire department our uniforms are plain black with a brass button on each shoulder, and a black tie over a white shirt. I have the trousers, but I could get the black skirt if you want. I can get it within a day or so. I could order it tomorrow during the day from the Station."

"I say the skirt would be nice. But it's up to you."

"Hon, I don't really care either way. I think it may make Pops happy, though."

"Then go with the skirt. That'll be worth it just for that."

We sat down on the couch and started cutting the photos apart with scissors on the coffee table. After we had them cut apart, we started putting them in piles. Some for us. Some for Pops. And some for Bella's family, even if they weren't really on board for this. You never know if they'll frame them or tear them up. Without warning, Bella got up and got her phone and scrolled through her contacts. She touched connect.

"Are you ready to say it yet? Are we really going to keep playing this stupid game? Would you rather I never call you again? If that's what you really want, then I'll obey your wishes... Now was that so damned hard? Well apparently it was or you would have said it last time I called you... Now, if we *were* to have a wedding, would you and Daddy come or not? I just want to know if you'd want to come. That's all I want to know. Damn it, it's not just to piss you off, it's because we're in love! It's going to happen, I just want to know if you love me enough to accept me for what I am and be happy for me and be proud of me...."

Bella's eyes were starting to get watery. I just shut my mouth and sat there, picked my tablet up off the table and tried to act distracted.

"If I'm such a screw up how is it that I'm a group director for a Fortune 500 company and I'm twenty-three years old? Because your preacher tells me that God loves everybody, but since I'm queer God doesn't love me. It can't be both ways... Whatever. So you'll know, we're getting married on Christmas Eve... No, not in a church, in a judge's chambers. Kathleen and I, Kathleen's father, and her stepmother... No, they're not divorced for Christ sake, she *died* you insensitive cow. Even if you were willing to come and could come I don't know that I'd want you there. I've had just about enough of you and your 'I'm better than you are' attitude. Bye."

Bella hit the end button. I just sat there for a second, not moving, not saying anything. I got up, scooted over right against Bella and sat back down. Still just holding my tablet. I was pushing hard into her though. I laid my head over onto her shoulder and kept doing what I was doing on my tablet, still not saying anything. I didn't try and hold her hand. I didn't try and console her. I figured mostly that she needed to cool down and she knew best how to do that, not me. So, I let her go.

After about ten minutes of silence, she reached over with her hand and started running it through my hair, playing with it. Making it stand up, shaking it out and making it fall back down straight, running her fingertips up into it. Then she let out a long heavy sigh. She picked her phone back up and opened the text app. She typed in a quick bit of data and hit send. My phone chirped to let me know I'd gotten a text message. 'I L Y.' I smiled. Neither of us moved for about half an hour.

Finally, I got up and put my tablet on the table and went into the second room, got into my bag and fished out a clean uniform. I went into the bathroom and brushed my teeth, put on deodorant, and went to the bedroom. I took off my street clothes and folded them up, placing them in the chair. I put on a clean tee shirt and my uniform. As a last thought, I went back into the bathroom. I searched through makeup. I found a light pink lip-gloss. I've never liked pink much for lipstick. I prefer shades of red, like the crimson I'd worn to the Policeman's dinner. Not that anybody else that knew me would have any idea that there actually was a feminine side to me. But this would be more subdued while at the Station and still maybe make me a little more feminine.

"Come on in and lie down with me for a little bit."

"I'll be right there," Bella answered.

"Okay."

About fifteen minutes later she managed to get the energy enough to get up and crutch her way into the bedroom and get up on the bed with me. She took her top hand and wrapped it around my bottom and rubbed it.

"If you didn't already have your uniform on I'd make you make love to me."

"I think if it were any other night than tonight, I'd do it anyway and just get dressed again."

"My mother took the wind right out of my sails. Honestly, I don't know what her gig is. She was never this way when I was growing up. I've had a couple of girlfriends over to the house. I don't think she was totally comfortable, but she got through it."

"Yeah, but now you're twelve hundred miles away, and this one might actually be forever. Her last possible chance to change you from the dark side back to the light. And some people get more mellow with age and wiser, while others get less able to handle life instead. I'm guessing she's the second type. Anyway, you've already been taken and adopted by Pops and Martha. You don't need other parents anymore. Even though it hurts, you have to just keep putting one foot in front of the other."

Tears started flowing down Bella's cheeks.

"I know," she barely managed to croak out.

I reached up and wiped her tears with my thumbs.

"Look at me, would you. I'm supposed to be all grown up."

"If you have any heart and soul, you'll cry from time to time for the rest of your life," I corrected her.

The tears started really coming down from both eyes, flowing non-stop. Bella buried her head in my chest and grabbed my arms with her hands and her body started silently but violently shaking. I said nothing, just held her tightly and rubbed her back up and down. Her movement subsided gradually. I pulled my head back where I could see Bella's face better. She was asleep. I knew that this wasn't my battle to fight, but it was hard not to just pick up Bella's phone, call her mom, and give her a piece of my mind. I managed to resist the urge. I decided to sleep until my watch went off.

When my alarm did go off, I slipped out of bed and got completely ready before Bella even stirred. She was really emotionally beat up. I sat down on the bed and leaned over her and put her hair behind her ear.

"Hey, sweetie. I'm going to work now. Give me a kiss."

"How long have you been up?"

"About forty-five minutes. You didn't wake up when I got out of bed so I decided that you probably needed sleep. And you have to work tomorrow morning so I left you alone. I just wanted to give you a kiss before I left for work."

"I'm glad you woke me up. I would completely freak out if you ever left without waking me up. So you know."

"I wouldn't dream of it. I'll see you Saturday morning, alright?"

"Okay. I love you."

"You can still back out, you know. It's not done until it's done."

Bella reached up with both hands and patted my face on both sides.

"But I wouldn't be able to live without my little chubby cheeks. I don't want to change my mind. I hope you don't."

"Chubby cheeks? What the hell?"

"Well, your do have rounded cheeks. You're not fat, you just have chubby cheeks. They're cute. You're cute," she said ruffling my hair.

"Goodnight. Go back to sleep. I love you."

"Love you too. 'Night."

Driving to the Station, I realized that the only time I hadn't had Bella on my mind since I'd met her was the morning we had the big warehouse fire. The whole time I was on scene it was all training and reaction. That was a good thing. The number one thing you can do to stay safe is to keep focused and alert. But other than that, no matter what I was doing I was thinking about Bella.

I made a mental note that during the day I needed to call Pops to see if he could get our marriage license. I could have had other people do it but I wanted to keep it hush-hush until it was done. And I needed to remember to call the uniform shop and make sure they had a skirt in stock. If they didn't I'd have them do an overnight delivery of it to get it on Monday. That would only give me one-day leeway, so that would be a last resort thing.

I pulled into the station, picked up my bag and went inside. We had our safety briefing and went to the bunkroom.

"Hey, Kathleen… You know Timmy Carmichael from the Eastern District PD? He told me that he saw you at the annual dinner," said Scott.

"Yeah? So?" I replied.

"He said that he saw somebody looking suspiciously like you was sitting at the table with Detective Sergeant, excuse me, that is Detective *Lieutenant* Kevin Pope."

"What's your point, dorkus?"

"He said that whoever it was had on a blue dress and heels. And she was *beautiful*."

"Don't be an ass."

"And lastly, he said that she was accompanied by an absolute angel in red. I wish I'd been there. I wish he'd taken a photo of it."

"Tell you what Scotty-me-boy, we are going to a party at Bella's office tomorrow and we're wearing the same dresses. Would you be happier if I had somebody take a photo of us with my phone? Would that satisfy your morbid curiosity?"

"I just forget sometimes that you have boobs."

Without thinking I curled my hand up into a fist and punched him squarely in the solar plexus. I don't think I fully knocked the air out of him, but I shut him up for a minute, leaving him panting a bit.

"I'm sorry, sometimes my filter is off. Shit just falls out of my mouth from my brain. I didn't mean to say you weren't every bit a woman. More like you're as absolutely capable as anyone in this Station, and still are a beautiful woman. I'll shut up now. I won't blame you if you turn me in."

"Scott, why would I do that? We're buddies. And that was only a love tap. If I was truly pissed, you'd still be on the ground," I smiled at him.

He held out his hand to me and we shook on it. He smiled back at me and patted my shoulder. Everybody had pretty much gotten in bed already. I wasn't far behind. The overhead lights were already out when I made my way in to lie down. But within five minutes I was snoring alongside everybody else.

I woke up at about a quarter to seven. I don't know why. I just woke up and went to the bathroom. At that point I was wide-awake and the first one in the canteen so I started both coffee makers. No decaf here, we just needed two pots for the volume. The smell was delicious. I couldn't wait until the black nectar was done with its fall from the filter into the voluminous stainless catch vessel, waiting to be shared with each and every one of our team. Except for John. Stupid tea drinker. Gack, cat on a hairball! I like tea maybe half a dozen times a year and that's my limit.

Within the next thirty minutes or so everybody had filled their cup at least once and two new pots were brewing. I'd hate to see what our annual budget for coffee, tea, and hot chocolate was. Then the alarms went off. Lieu went running into the CP and scanned the dispatch order. The radio came over the intercom giving us details. We were being called as secondary, or backup, in case we were needed, so we may not even have to work the fire. It was on the outskirts of downtown in a multi-story so both Engine 7 and Ladder 7 were being called in to back up Engine 8 and Ladder 8. Sometimes they call us and sometimes they call in 22, whether or not we work the fire. That leaves 18 close by for a second primary if needed or if there was a three alarm or more call.

Fortunately for us, today all we did was stand around and watch. Even 8 didn't do too much. It was an electrical fire, and there was some smoke damage but no real fire. We were released first and rode back to our Station with clean apparatus. I missed not being in the action, feeling somehow let down, but also feeling very happy that there wasn't going to be any cleanup. That would be a bonus for the day. It was a warmer day this morning. It was already about twenty-eight degrees out heading for thirty-three.

As soon as we got back I went online to check out getting a marriage license. Shit! Both of us had to be present and we had to wait for five days to pick it up. Damn, damn, damn! I walked up to the Lieutenant and motioned to him with my hand then I walked into his office with him following me. I shut the door and sat down across the desk from him. He took a seat and waited for me to talk.

"I need to take off for a couple of hours for some personal business. It's a matter of timing, or I would work something else out. Apparently, both Bella and I have to be present to apply for our license."

"Your license?"

"Our marriage license."

Carl's jaw dropped open. Literally. I stared at the floor for a minute not saying anything.

"You're serious, right? No joke? That's actually what you're doing? You know they do have a thing called courtship that can last up to quite a while, don't you? It's almost considered normal in some circles."

"Yeah. Do you think it would be possible? We were going to do it Christmas Eve but we didn't know about the waiting period."

He just sat there for the longest time.

"I'm good with that. Congratulations. I mean it, congratulations," he said as he held his hand out for me to shake.

After I left his office I took out my phone and send a text message to Pops telling him that we had a change of plans and why. I asked him to see if he would check with the Ramsey County Court and schedule it in for New Year's Eve instead. I called Bella. Fortunately, she wasn't on the phone with work and answered.

"Hi, baby. I was just about to take a lunch break and fix a sandwich. I'm glad you called."

"You won't be when I break the news. We can't get married on Christmas Eve. There's a five-day waiting period after buying the license before we can pick it up. So, I was thinking what about New Year's Eve? We could make that? If you wanted to?"

"If we can't do it the twenty-fourth, we'll pick the second-best day of the year? I'm okay with that, so long as we still are getting married."

"And one more thing: we both have to be present to pay for the license or we have to have a notarized request from the person that's not there. So, you have to find a way to let me come get you and we'll run over to the Ramsey County Courthouse this afternoon. My

Lieutenant has already let me off for as long as I need. He's not even charging me the time off. He's pretty cool that way."

"Sure, I can take off. When are you coming by?"

"Right now, if it's okay with you. No need to get dressed up. Sweats are okay. But you'd look really cute if you'd wear department sweats. And bring your sandwich and a drink with you."

"I'll be ready in fifteen minutes. Kathleen?"

"Yeah, sweetie?"

"You sound really disappointed."

"I just was really into the idea of having our anniversary be on Christmas Eve."

"It doesn't matter if it's the sixteenth of July. Just as long as we're together. I can wait as long as we have to, so long as we're living together."

"I'll be alright. Pick you up in a few."

"I love you."

"I love you too."

Jeff was making a big chef salad for everybody for lunch. He was still in the process when I walked up behind him with a paper cup. I quickly put some chicken and ham in it and a couple of wedges of tomato, along with some cucumber slices.

"Hey, get out of the food until it's ready. This isn't your mother's kitchen!"

"Sorry to run away from your highly talented skills as a chef, dude, but I've got to run away for a couple of hours. Family situation."

"Everything okay? Nobody hurt or sick?"

"Nothing like that, thanks. See you this afternoon."

I ran out to the truck and headed for my house first. I ran in, ignoring Tinkerbelle, grabbed my birth certificate, and headed to the apartment.

Bella was waiting at the front door when I drove up. I got out and opened the door for her. She made me smile. She actually was wearing departmental sweats just for me, including a ball cap. She was so darned cute it almost hurt. She ate her sandwich while we drove. I kept raising the paper cup to my mouth and eating.

"What are you eating?"

"Part of a chef salad, without the salad."

Bella thought that was funny. It took us almost twenty minutes to get to the Ramsey County building. After we got in line, I told Bella to wait and I'd be right back. I walked around the corner to keep from bothering anybody. I called the uniform shop. They had a skirt in stock, so I had them pull it and put my name on it telling them I'd come in tomorrow. She reminded me they were only open until three on Saturdays. I went back and got in line with Bella.

"What was that about?"

"Picking up a skirt tomorrow. Even though we can't use it for another week."

"Oh, will you quit pouting? I agree, Christmas Eve would have been perfect, but hasn't everything else so far been pretty perfect? Really?"

"I'm okay. Really."

"Your voice says yes but your pouty face says no," she said, reaching up to give me a kiss.

I noticed a couple of people looking at us. One guy held out his hand and gave me the thumbs up. I leaned down into Bella's ear and whispered what happened. She asked me which person it was and I told her the man in the Vikings stocking cap. She turned around and looked his way. He was facing us, so he saw her when she waived at him, giving him a smile. He waved back with a smile.

"Now, something that would definitely *not* happen in Houston very often," said Bella.

"You mean there aren't any gay people in Houston?"

"Tons. But PDA is frowned upon greatly. Interracial couples are fine. White, black, Hispanic, Asian, whatever. But same-sex? Not ready for prime time."

I thought the line would take forever. It took almost an hour until we got up to the front. The lady in the second window finally waved her hand to take the next person.

"What can I do for you?"

"We need to get a marriage license," I said.

"I need to see two forms of ID for each of you. Driver's license or passport and birth certificate."

"Oh, you don't have your birth certificate?" asked Bella with a worried look on her face.

I reached inside my coat and produced it.

"I ran by the house on the way over. Ha!"

"Thank goodness."

We both handed over our licenses and birth certificates. The woman disappeared for about ten minutes and came back with our documents and a receipt for the marriage license.

"You can pick up the license in five days. After that, you have six months from the date of issuance to use it and if you miss that deadline you'll have to re-apply. Do you have a certificate of premarital counseling?"

"No. I didn't know we needed one."

"The fee is forty dollars with the counseling. So, in your case that will be one hundred fifteen and our location does take credit cards, as well as checks and cash."

Bella reached into her purse and pulled out her billfold.

"I can get this," I said.

"Don't be silly. After all, to be completely honest, this was my idea, wasn't it?"

"Let's just say it was mutual. And you can pay if you like, sweetie."

The woman went away again for about two or three minutes, returning Bella's card along with a credit receipt and a receipt from the county with the transaction number. I took Bella back to the apartment so she could get to work and I drove back to the station.

"Everything alright, Pope?"

"A-okay, Lieu. Thanks a million."

"Hey, Kathleen! Somebody brought something by. I think it might be for you. Well, sort of," said Oliver.

"What is it?"

He handed me a large manila envelope, sealed, and marked Bella on the front.

"Who left this?"

"A reporter from the paper."

"Huh...."

CHAPTER NINE

I was eaten up all day with the contents of the envelope. What was it? An exposé on me for my future bride to throw her off the trail? I didn't say anything about it when I talked to her that evening. I bided my time until shift change. We didn't have any other calls during the shift and finally, quitting time rolled around. It seemed like it took an eternity. I put my stuff down and went into the bedroom. Bella was sitting up reading a book, with the lamp on.

I set the envelope on the dresser, and then proceeded to get undressed.

"Whatcha got there?"

I didn't say anything; I just continued to get into my nightclothes. I went into the bathroom, brushed my teeth, and peed. I went back into the bedroom, picked up the envelope, sat down on the bed, and handed it to Bella. She gave me a puzzled look.

"What's this?"

"I don't know. It's sealed and it's in your name."

"How did you get it?"

"One of the guys said a newspaper reporter gave it to him."

Bella opened the envelope. Inside were several photographs, with a cover page printed off with an explanation. The reporter had been covering the downtown fire this morning. He'd apparently been told to look out for Engine 7 and look for me. Timmy Carmichael, after having seen us at the dinner, had given the reporter the request to keep an ear out for my Station on the scanner and get some photos of me in action. Why in the hell Timmy didn't come over to our table was beyond me. He and I aren't particularly friends, but he knows Pops pretty well. Bella pulled off the cover sheet and there were about a dozen photographs of me in bunker gear around our truck, on the street, talking with a firefighter of Engine 8.

"Ooh, it's my little firefighter... How cute you are! I mean, I saw you in your gear the other day, but this is different. You're in the middle of it."

"We didn't actually end up doing anything. We were just a backup in case."

"It doesn't matter. Tell whoever it is that got these for me thank you very, very much."

Bella hugged the photos to her chest, smiling at me.

"I'll always worry about you, that's just the nature of having someone you care for in the line of danger in any situation. But I'm so proud of you. I wouldn't trade you for any of the golf and country club types that my family hangs out with. I love you so much."

I gave her kiss and took the photos from her, placing them on top of the envelope on the dresser and crawled into bed. I took her book that was beside her and placed it on the table. I pulled the covers back from her, and straddled her body with my legs. I leaned down and interlocked my hands with hers and put my face into hers. We feasted on each other hungrily. We eventually wound up bare skin to bare skin. Later, we pulled the covers up, turned off the light, and spooned together.

I woke up with Bella's leg over me and her grinding her pelvis into me.

"What are you doing back there?"

"Remember how your grandmother always thought that you were still two years old. Even when you wore size six women's shoes she would hold them up and say, 'look at her little shoes'? In her eyes they would always see you as that little girl?"

"And what does that have to do with your little bump and grind going on?"

"When I'm old and grey and in a nursing home eating oatmeal three times a day, I'll still have the memory of you standing in my bedroom, wearing your purple tank top and underwear. I was just thinking about that, that's all."

"I see. Let me help you out with that," I said turning over to face her.

And I did. Help her out with that, that is. When we were finished with our little 'happy time', we got up and dressed for our day out. Bella said she was feeling pretty good and wanted to go out with me to do our errands. We went to the post office, which was busier than hell, being right before Christmas, and mailed the photos of us to her parents, her brother, her sister, as well as a few of her friends and my cousin and aunt. We went to the uniform shop and picked up the skirt. I went ahead and tried it on to make sure I wouldn't have to exchange it. It fit perfectly. And we went to the cleaners to get our dresses. The last thing we did was getting Bella another pair of tights that could be stretched over her cast.

"By the way, there's a pervy guy that I work with that is good friends with a cop. It's weird because the cop knows Pops and he didn't come over to the table. Anyways, he tells the guy at my station about me wearing a dress. And the fact that he thought I was beautiful. And the fact that I had an angel in red on my arm. I promised him I'd take a couple of pictures tonight with my camera and prove to him that I'm a girl. He's pretty cool, over all, but he just pushed a button I guess and I punched him right in the gut."

"What button did he push?"

"He said he forgot that I had boobs."

"Bigger than mine I might add. They're definitely obvious, even in your uniform."

"But you can see how that sort of set me off, right? Anyway, he kind of caught me off guard with that remark."

"And neither of you got in trouble?"

"Well, I'd never turn anybody on my team into HR unless there was some true harassment. Scott just wasn't thinking when he spoke. And it wasn't that bad. It's not like he was hitting on me. His wife is pretty nice to me at picnics in the summer and stuff. And fortunately, I didn't hit him full force. I really held back for the most part. I did get his attention, though," I laughed.

"I would imagine. I bet you're every bit as strong as most of the guys you work with."

"Overall that's true. But there's this guy, Ambrocio, who we all just call Greek, who is built like a side of beef hanging on a hook in a meat locker. He's as solid a man as I've ever met in my life. And he can bench press over five hundred pounds. No joke. And another guy that's in the Special Forces Unit for the National Guard. Have you ever seen the movie, The Green Berets?"

"Of course. Who hasn't?"

"Remember the guys that are introducing the guests and reporters to the members of the Green Beret's functions that's the Swedish guy? Built like a mountain, slight accent?"

"Yeah. I think so," Bella said after thinking for a moment.

"This guy is like the Swede but about twenty percent bigger and stronger. I couldn't compete with those two. But most of the guys, yeah. I'm right up there with them."

"I'm so glad I got photos of you. I'm going to scan them and send them to my family just because. I'll email them and tell them all about you. Maybe if they get to know you, to know that I'm marrying a real live hero, they'll give me a little more credit."

"Just don't get your hopes up too high. If it happens, it happens."

"I know. But as mad and frustrated as I was the other day, I somehow still feel the need for validation from them. And I *hate* that. But it's just the way things are."

Soon we were back home. We both needed a fingernail polish touch up. My fingernails have to be kept short for work, but I put a clear coat on them quite often. I still had on the crimson red to match the lip-gloss I wore going out. We did each other's nails while chatting like a couple of coeds. We talked long enough to let the paint dry.

"Party starts at seven, right?" I asked.

"Yup. I guess we ought to start getting ready."

I pulled my underwear out of my bag at the same time Bella pulled hers out of the dresser. We both laughed, since we both pulled out blue, and almost the same shade. We couldn't have gotten it better if we planned it. Bella went into the bathroom and put on her makeup first. This time I'd see her build up to the finished product, and so would she. But it didn't make it any less magical for me. I'd just wanted to surprise Bella that first time.

Bella came back to the bedroom and sat down on the bed. I helped her get her tights over the cast and on.

"You know what?"

"What?" I asked.

"You're hot in that underwear. You can wear that around the house anytime you want."

"It's not as comfortable as my other skivvies. I think I'll keep these for special occasions."

"Aww. That's too bad."

I went in and put on my makeup. I've always been very lucky about my skin. My skin is very clear, if a little pale. And my cheeks are always a bit ruddy, not quite like I'm wearing a little rouge, but making it where I don't have to. It's smooth enough that I don't wear a foundation. I put on eyeliner, mascara, a little eye shadow, and lip-gloss. That makes my routine, when I dress up, pretty quick to finish.

"I hate you."

"Why would you say that?" I asked Bella.

"It takes you no time at all to throw on your face and you look perfect. It's not fair."

"Don't tell me you have to get up an hour earlier than necessary every day to put on makeup? That's disgusting."

"No, only about fifteen minutes."

"Whatever. Let me get your dress for you...."

I put my arms through the dress and got it ready to put over her head. She put her arms straight up to allow me to drop it down. Then she stood up and it fell down around her body. I reached behind her and zipped it up. She sat on the bed and picked up her shoe and I put it on for her.

"I can do that you know."

"Yeah, but even after you're all healed up it's the kind of thing I'd do."

"That's sweet."

I picked up my dress and was about to drop it over my head. I was facing away from Bella, for no particular reason, and I felt her hands on my butt.

"Are you trying to start something again?"

"No. I just like your bottom."

I clenched the muscles in my butt. Bella feigned a moan.

"Stop that or we won't go! Stop it right now."

"Then get your hands off my ass, Chiquita."

I got my dress on and Bella leaned over and zipped it up for me. I brushed the material down over my body, smoothing it into place. I sat down on the side of the bed next to Bella and put on my heels. They weren't particularly high, less than three inches. But much higher than I was used to. I was amazed I managed so well with them on Wednesday since I absolutely rarely wear them.

"Hey, Bell?"

"What, baby?"

"I don't go to mass anymore. But I do like going to Midnight Mass on Christmas, because its only function is the birth of Christ. Would you go with me to that?"

"I think we can manage that with no problem."

"I wish we could have gotten married next week."

"Darling, you're going to have to let that go. You're just going to have to. I know how much you wanted it, but it's just not going to happen. No matter how much you wish it would."

"I'm sorry," I said.

I don't know why I couldn't let go of this one. Both of us put our keys, billfold, and lip gloss in our clutches and sat down on the couch waiting until it was time to go. We watched the news and then something on the Discovery Channel. Finally, I looked at my watch and it was about six-thirty. We got up and headed for the garage. There was a parking garage next door to her office building making it easy to find a place to put the truck. I dropped Bella off on the front curb in front of her building and then went and parked the truck. I got back to the building and found her leaning up against a wall waiting for me.

"You okay?" I asked.

"Very much so. Tonight, will be a breeze."

"Let me know if you get tired and we need to kick this scene."

"Will do."

"What do you want to do for your name?"

"Do what?"

"Pope. Ward. Ward-Pope. Have you thought about it much?"

"Wow. That was random. Pope, of course. Is that okay with you?"

"Fine. I'm not that particular. But Pops would like it."

"Okay then."

"All right then."

We rode the elevator to the top floor. We stepped off the elevator into a wide-open room. There were tables all along one wall with food and drinks. There were chairs lining the other three walls. Christmas music was softly playing over a PA system. The lights weren't dark, but not bright either. Like they had only switched on every other bank of them. It was quite nice. I carried both of our purses over my left arm, and held a glass of wine in each hand, making it easier for Bella to walk with her crutches.

From our right, an older gentleman and a woman who was probably his wife approached us.

"Ms. Ward. Happy to have you with us tonight. How are you?"

"I'm well. But you might not want to get too used to using that name."

"Why not? Are you going to change it?"

"I'm getting married in a week and a half. Mr. Parker, may I present my fiancée, Kathleen Pope. She's a firefighter here in St. Paul. And please, call me Bella."

"Well congratulations. And this is my wife, Carina. Thank you for coming tonight. My, my, a firefighter. How exciting! Thank you for your service, Kathleen. Anyway, both of you have a wonderful time. Oh, and get well soon. I heard about that from Reynolds."

We walked off in another direction.

"Are you going to have to tell everybody and their dog what I do every time we meet them? And who was that guy?"

"To answer your first question, no. But it was based on my answer to question two. I manage a group. There are four groups in our division. Many others in the company, but my division has four. McNally is the Assistant Vice President for our entire division. Reynolds is the Vice President over him as well as five other divisions. And Mr. Parker is the Executive Vice President of all accounting and investment divisions. He's the one to impress. Big time. And the fact that he knew me on sight was a good sign. You were right, Kathleen. Not being here wouldn't be noticed but being here would be."

We ended up running into both Reynolds and McNally with their wives. And I got to meet Bella's Admin Assistant, Courtney Braun and her husband Craig.

"Hi, Courtney! How are you doing?"

"Hi Bella. This is my husband. And this must be Kathleen. I've got to tell you, she probably works harder now that she's met you, but she's a lot happier. I can tell that, even doing everything over the phone and internet. She's keeping everything right on track. She's really impressing some people."

"I hope she isn't as mean to you as she is to me at home!"

"Oh, stop it. She's sweet to me. Always has been. She's the only boss I think I've ever had that knows it's easier to attract more bees with sugar than it is with vinegar."

"So, Craig. Are you going to be all right being dragged around getting introduced tonight to everybody? Maybe we could get a beer and go off and sit down somewhere," I joked.

"If only you knew how good that sounds," said Craig.

"Oh, shut up. He'll be fine once everybody starts eating and he gets to pig out. Then he'll be happy as a little clam. We'll see you two before we leave. Bye for now."

"She sure seems capable."

"I couldn't have asked for a better AA. She's a brilliant combination of old school discipline and business style, mixed with a real understanding for change and for the technology that accompanies that change."

"And of course you've let her know that?"

"Of course. I encourage her every chance I get. I don't shine if she doesn't shine. We're a team."

We moved around the room meeting people. I refilled our wine glasses once while Bella was talking to some old woman that did something somewhere. I frankly couldn't keep up with who did what and what their names were. People were starting to eat, so I put down the wine glasses on a cleanup tray and filled up a plate with food. I found Bella and we shared the plate. When it was empty, I went back and filled it again. After I threw the plate away, I was introduced to yet another person, but at least this time it was somebody in management at about her level.

I'm guessing the woman was about forty or so. That made it even more impressive to know that Bella was on par with this woman but half her age. Her name was Lilly.

"Lilly, could I ask you for a huge favor?" I asked.

"I'll try? What would you like?"

"Would you come out in the hallway with Bella and I?"

"Sure," she replied.

Once we were in the hallway, I had her take half a dozen photos of the two of us together after setting down the crutches where they weren't in the photo. I had Bella leaning against me for support.

"Thanks ever so much. It's just that I don't really have much of the two of us together dressed up."

"Don't worry about it, happy to do it."

We went back inside and milled about talking to various people, drinking a bit more wine, until about eleven o'clock, then went to the house. We went inside, got dressed for bed, and went straight to sleep. Tomorrow would be moving day.

I'd asked a couple of guys on my shift to give me a hand for about an hour or so on Sunday. It wouldn't take much time. Mostly clothes, truthfully. I got a dozen boxes from the basement and a roll of tape and put it in the back of my truck. I normally have the third-row seat in the garage anyway, but I took out the second-row seats as well to have more room to get boxes in. I drove over to the apartment and got to work.

I taped the bottom of the boxes and took several into the bedroom. I put everything from the top two drawers of the dresser in the first box. The third and fourth drawers each got their own box since the drawers were deeper. Another box held most of Bella's shoes. The last three pair started another box and I started taking everything off the shelf in the closet and started boxing that up.

The guys from the Station were downstairs and called my phone to let me know they had arrived. I buzzed them up and then went to the front door and propped it open so they'd be able to get in. I kept working on the bedroom. It took two boxes just for her CD's and DVD's. I had the guys start taking everything from the fridge and pantry and start boxing that. I was parked in front today pretty close to the main door. John was there and I had him start taking the boxes down to put in my SUV. After we had one layer of boxes toward the front of the truck Oliver started taking the hanging clothes and laying them down over the boxes in a neat pile.

The kitchen was done so they took those boxes down to the truck. Even with two layers of boxes, the kitchen and bedroom items pretty much filled my truck. Oliver had a four-by-four pickup with a topper on the back of it. We started loading everything from the office into the back of the truck after laying down a wool blanket that he carried.

All of the stuff from the drawers went in a couple of boxes, but there was her laptop, her printer, her power strip, her external monitor, mouse, and keyboard. We worked for less than the hour I promised them it would take, and were ready to caravan over to my house. I took one last walk through the house and made sure everything was gathered up. It wasn't critical, because we would come back to clean, and we undoubtedly would let Bella check through everything.

The last thing I did was going through the bathroom and gathering up everything from the counter along with the towels and washrags so I could wash them. I remembered at the last minute to pull the sheets and mattress cover off so that I could wash those too.

John drove Bella's car over to the house with Oliver planning on taking him back to the apartment to get his truck. It's a thing with firefighters: ninety-five percent or more drove pickups, SUV's, or specifically Chevy Suburbans. I went inside the house and picked up Tinkerbelle and took her to the bathroom, putting her inside and shutting the door where she could get to her litterbox but be kept out of the rest of the house.

Bella was asleep on the couch when I walked in. I stood over her with my hands on my hips.

"Yes, I heard you come in. I'm just resting my eyes."

"Bullshit. You were asleep."

"Okay, you caught me. Now give me a kiss then leave me alone."

I leaned down and gave her a dozen kisses or more, then started bringing in all stuff we brought home. We started by taking the hanging up clothes upstairs and put it in the second walk-in closet, which I had cleared just for Bella, in the master bedroom. When we got upstairs with the first load, Oliver looked at me.

"Jesus, she is *smoking* hot. I wish my wife was that good looking!"

"I'll have to remember and tell her that next time I see her."

"You will not. I'm just saying... I'm not saying there's anything wrong with you at all, Kathleen, but man or woman, you hit the damned jackpot!"

I had to laugh at that.

"You don't know the half of it. On the one hand, she's the smartest person I've ever met. On the other she's the most innocent person in the world. I don't mean dumb, I mean she's just so... Childlike. Don't say anything but quite frankly I'm glad that I impress her. I wish she knew for real how much she impresses me. Now let's get all the boxes inside and I'll introduce everybody. I can unpack it all myself later this afternoon."

We finished getting everything inside and everybody gathered in the living room. Bella was sitting in the corner of the couch with a fleece blanket covering her lap.

"Belladonna Ward, John Miller, Oliver Davis, Scott Dunn. Everybody, my girlfriend, Bella."

I'd started to say fiancée, but caught myself in time. Everybody of course said 'pleased to meet you' or an equivalent. Hands were shaken all around.

"Anybody want a beer?" I asked.

"I've got to go do the family thing," said John.

"I'll take one. But just one. I can't stay too long," Scott chimed in.

"I'll have to take a rain check Pope. I'm in the middle of laying new tile in the main bathroom. I won't get any grouting done this weekend but I was hoping to get all the tile down and on the walls. I'm going to go ahead and take off. Thanks, though. Bella, good to meet you. I know we'll run across each other soon. Hopefully by then you'll have two good ankles to walk on," he laughed.

"Here's to that!" Bella said holding up her beer in a salute.

"Thanks for coming by guys. See you tonight at work."

"So, Bella, Kath says that you do something in business. What exactly do you do?"

"Have you heard of the company Pfister-Blankenship?"

"Sure. Almost everybody around here has. Of course, when you're a firefighter in St. Paul you pretty much know the companies that own their own high-rise."

"I'm the manager of one of the accounting groups."

"You're a manager? Your nose is growing, Pinocchio. I want to see your driver's license to see if you're even old enough to vote!"

"I get that all the time. But believe me, I'm older than I look, and I've had lots of training," Bella laughed.

"To tell you the truth when I first saw your pictures on Pope's tablet at work I thought she would get arrested by the vice squad for dating a high school girl."

"You're too funny. Hopefully all the ribbing I get now will pay off when I'm old and don't look it."

"Bella, Scott is the dude I punched out at the Station," I said.

"You told her about that?"

"Sure. I've told her everything since we've been together."

"I have to say, you two sure have moved fast. I mean, to move in and everything. It must be serious."

"Scott, can you absolutely keep a secret? I mean swear on your mother's grave kind of secret?"

"You know I can. I mean, I can act stupidly sometimes, or at least say stupid stuff, but you can trust me one thousand percent."

I don't know what possessed me, but I just felt like I needed to shout it out at the top of my lungs. I went over to the couch and sat next Bella and pulled the blanket over my lap too and put my arm around Bella. I leaned in and gave her a couple or three kisses quickly. Then I looked straight at Scotty.

"Go ahead, Sweetie. Show him."

Bella had been holding her beer with her right hand, but her left hand had been under the blanket in her lap. Not intentionally, just because it was chilly. She flipped the edge back as she brought her hand out and not so shyly shoved it out for Scott to see, wiggling her fingers to show off the sparkle in the diamond.

"We're getting married on New Year's Eve," I said with a grin.

Scott just stared. He didn't move. He just let it sink in.

"I'm blown away. Oh my God. I have no response. No words."

"Good? Bad? Indifferent?"

Bella just sat there smiling, holding my hand under the blanket.

Finally, Scott spoke, "I promise that I won't say anything. Are you planning on telling anybody else?"

"Sure. After the fact. But we're going to have my parents as witnesses and go in front of a judge. No big deal. In and out and nobody gets hurt. I'll bring a couple of pictures to work after we do the deed. I'm taking off the first day of January so we'll have a couple of days off alone. I think for our honeymoon we may drive up the North Shore and maybe stay the night at Two Harbors. Drive up to Thunder Bay for the afternoon. Bella can't walk around much but it would be cool to see the woods covered in snow, I think. Nothing solid. Just going to play it nice and loose."

"Well, thanks for telling me. That means a lot that you would tell me first. And by the way, I'm really sorry for being so stupid at the Station house the other day. Really."

"Pish-posh. It's already forgotten. Let it go."

"Well, thanks for the beer. I have to take off. My wife has somewhere she wants to go this afternoon. I hope it's not crafting. I hate that shit. That's what she has a sister for. And my sister, for that matter. Both of them like that sort of thing. But Clarice thinks it's great 'alone time' for the two of us. I'd rather go to the dentist. She likes fishing; I wish she'd go fishing with me more and do that crap with the womenfolk instead."

"Well thanks for giving up part of your day off to help me and my lovely bride-to-be. It's greatly appreciated."

"Hey, you do stuff for people all the time. It's the least I could do."

"Thanks, Scott. Come give me a hug. It's hard for me to get up," said Bella.

He did, and then made his exit.

"How are we going to get my car home?"

"It's home. John drove it here and Oliver took him back to the apartment to get his own truck. Sweetie, it's official. We live together. You're home. Let me go let kitty-kitty out of the bathroom, then put up the refrigerator stuff. Everything else we can work on later."

I leaned down and kissed Bella over and over and held her tightly in my arms. I was really going to get used to this. One thing I wanted to do before I got started on anything else. I got Bella's purse, then went into the kitchen and picked up my extra set of keys to the house and my truck and put the ring through Bella's keys.

"There. *Now* it's official. You're a U-Haul Lesbian! This is your house. I hope you really don't mind living here. It's all I've got but what I have is yours."

"Kathleen, don't ever think that anything about your life is substandard. Don't try to 'live up' to anything for me. Just be yourself, always be yourself. It's *you* that I'm in love with. Remember, I walked away from my parents' lifestyle. It just wasn't for me. I could have had that. Hell, my parents even tried to set me up with a doctor. He was actually a total hunk. And made a huge amount of money. He was a neurosurgeon. There was only one major flaw with him."

"And that was?"

"He had a penis. Ick."

We both laughed until our sides hurt. I let Tinkerbelle out and began putting up cold food. Then I went through the pantry and cabinets and put anything that was old in an empty box to give to the food bank. I started loading all the rest of the dry goods where I'd created empty spaces. The next thing I did was to take all the computer gear in the office. I cleared off my desk and set up Bella's equipment so that she'd be able to work tomorrow right out of the gate. I did the bathroom stuff next. Then I went to the bedroom and consolidated the small dresser removing a lot of things and putting them on the bed in the guest room for the moment.

I moved everything from the big dresser to the small dresser or to the guest bedroom, and then put everything from Bella's old dresser into the large dresser. It was bigger than her old one so I kept the bottom drawer for several pairs of sweats and shorts. I went downstairs and told Bella that it was all in the dresser and she'd need to find time to arrange it however she wanted it. I put all the CD's and DVD's along the outside wall of the living room for the moment. That had almost all of Bella's things put at least temporarily away.

"You know girl, you travel pretty light. But there's more stuff than would fit in your Lexus. How did you get it all moved up here from Texas? Or did you buy it all here?"

"Pfister actually paid to move what little I have up here. There's more at my parents' house but I kind of left in a huff. And like a thief in the middle of the night. Well, actually afternoon. Mama and Daddy were both at work, and I got some movers in and grabbed the basics and absconded. I spent the night in a hotel in Tulsa the first night. Then drove to Joplin the next day and turned north until I got here. The apartment was waiting for me. And of course I had some clothes and my makeup with me. That's my story and I'm sticking to it."

"You never told me that. And you wonder why they're so pissed off at you?"

"That's not the reason they're pissed. They're pissed at the underlying cause. I just avoided the inevitable confrontation."

"Well, I've got a website that I'll forward to you in email that's a local company where you can design our announcements online, they print them, and you go by and pick them up. Or they send them if you want, for a little extra. You can do that when you have a chance, and even though we're going to send them out as an after-the-fact thing, we can go ahead and send some to everybody in your family. If that's okay with you. But don't do it to needle them. Do it to inform them that this is the way life is going to be. And you should probably list both my parents and your parents, even though yours won't be there."

"You're right, of course. I just have trouble staying objective about it. Let me tell you something. I was in the first grade and I thought I had a crush on a girl. We had a beautiful teacher. Her name was Miss Cabiness. I mean, so totally beautiful. And it was only her second-year teaching. She was really young. One day we were giving oral reports on something or other. I don't even remember what. But after I gave mine she gave me this giant hug before I went back to my desk. I lost my girl crush on my classmate. I wanted to marry Miss Cabiness. That's when I really knew that I liked girls. And my parents knew it within a couple of years of that. And that was seventeen years ago. They still don't get it."

"Then they're never going to get it. Get over it. Move on. Keep loving them as much as you can for what they are, your family, and surround yourself with people who will support you. What about the three guys I had over here today? Totally non-judgmental. Totally supportive. I'm just saying…"

"What would I do without you?"

"You'd do just fine, I imagine."

"But life would be so mundane. You give me fire, and I don't mean your job. I mean a reason to keep moving and going and everything. I miss you when you're gone for a whole day, and even on your days off when you're out at the gym and doing whatever. It's really strange, and counterintuitive. You'd think being distracted all the time my work would suffer. But I think about you non-stop while I'm working and I can do a better job with you by my side than before I met you. You're a miracle worker. And a pretty darn good cook. And as a lover, you're at best passable."

"I'm going to make you pay for that one," I said as I jerked the blanket off of her and jumped on top of her, tickling her ribs.

"Stop, I give, stop…I take it back, I take it back…"

We laughed and kissed and hugged and then just to prove her wrong, I started unbuttoning her shirt. She lay back and gave me a free rein.

CHAPTER TEN

Monday morning at five-fifteen, the alarms went off. They rolled Engine 7, Engine 9, and Engine 17. Along with the three main pumpers they rolled both Medic 9 and Medic 17. There was a natural gas leak. We were being moved onsite as a precaution, in case there were any trapped pockets that triggered explosions. And of course, the Medics for any burns or other injuries. The gas company had about twenty people out trying to determine the exact source, along with five people from the Forensics and Arson team with chemical sniffers. There were also four or five ambulances from hospitals and private services in the area.

There must have been about fifteen police squad cars out evacuating people from houses. Fortunately, it was almost thirty degrees. It would have been especially brutal if it had happened when it was below zero. Once the people were out of their houses, they were led upwind and away and loaded on Metro buses to a holding point in two churches several blocks away. It was also fortunate that it was a weekend and not a weekday, which would have put even more of a burden on the families.

Our job was pretty much to enter the area and wait. And unlike every other instance where we leave the engines on the vehicles running, this time, they had to be shut off due to the possibility of an ignition hazard with the natural gas. It got very cold just sitting there. And we had to wait until not only the situation was resolved, but also until they made sure there weren't any residual depressions filled with gas. Since it's heavier than the ambient air, it wouldn't necessarily disperse.

It was after four in the afternoon when we were given the all clear to return to our respective Stations. I think there was a simultaneous cheer from everybody all together. I was impressed though, to see that District Chief 3 was still there in his Suburban. The Lieutenant was there, but they figured it was a big enough deal that the Chief was there as well, and instead of bailing, he waited with the rest of us. I'm not sure what the other two Chiefs are like; I haven't heard one way or another. But he and our Lieutenant are both top notch.

When we got back to the Station, hot coffee was waiting for everybody, and as soon as we'd slugged down a cup, we all headed for the showers to get doused in hot water for about fifteen minutes. While that almost did the trick, I was still a little chilled when I got off at midnight. I ended up not getting to call Bella until almost six-thirty.

"Hey, stinky. Did you chase any firebugs today?"

"No, but we did have to babysit a gas leak. We were there 'if needed' without our engines running. For hours. Ugh."

"I thought you always ran your motors the whole time. They're diesel, aren't they?"

"Spark hazard if a cloud of gas came by. Remember that it's colorless. Did you know that natural gas doesn't have any color, any odor, or any taste until they add methylmercapto? That's actually what you smell, not the gas."

"Sounds absolutely awful. Are you warm enough now, baby?"

"Almost. Everybody had a cup or two of coffee or tea and then took a hot shower. Best medicine you could have."

"Except to crawl under the covers with me."

"I think you would have kicked me out after about ten minutes because I would have been so cold against you. So, what have you been doing today?"

"The wireless wasn't working with my laptop here. I turned off the power to the modem and router and then turned them back on in order.

That rebuilt the IP address tables. So, I'm good to go. I scanned in the photos of us from the studio, from the Christmas party, and the ones of you from the non-fire downtown. I wrote an email to each member of my family and attached the photos of the party and of you. See? I'm not totally giving up yet. I was just upset the other day."

"I know you were. But I had to just give you space to calm down in your own time."

"I'm glad you did. I like the fact that you don't pressure me. You're so... Grown up. You're my first girlfriend that... No, let me rephrase that. My previous girlfriends didn't understand that really. But my fiancée, now, she's a pretty smart cookie. Oh, by the way, I went online and built our announcements. Check your email. You can save a .jpg file of them to compare. It has a watermark on it of course so you can't use it as is, but that way you could look at them and tell me what you think before I order them."

"I trust your judgment."

"Pull out your tablet while we're talking and check it out."

I did. What I saw about sent me into a tailspin. It announced that we'd gotten married at the Ramsey County Courthouse, with the date of December thirty-first. It said that Belladonna Elizabeth Ward Pope was wed to Kathleen Marie Pope. It listed the parents of Bella along with my parents. I was really surprised she did end up adding her parents, and it was nice that she listed Martha as my mother. Pops would really like that. There were three designs with the same wording.

"They're perfect, Bell. I like number two the best."

"I was hoping you'd say that. I already ordered them," she laughed.

"You are *such* a brat!" I retorted.

"I'm kidding. I wouldn't do that without asking you, my love. You're so gullible. Ha ha. This says that if the order is in place by seven o'clock in the morning they can be picked up by three-thirty in the afternoon. If we want to pay a little extra for rush. I do. Sound okay to you?"

"Sounds perfect. I'll call you later tonight. Unless you need anything, and then call me. I love you, sweetie."

"I love you too. See you in a little while. Mwah."

It was fairly dead. I called Scott over, along with a couple of the other guys.

"Here it is. I'm warning you all, if you say one damned word, I'll punch your lights out. If you don't think I will, ask Scott."

"She did. She punched me right in the gut. Straight punch. No hesitation whatsoever."

I pulled up the photos on the tablet and began scrolling through the ones of us from the studio. Everybody thought they looked cool. They all made comments that we both looked beautiful. Then I got to the half dozen photos from the party.

"Holy shit, Batman! Is that you? Honest to God?" exclaimed Oliver.

"I told you to shut up. I just wanted everybody to know that I do have a girly side to me, too."

"Those images are burned into my retinas. You're both right off the red carpet on Oscars' night."

I think I may have blushed at that. In fact, I know that I blushed. Not only could I feel my face on fire, but everybody around me thought it was necessary to point it out to me. Rat bastards. Even though the Chief doesn't work shifts and works through the week, he had been here this weekend for our run. He'd joined up with the crews about nine in the morning. But he was still at the Station finishing up paperwork. He and the Lieu came over to see what all the commotion was about. So, I started from the beginning with the photos.

"Kevin has got to be so proud of his little girl. And I know that your mom would have been too. I still remember my wife and I sitting down to dinner with your family when you were a youngster," said the Chief.

"Thank you, sir. It's very kind of you to say."

"Nonsense. You make us all proud of you with the work you do here as well. Your whole family has been devoted. Even as a housewife, your lovely mother supported all our functions, our charities, and special little projects for one or two of the guys in need... I'm just glad you didn't stay with the police department. I was afraid that even though you wanted to be a firefighter from the age of ten or twelve we were going to have a turncoat in our midst and your father would take you over to the dark side."

"No, sir, that never would have had a snowball's chance. I've always wanted bunker gear. Not a Second Chance and a flashlight. That's sissy shit," I laughed with him.

FALLING INTO FIRE

The Lieu looked at me when he was sure that nobody else was looking and gave me a wink. I probably shouldn't have told Scott we were getting married but even tonight I wanted to show everybody my announcements and didn't. I was like a pressure cooker that was boiling and the valve was stuck shut. I called Bella about ten after ten just to talk to her and calm myself down. I told her I wanted to shout it to the world.

"We need to go and buy a simple gold band for me. That way I can wear it to work. It can't have anything in it or protruding at all or I'll have to take it off every shift. I want a ring I can put on and never have to take off."

"Well, if I get one that I never have to take off, then you should have one too. We can go tomorrow night after I get off. And tomorrow afternoon you can go get the announcements. If you want to. After you go to the gym and everything."

"I'll still go to the gym sometimes, but I have a treadmill, a weight bench, and free weights in the basement. I'll only have to go to the gym a couple of days a week. The rest I can do from home. I forgot that you haven't been all the way in the basement. You Houston people don't have basements much, do you?"

"Not for the most part. Different kind of bedrock. Based on sandstone. Used to all be an ocean down there, you know."

"I should know that. My electives were mostly geography. Sorry. Lapse in memory. I'll be home in a couple of hours. Why don't you try and get some sleep? You'll be tired tomorrow if you don't."

"I may just do that. Hey, by the way, I've had a shadow all day. And I mean all day."

"You mean Stinkerbell?" I laughed.

"Don't call her that! But I do. She's adorable."

"That's cool. Love you, sweetie."

"Love you. See you in a bit."

I had already changed uniforms once today and had a shower after we got back to the station, so tonight I didn't need to change. But I did brush my teeth and bush my hair out. I put on a little neutral pink lip-gloss and went into the day room. John looked up from his newspaper to see who came in. Only half the lights are on in the dayroom after hours, so that you can see with no problem but they're not glaring at you. Even so, he smiled at me.

"Lookit. You're wearing girl stuff again. I must say, Pope, this new girl of yours has certainly changed you."

"If you mean she's made me totally happy, that's affirmative."

He looked back down at his paper and kept reading. I smiled to myself. I've always been a tomboy and that wouldn't change, but I kind of liked being treated this way. It made me feel good about myself. I weightlift and exercise knowing it only makes me look less feminine but it's what I have to do to be the best I can at what I do. And I don't mind it at all. In fact, I'm proud of my body, to tell you the honest truth. Very much so. Even so it was just always something I tried to ignore, and was usually successful at.

The end of shift was slow coming. It was as if somebody put the batteries in the clock backwards. But finally, C shift was coming in and I was warming up my SUV. I had to make a mental effort to keep my foot off of the gas pedal driving home. I didn't need to get a ticket. That would have just made me get home later anyway, thus defeating the purpose of hurrying home. This was the first night off shift coming home to Bella in 'our' house. And even though I was only half way home, I couldn't keep the smile off my face.

A few minutes later I was opening the lock on our door and slithering in. I set my bag down by the front door on the right side where everybody took off their muddy boots on the plastic runner. I crept up the stairs, but they creaked like dickens being an older house.

"Hey, lover. Welcome home. Isn't this so cool?" Bella called out to me when I was only halfway up the stairs.

"Hi, sweetie. I have to admit this is pretty special."

I entered the bedroom and the light was on and Bella was sitting up reading a book.

"Didn't you even try to get a nap in?"

"I couldn't tonight. I promise you I'll get better at it. It's just too new and I was so excited that you were going to be home. I couldn't have slept if you put a gun to my head, so I decided to just relax and read a little."

I sat down on the edge of the bed. I picked up Bella's hand in mine and looked her straight in the face.

"I don't want you as my lover or as my girlfriend. I want you to be my wife. Forever. Until death do us part. Are you sure that's what you want?"

FALLING INTO FIRE

"Of course. Isn't that what you want? You didn't ask me to go steady with you. You didn't ask me to move in with you. You asked me to marry you. That usually entails the whole ball of wax, doesn't it? Are *you* sure?"

I got up on top of the bed and moved over next to Bella. I took her face in my hands and kissed her over and over. Softly. Gently. Over and over.

"I love you Bella. I don't think I would be able to live without you now. One of my strengths is that I'm so independent. I still am, as far as being able to function on my own. But mentally, without you around me I would fall to pieces. I'd go into a depression so far that I would literally be unable to do anything. Everything that I do in life from this point on, I do for us. Not for me. Even if it's something that I do on my own it's something that in some way makes us stronger as a couple. Having you beside me is just too good to be true."

"Do you think I don't feel the same way?" she asked.

Bella pulled the covers back on my side of the bed. I took off my uniform and put it in the hamper. I climbed in bed next to Bella and pulled the covers up over my shoulder and got as close to her as I could without being inside her skin.

"Turn out the light, sweetie," I told Bella.

She turned the lamp off, and in the darkness, our hands began to explore each other in the most exquisite fashion. Sleep was not found quickly. I knew it would be hard on Bella in the morning, but quite frankly neither of us cared at that particular moment in time.

The next day I was putting things up in the kitchen. The desk in the office is against the adjoining wall so you couldn't see into the rest of the house from there, giving Bella privacy for her work. I had already started washing the sheets and had the towels in a basket ready to wash next so that I could put them back in the apartment. I also had a couple of baskets of laundry for Bella and I. I was being domesticated. I didn't mind the extra clothes since it didn't take any more loads. You still have to wash the right stuff in the right temperature and it takes so many loads. And besides, I enjoyed doing things for Bella. A lot. After I put the first load in, I told Bella that I was going out for a little bit.

I went over to Edgars' Jewelers hoping they'd be open. Thankfully they were. I went to the necklaces and found some pendants that were single letters in script. I picked out one that was a capital 'P' for Pope.

It was in white gold with a diamond at the top, about an inch tall, and got a twenty-two-inch white gold chain to go with it. I had them wrap it for Bella for Christmas. Then I asked about a plain white gold wedding band. Eight millimeters wide. And only ten karats to make it harder, less likely to scratch so easily at work. I had them wrap the ring separately so I could go ahead and give that to Bella to give to me.

When I got home I first went to the basement and started a second load of laundry. I went upstairs to the kitchen and got out everything for making sandwiches. I already had Bella hooked on one of my favorite sandwiches. Beef cotto salami on wheat bread, and Green Goddess dressing instead of mayonnaise or mustard. A couple of pieces of red leaf lettuce. And a slice of tomato. I made two of them and cut them from corner to corner, putting them on plates. I added some cheese puffs and grabbed two sodas. I took them in the living room and set them on the coffee table, turning on the television. I walked into the office and tapped Bella on the shoulder. She was just looking over some things for the week's schedule. There weren't very many people working on Christmas Eve I knew, but Bella was, like a trooper. I made the motions with my face and hands of eating and jerked my head in the direction of the front of the house. She held her hand in an 'okay' sign and I went back into the living room.

Bella joined me about twenty minutes later.

"Why haven't you eaten yet, baby?"

"I wasn't that hungry, so I just waited for you."

"You're so sweet to me. Give me a kiss."

We ate in silence, with my feet up on the coffee table and her legs propped over mine.

"You're pretty," I said to Bella.

"Hush."

"I mean it. You are so pretty. How did I end up with you?"

"I could say the same about you. In fact, I do say it to myself several times a day. I do. Every time I look at you, every time I feel your body against mine, with or without clothes on, you send shivers down my spine. You electrify me."

"It's too bad we can't take off two weeks and go somewhere warm."

"You're changing the subject. And besides, what good would it do if I can't get around very well. If we went to a beach somewhere I'd just get sand in my cast and I'd be in a world of hurt."

"I guess. At least I have off the First of January. That'll give us a few days off together without interruptions."

"I already have off the thirty-first through the third. I'll get off on Monday too and that way we'll have almost all week off together. Oh, go in and get the calendar off the printer."

I set my sandwich down and went into the office. There were two legal size pages with a month's activities on each, one on top of the other. The top one was December, the bottom one was January. On the top one was our wedding day, and both had days off that Bella had scheduled, holidays, and had a big red 'x' in the top right-hand corner of each square that I was on shift.

"Put them on the fridge for me if you would. I don't know if you have any magnets or not, so you can tape them up for now if you need to. But that way I can keep up with when you work."

"You're so organized that you can't stop, can you?" I laughed at Bella.

"I just like to keep on top of everything."

"Oh my God. Is the house now going to be re-arranged?"

"That's different. I'm talking about keeping up with your shifts. I'm not used to a three-day week. I know I'd be forever getting it wrong."

"Don't worry. It took me almost a year to quit being afraid that I'd missed a shift. And as far as rearranging the house goes? Knock yourself out. Whatever you want to do. Change the furniture? Paint a room? New paper in the kitchen? I know we haven't talked about it but I'd actually planned on living here for a while. It's a lovely neighborhood, it's fairly close to Pops and work both, and it's big enough. If you want to move and we have enough money, then we can do that. I like my house, but it's just a house for goodness sakes. And I only moved in about two years ago."

"May I ask you a question?"

"Sure."

"Did…Melanie ever live here with you?"

"No, sweetie. I got the house the second week of November. It was already in the works, but it hadn't closed yet. And she and I split on Halloween night two weeks before. You're the only one who's ever lived in the house with me. Does that make you feel better?"

"It shouldn't, but it does. I mean, I'm not usually jealous or anything, but it's just more special knowing that I'm the only one."

I turned Bella around where she was in the corner of the couch sitting sideways. Then I grabbed her behind the knees and pulled her slowly until she was lying flat on the couch. I lay down beside her and ran my hand through her hair, smelling it.

"Quit sniffing me. You're not a dog."

"I'm just smelling your shampoo. I like it."

"You're silly."

I didn't answer her. And I didn't stop brushing her hair with my hand. And I didn't stop smelling it.

"Don't forget we have to take you back to the orthopedist on Friday."

"I hope he gives me a removable cast."

"Don't count on it. You messed it up badly. You may end up doing the whole stretch in a hard cast. Hopefully they'll at least be able to give you a walking cast at some point. Maybe not, being that the damage is in your ankle. You know, I always used to think that fate was an evil thing. Because I related it to every old relationship I ever had. But now I feel that I understand fate better. Fate brought us together."

"No, you brought us together. You danced your way right into my heart. Somebody you hadn't ever laid eyes on. You swept me off my feet."

"I'll cop to stealing your heart but you swept yourself off your feet. That's why we met," I joked to her.

"Point made and taken."

I put my finger over her lips to quiet her. Then I replaced my finger with my lips. We kissed and held each other for about fifteen or twenty minutes, when she said she really needed to get back to work.

Bella went back to work until about four o'clock and then came into the living room and we watched TV for a couple of hours. I told Bella to get up and get dressed so we could go out for dinner. She asked where we were going, but I ignored her. I went out to get the SUV and helped her in.

Once we arrived, I went around to the passenger's side, reached in and took the crutches and held them up for her in one hand and reached out with my other hand to support her getting out of the truck. Bella made a loud, primal, grunting sound, but swung her legs around and stood up on the pavement. I gave her the crutches and we went inside. It was very dimly lit affair, with a long 'L-shaped' bar and several tables, with a pool table at the far end. There weren't but about a dozen people in here tonight. We took a table away from the front so there wouldn't be so much cold air off the glass. Our waitress showed up as soon as she finished taking beers to the next table over.

"Hi. What can I get you two to drink tonight?"

"Two draught, dark lagers," I ordered for both of us.

"Do you want a menu or do you already know what you want?"

"Two walleye dinners, but instead of potato fries would you substitute fried mushrooms, please."

"No problem. Be back in a jiffy."

"So, this is it, is it? I'm going to lose my mythical 'Walleye Virginity' tonight?"

"In the most indescribable way. And nobody does it better than this little hole in the wall."

"Is this where the burgers came from?"

"No, that was a different place. And the fish from there isn't bad. But for the best fish you come here."

The waitress brought our drinks to us and set out some condiments.

"Excuse me, but could you bring me a small bowl about half full of mayonnaise so that I can make up a little sauce for the mushrooms, along with some soy sauce if you have any?"

"Sure thing. I'll go check."

"What are you doing, Kathleen? I'd be too embarrassed to ask for that stuff."

"It'll all be worth it. You'll see."

The waitress brought everything to the table for me and smiled at us. I added a small squirt of mustard, some Worcestershire sauce, a little bit of soy sauce, and some salt and pepper.

"It's best if you add a little garlic, but it'll be okay."

We talked for a little while waiting for the food to be brought out. Finally, it arrived at the table.

"Be careful there, everything just came straight out of the fryer. It's hot. And would there be anything else for you for now?" asked the server.

"Thank you, we're fine."

"Let me know if you need anything."

I watched Bella's face as she stared at the food. She finally picked up a fork and started breaking the fish apart so it would cool, and stabbed one of the mushrooms, dipping it in the sauce I made. She put it in her mouth, but immediately took it back out. She fanned her mouth and blew on it for a half a minute, then tried again. This time it was okay.

"Jeez! This is fantastic. Man."

"Told you it would be worth it. Wait until you try the fish."

After giving the fish a few moments to cool off, she put a bite into her mouth.

"So, is it as good as catfish?" I asked her, although I suspected I knew what the answer would be.

"Oh, this is much, much better. It has a much lighter taste. By the way, just to make sure it got there in time, and to make sure that they wouldn't find out about it some other way, I sent the sample of the announcements to my mom and dad. I don't know how they would get notice, but you just never know. Stranger things have happened. Dad does have several friends at the Mayo. And that's a pretty tightly knit group. I don't have any clue how one of them would find out but if they did... Well let's just say I'd rather them hear it from me."

"That's fine. It was probably cleansing to do so anyway, wasn't it? Admit it."

"A little bit. I'll still send everybody a real one."

"Of course."

Bella and I ate our dinner slowly and talked about our pasts, filling in little bits and bobs from here and there about growing up. Bella paid the check and we went back home. Just before we'd left the house, while Bella was in front of me and couldn't see, I'd quickly put both packages in the tree. We came back inside, got out of our coats and gloves, and sat down on the couch. It didn't take her two seconds to spot the presents in the tree.

"Okay, now I'm pissed. You got me something and I didn't have any ability to go out and get you anything."

"No, one of them is from you to me, and the other one is for you."

I got both packages and gave her my wedding band.

"That's the one from you to me. Don't worry, I slipped your credit card out and paid for it with your account."

"Aren't you the clever one? So here, I guess, is your Christmas present. Enjoy it."

I took it and feigned surprise.

"For me? I wonder what it is?"

I opened the outer box and removed the ring box. I opened the ring box, and showed her my wedding band.

"I want you to keep it for me until we get married next week. How sweet does that sound? Next week? And this is for you, my sweet lover."

I handed her the long package. She unwrapped it and opened the box.

"Oh, it's got a 'P'. It's perfect. Thank you, baby," she said hugging me.

"Next year we'll both be ambulatory and have more time. We'll do a little better than this year."

"Kathleen, I think all in all we've done okay this year, don't you? And by the way, go up to my dresser and get your present out of the top drawer."

"How did you get me a present? Just one sec," I said as I scooted up the stairs and back down holding a flat wrapped package.

I dug into the paper, and when I opened it I was stunned. It was a picture frame around an eight-by-ten cropped photo of us in our dresses from the party. A sterling silver frame. And there was a small flat spot in the middle of the bottom for engraving. It said, *'Kathleen & Bella, 06 December 2013'*.

"I wasn't sure whether to use the sixth or the seventh. On Friday, we both got girl-crushes on each other. And on Saturday, we officially connected I guess you could say. But I knew when you were holding my hand in the ER that it was meant to be. Maybe that's why I didn't put up much of a fight when you offered to come over. I was just afraid you were only trying to be nice and that the next day you would be gone from my life forever."

"You remember me holding your hand in the ER? You were completely out. I was sitting there holding your hand wishing I could do it forever."

"I not only gave you permission, but I expected it as well."

I put the photo frame on the coffee table, turned to Bella, and pulled her up onto my lap.

"Merry Christmas, sweetie. I love you so much."

"Merry Christmas, Kath. Don't worry. I'll be here for you, forever and a day."

We squeezed each other in the tightest of hugs.

"How would you like to go upstairs and watch White Christmas with me?"

"I'd love to," I told Bella.

I sorted through her boxes of DVD's and found it then took it upstairs after turning out all the lights downstairs. The Christmas tree looked beautiful in the darkened room. Bella was right, this was a pretty all right Christmas. I still wished that today we could have gotten married. Next week, though. Seven short days.

Tomorrow we'd go over to Pop's and Martha's place. I should stop that, I thought. I should just start calling it my parent's house. I decided to take one of the announcements over to give to them tomorrow. I'd already bought Martha a new sweater and Pops two new ties for work back at the end of November. Small gifts, but ones that would be used. The biggest thing was just getting together for food and family.

"Hey Bella?"

"Yeah, babe?"

"I'm glad you wrote the announcements out like you did. I'm going to start something tomorrow even if I don't quite believe it myself. At least yet, anyway."

"What's that?"

"I think I'm going to start calling Martha 'Mom'. It won't hurt anything, and Pops will know that inside I still don't accept anybody as a substitute for my real mother. I don't know why I hang on so tightly to her. I can't even remember her. I know her by pictures and by Pop's stories, but that's it. Somehow she has this bigger than life image in my head though."

"I know they'll both appreciate it. You'll be doing a good thing. I'm proud of you."

"Let's get some sleep."

"No, I don't want to."

"What do you want to do?"

"I want you to undress me."

"Will that make you happy?"

"It depends on what you do after you have me undressed."

"What should I do then?"

"I imagine you'll figure something out."

Without lifting the blankets up and letting in the cold air I stripped off both of our clothes and then pulled Bella up on top of me where she sort of straddled me. She dipped her head down and dragged her hair across my face.

"Stop it," I said as I blew her hair trying to get it off my face.

Bella giggled at me.

"Do you want me to get a pony tail holder?"

"No, just put your head on the side of mine."

"I don't want to. I want to sit up."

Her hands began to explore me. After all, it was just hair, right? Was that so bad? I think not. In fact, when she came down with her face again and mine was awash in her hair once again, I relished its soft feeling and sweet smell. We made love from late on Christmas Eve right on through early Christmas Morning, finally falling asleep at about two-thirty.

When I woke up in the morning it was about eight-thirty. I was beginning to realize that Bella doesn't wake up much without the alarm going off. She'd sleep until eleven or noon if left alone. I kissed her and told her I was going to make some toast and jam and some hot tea.

"Sounds good. I'm going to wait here for you, nice and warm."

I finished making breakfast and got a couple of trays out. Unlike Bella's apartment, I had two breakfast trays meant for a bed. I loaded them up and went upstairs.

"Sit up, sweetie."

Bella pushed up placing her pillows behind her. I put both of the trays down on my side of the bed. Then I took hers and put it across her lap. I picked mine up and twisted around sitting down and set it over my lap and we dug in. Neither of us said anything for the most part, we just enjoyed eating.

"What time are we supposed to eat Christmas dinner at your parents' house?"

"About noon. Some people do the family gathering dinners about two or three in the afternoon because there's so much food it takes longer to make everything. For us it's fairly simple so it doesn't take so long to make or eat, thus letting us start up earlier and freeing Pops and I to duty if necessary."

"I feel bad that we really didn't get anything for your parents for Christmas. It's just all been so hectic."

"Don't worry, I already did before I met you."

I told her what I'd gotten and she felt somewhat better.

"What time are we going over?"

"About ten-thirty. Finish up your breakfast and I'll go do the dishes."

I took the trays to the kitchen, loaded the dishwasher, and wiped down the countertops and sink. After I was done I went up to the bathroom and got ready. Bella was already in doing her morning routine. I walked up behind her while she was brushing her hair, and put my arms around her from behind.

"Mind if I join you?"

"Don't be silly," said Bella.

We both got ready, Bella with a medium amount of makeup for daytime and me with eyeshadow and lip-gloss only. We returned to the bedroom to get dressed.

"What should I wear today?" asked Bella.

"I'm wearing a pair of jeans, some tennis shoes, and a flannel shirt over a tee shirt."

"Oh, ok. Neo-lesbian."

"No, you putz, modern North Woods!" I said, punching her lightly in the shoulder.

"Your idea of a tee shirt for Christmas says 'I Can't Think Straight'? Holiday notwithstanding that would never ever go down in a million years at my house. Your Pops much be really cool about you being out."

"Totally. And he carries a gun. He'll shoot anybody that gives me a ration of shit," I laughed.

"So, flannel. Does this mean we're officially dykes?"

"No, it means we're officially Minnesotans. Just grab one of mine. There's one in there that's red and green for Christmas. That would go well."

Bella put it over a black tee over a pink cami. And we were ready to go. I went into the second bedroom and reached up into the closet on the shelf and got the presents for Pops and Martha, and started the SUV remotely. I went into the kitchen and got out a twelve pack of beer, and a pecan pie I'd bought last night at the pub. We got in the truck and made the short ride over to Pop's place.

CHAPTER ELEVEN

He was practically waiting on the porch for us, welcoming us in.

"Come in out of this cold air. Get warm again."

We took off our coats and hats and gloves and boots. Then Pops eyes looked directly into Bella's eyes.

"Keep in mind that I'm a cop. Not just a cop, but a detective and a darned good one. If I absolutely needed to I could dispose of a body so that no would ever find it. Ever. Just remember that if you ever even think about breaking Kathleen's heart."

"Pops, leave her alone. Bella, ignore him. He's trying to act like a concerned father, but he only comes off acting like a complete fool."

"Uh, actually, he's pretty convincing, to tell you the truth," replied Bella.

Everybody laughed except Bella. With her it was more of a single, little 'ha' at best.

Martha came in and gave everyone an ETA on lunch, noon as planned. I got up and walked over to her.

"Hi Mom," I said as I kissed her cheek.

You could have knocked her over with a feather. And Pops too.

"Hello. And you too, Bella. Welcome to Christmas dinner."

"Thank you, Martha. I'm totally happy to be here."

Everybody moved into the den to open presents first. The first present given out was the announcement for the wedding. Pops smiled broadly and Martha actually got a little teary eyed at the mention of the two of them as my parents instead of father and stepmother. It was the first time I'd ever done that in my life.

Then we gave them the sweater and the ties. Up next, I got a ceramic figurine about ten inches tall, that was a fire hydrant with a Dalmatian lifting its leg up and peeing on it. Everybody thought that was cute. Pops stood up and addressed Bella.

"We don't really know much about you yet other than the fact that you've managed to steal Kathleen's heart. But I heard a rumor when chatting it up with her one day, that your life here was missing one small thing. With that he got up and went into the back of the house. He came back holding a cat transport carrier. He set it in front of Bella, and she peered into the wire front.

"Ivan! Oh, my wonderful Ivan! Now Tinkerbelle will have a friend. How did you do this? How did you get my lil' kitty here?"

"Like I said I heard you had a cat and that you pretty much had to leave him behind, so I simply asked your father for the cat. It carries a lot more weight I guess when the request comes from the police department. So last week I had him flown up on a Delta flight. He's been playing around our house here for a few days. I was hoping that you two wouldn't come over and ruin the surprise."

"Next to getting Kathleen, this is the biggest present I could ever have hoped for. Oh, Mr. and Mrs. Pope, I can't thank you enough."

"Please, don't call us that. You can call me Kevin, but I prefer Pops. Kathleen calls me that even in my office. And Martha. Okay?"

"Okay, I promise."

Ivan was running his motor and letting Bella just hold him and scratch him. The light part of the fur on Ivan was lighter than most Siamese, and the chocolate points were dark, dark brown. And he was huge.

"How much does he weigh, anyway? He's huge!" asked Pops.

"Nineteen pounds. And not an ounce of fat on him. Amazing, isn't he. He's brilliant. He's my itty-bitty kitty."

"Itty Bitty, he ain't," I quipped.

FALLING INTO FIRE

She put him down to run around since lunch was just about ready. I got out the envelope with photos in it. We had already given the photos from the studio to them but I gave them photos of us at the Christmas party and a couple of me in gear out on scene. Martha made the comment that she'd never seen a picture of me in my gear. Only in my regular uniforms.

We had a grand lunch of salad with mushrooms, olives, and tomatoes covered in Feta and Asiagio cheeses. We followed that with meatballs covered in a tomato based sauce and dusted, again, with Feta cheese. Our main dish was baked potatoes and ribeye steaks. To top it off, we ate ciabatta rolls and drank red wine. Not the standard turkey or ham that most people had. We ate until there was no more room. Martha and I cleaned the kitchen while Pops and Bella talked to us. We put leftovers in the fridge.

After we got done in the kitchen we made our way back into the den. Walking past the living room Bella spied the front window.

"Hey, you have a cute police logo sticker on your front window."

It was a four-inch square with the St. Paul Police Department logo on it in black and gold.

"Sweetie, haven't you noticed the one on our front window?"

"I guess not. The only time I'm around the front glass it's been dark."

"Ours is a St. Paul Fire Department sticker and it's red, black, and gold. Every cop and firefighter in the city has one on their house."

"I guess I just never paid attention."

All the while that Bella was talking with us she was playing with Ivan, who had obviously missed his mommy very badly.

"So, Pops... How did you and Daddy get along?"

"He wasn't too bad. I thought he was a bit of a stuffed shirt. I merely pointed out that it was your cat and that it hadn't been sixty days therefore it wasn't abandoned and he couldn't therefore claim the cat. I told him that I would be happy to pay for the transportation to fly the cat up here. Or I would go down there, go to a small claims court, and win the cat back. His choice. I don't think he likes me very much. He acts very much like somebody that's used to getting his way."

"That's him to a tee. That's why I literally snuck off in the middle of the afternoon when everybody was away when I got this job locked in. I wanted to avoid the drama."

"So, I take it that in their eyes you'll grow out of your desire to be with other women and come to your senses magically and fall in love with a man and want to settle down and raise a family."

"You got it, Slick. There are a lot of gay girls and women that come to realize it late in life. Even in their fifties and sixties. There are girls that date boys through high school and even college, even having intimate relations with them, but end up feeling something's missing. But I've known since I was in first grade that I was different, and I told my parents when I was in third grade. I've never dated a boy in my life. Not even once. I've had friends that are boys, certainly, but not romantically. And still, they won't listen to me. I honestly don't know what it's going to take."

"I would say at this point it's not worth the effort. Send them a Christmas card and a card on their birthdays. Other than that? Maybe a text message once in a while. Keep it short and sweet and just a statement of hello, without letting a dialogue develop. That's what I'd do, anyway."

"I can see where Kathleen gets her common sense, Pops. That pretty sage advice."

"I just call it like I see it. I've been a detective for years. And as elaborate as you see things on the television and in the movies, most crimes are pretty straightforward. The same could be said about relationships. They are what you make them. If you make it drama-free, then none will show up."

"Well, lunch was great, Martha. Really. I'm so happy to have a family to spend the holidays with you all. I would have survived, but it wouldn't have been very pleasant. I've had such a good time today. I think we're going to head home and let Kathleen take a nap before she goes on shift. We're still on schedule for New Year's Eve, right? Ten minutes with a judge?"

"Smooth sailing. I just wish one of us would have known about the waiting period. You two would have gotten married yesterday."

"Don't rub it in, Pops. As Bella keeps telling me, let it go. I don't seem to be able to, but she keeps saying it."

I smiled at Bella as I was saying it. She smiled back at me and held her hands up to me. I crossed the kitchen to where she was sitting and reached out my hands to hold hers.

"Get a room, girls," said Pops with a laugh.

"We've got one Pops. And we're going there from here."

FALLING INTO FIRE

I started the SUV to get it warming up. Martha made me take some of the food with us, saying it would just go to waste if we didn't. We captured Ivan and put him in his carrier. After the truck had been running for about fifteen minutes, I took Ivan and my statue and loaded them in. I came back and got Bella buttoned up in her coat and gloves, with her one boot she could wear, and handed her the crutches. Martha and Pops both gave Bella a hug and a kiss, then they came over and gave me one as well.

"Thank you for what you did. I know it means so much to Martha. More than you know."

"Pops, you need to thank Bella for that. I mean, I don't mind it, but it was her brilliant idea. I'm telling you, she's wonderful."

"Bye kids," Pops and Martha said in a chorus.

"That was fun. This was so much better than spending the week home alone. And now I've got my baby with me."

"By 'baby', are you talking about me or Ivan?"

"Yes."

On the ride home, I reached out with my hand and took Bella's while we sat quietly listening to music on the radio. We pulled up to the house, and I grabbed my statue and Ivan. Bella got out, on her own, without too much difficulty and we started up the stairs on the front porch.

"Hey, a fire department sticker. You were right. I just never noticed it before."

"Did you have any reason to doubt me?"

"No, it just surprised me."

We got inside and I put Ivan down. We hung up our coats and got out of our boots. I put all the gloves in the coat pockets. Then I leaned down and opened the door of Ivan's carrier.

"Let me take him up to the litter box so he'll know where it is. Then we'll show him the food. Keep an eye out and make sure that Tinks doesn't get jealous and hiss too much. She's never been around any other cat, so I don't know how they'll handle this."

"Ivan's been a loner, too. Hopefully this won't get too interesting."

I was showing Ivan the food when Tinkerbelle showed up. Both the cats started sniffing around each other without making any real noises. Then Tinkerbelle did something amazing. She starting giving Ivan a tongue bath on his face and Ivan's response was to start purring loudly. Bella and I looked at each other.

"That was easy," proclaimed Bella.

"I think I really am going to take that nap now. Wanna come upstairs with me and lay down a while? Or maybe read your book?"

"I'd love to come up with you and read. That won't bother you, will it?"

"Not at all. Usually I take a nap on the couch and it's really bright in here."

"Would you rather take a nap on the couch?"

"Nah. I would much rather be in bed with you."

We went upstairs and lay down in the bed. I put on some relatively quiet music and was sawing the big logs within about ten or fifteen minutes. I awoke slightly, noticing that Bella had crawled up next to me and snuggled in tight, but I was back out within seconds.

"Snugglepuss. Do you want to eat a salad or a sandwich for dinner?" Bella asked quietly in my ear.

"Mmph…."

"Baby, open your little peepers. Are you hungry at all?"

"I could eat something light."

"How about I make us some salad?"

"Okay. I'm going down to the basement for about a half hour or so."

"I wouldn't want those big muscles of yours to lose any tone by not exercising for two days in a row. You missed yesterday I noticed."

"Bite me."

Bella leaned over and bit me on the back of the neck, playfully.

"What was that for?"

"You said to."

"Ah. I got it. Sorry, I'm still half asleep."

I looked at my watch. I'd managed to sleep until almost seven o'clock. I never do that. I put on some shorts and a tee shirt along with some sneakers and went to the basement to work out. I jogged on the treadmill for half an hour, then moved to free weights and pushed three reps of twenty-kilogram weights. I finished up, wiped down with a towel, and then hung the towel up on the bar of the weight bench. I headed upstairs and took a shower. When I was getting ready I used just a little eyeliner and some neutral pink lip-gloss.

As I was walking into the dining room, Bella was just finishing setting the table. And our salad also had some chicken that she'd cut up in small pieces, given an egg bath, and rolled in breadcrumbs, then fried in olive oil. It both looked and smelled delicious.

"Well don't you look pretty tonight, my little firebug."

"You really didn't have to do all this. A simple salad would have been fine."

"Salad schmalad. I've also got some mushrooms cut up, some shredded Romano, some olives, some tomato wedges, some slivers of bell peppers, some slices of that thick ham for sandwiches you get, and your choice of dressings. Aren't I just the good little homemaker?"

"Promise me you won't quit your job. At least not yet."

"You don't have to worry about that anytime soon. Not at all. Say, let's say that A Shift is on, and there's a fire that they respond to starts at twenty-two hundred. Then you show up at the Station and all the tucks, sorry, 'apparati', are out and so are the people from that shift. What do you do then?"

"We're not a science lab. And the English department isn't correcting our grammar. More than one is still called apparatus, just like more than one is still called deer or moose. But to answer your question, somebody takes the replacement crews out on scene in the Suburban's. Then we take over the fire and the other team is brought back in."

I'd already had wine for lunch and since I was going on shift, I poured some iced tea for us.

"We need to talk about money a little bit," began Bella.

"Okay, that sounded both ominous and a little random. But it's your turn, go ahead."

"I've been thinking about it a lot since you brought it up. My car lease is up in April. I'm going to see if we can find something from somebody that sells Lexus as well as other cars. Maybe even the same owner with other dealerships. A lot of the time if you buy a new car they'll give you a couple of months off your lease agreement. I've been looking, and I really like the looks of the Subaru Outback. What do you think about them?"

"Dave on A shift has one, but his is about five or six years old. He got it new right after I hired on. He loves his. Totally. He hasn't had any real problems with it. It's been very dependable and handles the bad weather brilliantly."

"The other thing is I've been thinking about the house."

"You want to move, don't you? I told you that I didn't mind. There are a lot of nice neighborhoods around, some closer to your office, that are still reasonable priced and the market's still a buyer's market...."

"Would you shut up? Damn it. When you go on a tear, you do go on, don't you?"

"Sorry. You were saying?"

"If we make the monthly mortgage payment, then make an extra payment applied to the end of the note, then we can actually pay off the remaining twenty-eight years in only twelve years. Just think, we could own our house outright in twelve years! Why would I want to move into something bigger or newer and waste all that money? Babe, this is home. Me and you. Home," Bella said rubbing her fingers along my jaw line.

I reached up and took her hand in mine and kissed it several times.

"Dig in. Dinner's ready," Bella said, taking all the small bowls of the salad components and setting them on the table.

I was really happy that Bella wanted what I wanted. And it was going to be even easier with her paycheck. Even if it had been the same amount as mine just having two checks would have made life so much easier. Firefighters don't make that much.

"Say, Bell. I haven't told you this yet, but you know that once I finish my Paramedic training I want to move from the Engines and Ladders to the Medic teams. I want to stay with the fire department, not go to work for a private company or hospital. Unless it was maybe one of the Children's hospitals, either the one here in St. Paul, or even the one in Minneapolis. But if I could get on an air ambulance, all bets would be off. I think that's my ultimate goal. I'll always be on shift work. And there will be long days and more commonly long nights."

"Baby, I'm good with that. Just as long as you come home safe and sound to me."

"I just hadn't said anything about it before."

"I pretty much knew that you'd want to be a Paramedic if you were putting in the training."

"For tonight I'll just try and get through the shift with a minimum amount of fuss."

Bella held up her glass of tea.

"Cheers."

"Cheers."

FALLING INTO FIRE

We went in on the couch and put a blanket over us and watched a movie, then switched to television after it was done. At eleven fifteen I started the truck and went upstairs to get dressed. It was almost up to thirty degrees and was only supposed to drop down a couple of degrees tonight so I skipped the long underwear. I touched up my lip-gloss since I had eaten, then thought about it and put the tube in my shirt pocket.

I picked up my billfold and put in my front pocket and took my keys. I scampered back downstairs and put on my coat and gloves. I walked over in front of Bella in front of the couch and leaned in for a hug and a kiss before I left.

"Would you promise me something, Kathleen?"

"I'll try."

"Promise me that you'll never leave for a shift without giving me a hug and a kiss. Ever. I'd hate for something to happen to you and regret not getting that one last kiss."

"Oh, sweetie. I promise. Forever and a day, I promise."

I gave her an extra hug and kiss then headed out the door. I pulled into the Station about ten minutes till, later than normal for me. I was usually a half hour early. We were halfway through our briefing when Oliver shouted out to the whole team.

"Look. Kathleen's wearing makeup. Holy crap."

I just held up my middle finger to him and left it in the air for an incredible length of time. Everybody laughed of course, but I did catch a load for having on makeup. I had no intention of wearing lots of makeup, but just a little eyeliner and lip-gloss wouldn't be so bad. Especially since the color of the gloss was almost the same color as my lips anyway. It's not like it was scarlet-orange.

"Pope, what Oliver was trying to say, albeit in a not so politically correct manner, is that while it would be wrong, according to the Human Resources Office, to tell you that you look especially nice, he would have," offered Scott.

"Well, Oliver, thank you. And you too, Scotty, for that brilliant translation," I said in return.

"Uh, if nobody objects could I continue our briefing then we'll hit the lights for the evening? If that's all right with you guys? I mean, they gave me these cute little bars to wear on my collar that say to everybody, 'guess what, I'm in charge', but if you need some more time, I can certainly understand," Carl said winking at me.

"No Lieu, you go right ahead. We're all ears."

"Actually, half of you are all assholes," said Carl.

Everybody laughed really hard. Carl was usually so serious so when he said or did something funny it always came off funnier that it really was. He finished our briefing and told us to get the linens on our bunks so we could kill the lights in fifteen minutes.

We had a nice quiet night. There was something that came up for Station 23 in the northwest part of the city, but that was it. Then we got the alarms going off just before nine o'clock. There was a two-hundred-unit apartment fire over on the east side of St. Paul. We rolled every apparatus from Stations 7, 9, and 24. This was a big one. One whole end of the first building was in flames on all four floors. We got the three Engines hooked up and the two Ladders from our Station and 24 and started pouring water into the building as fast as we could. We were fighting with ladders from the exposed ends and we went inboard two units and started suppressing up-fire from the blaze to make sure it would at least be contained to the current perimeter until we could get the flames extinguished.

By God, this was a fire for sure. Everybody was full of adrenaline for this one. There were a lot of people that would have to be put up in temporary housing. It wasn't helped by the fact that this was an older building, didn't have any sprinkler system, and was built more cheaply than a lot of other buildings. We were still working on hotspots and clearing the roof off at four o'clock in the afternoon when the sun began waning. After we finally succeeded in putting out the fire, we packed up all of our gear and headed for our respective Stations. By that time, it was six o'clock and well after dark.

We rolled into Station 7, backed in carefully, halfway through bay doors to get lined up, then we went back in front of the station to clean the vehicles, closing the bay doors. We started the arduous task of cleaning and refolding hoses, inspecting them as we went under flood lights, and washing down the apparatus. Both trucks worked on the hoses first, but when it came to the trucks, ladder and our group got into a little competition to see who could get done first. Tonight, we lost. Crap. We finally finished, backed the apparatus back into the station, and closed the doors once again.

Next up we had to all go through a thorough wash-down. I drew Scott for my scrub buddy tonight.

"Hey, Pope. I'm really sorry about last week. And just to let you know, I do think you look really pretty when you throw on a little makeup. You're a pretty woman. And a kick-ass firefighter. Just so you know."

"Look, Scotty, I know you didn't mean it. And I really didn't mean to slug you. And you have to admit that I couldn't have been too upset, I didn't punch you that hard. But the truth is it never meant anything to me before to look nicer. I'm neither completely nor a complete butchy, if you hadn't noticed. But Bella has just had so much of a profound effect on me. I can't explain it."

"Yes, you can. The proof is in New Year's Eve," he winked at me.

I started brushing down his coat and boots with soap and water, then he washed me down in return. We moved over and the next pair came up to the decon station and started the same procedure. I carried my gear over to the wall inside the bay and stacked it where I could get it right back on if we were called out again. We had pizza ordered already so we wouldn't have to cook anything tonight. If it had just been Engine 7 or Ladder 7 out, the remaining crew would have fixed dinner. Usually we go out as a pair, so it's a matter of who would get pulled out of cleaning early to cook. In tonight's case, it was a really messy, smoky, dirty, suety fire. Everything was terribly dirty.

Lieu walked into the area and pointed a finger at me.

"Pope. My office."

Shit. What did I do now? It was always something simple, but I still felt as though every time I was being called into the Principal's office.

"Sit."

"Aye, aye," I said taking a seat.

Carl took a manila envelope from the top of his desk and handed it to me. It was sealed and marked 'Bella Ward'.

"Are we going to expect to see these keep coming in but addressed to 'Bella Pope'?" he laughed.

"Honestly, Lieu, I didn't know what the first ones were until I got them home and gave them to Bella to open. After all, it was sealed and it was marked for her. And I still don't know which reporter is doing it or who put him up to it. Well, actually who put him up to it may well have been Tim, a cop. Honestly, that's all I know."

"Don't worry about it. I think it's sort of funny."

"How do you even know what's in it?"

"Your dad and I were talking at City Hall earlier this week. We just happened to run into each other. I see him every once in a while. We end up having departmental meetings on the same days quite often."

"Thanks, Lieu."

I took my envelope and went into the day room. I laid the envelope on one of the tables. Scott was sitting in one of the padded chairs watching television. I cleared my throat a couple times. Then I did it again, very loudly. He finally looked over. I pointed my finger at him, then at the ground right at my feet rather emphatically. He stood up and came over to me.

"Spill it," I demanded.

"What are you talking about?"

"Your friend the cop knows a reporter, am I right? You're the one that started this."

"I thought it would be nice for Bella. Richard takes photos of me sometimes and gives them to my family. My parents and my wife, my sister, everybody loves them. All I did was to give him the tip. And every once in a while, you end up getting your photo in the local paper. Trust me, it will happen. It'll be something to give to your children someday. If you're planning on having children."

"Yes, eventually we'll have children. And thanks. Bella really, really liked the first ones. I'm sure that today she'll get to see me really dirty and really working instead of standing around watching the sidewalk freeze over."

"No problem."

I reached out quickly and gave him a shoulder-bump of a hug.

I found a quiet corner of the Station and pulled out my phone. I decided to text message Bella instead of talk out loud so that I could get a little more intimate. We chatted for almost thirty minutes.

It had been a very interesting day for Bella. A little after noon, somebody rang the doorbell. She hobbled over to the door, and a youngish woman she'd never met before was standing on the porch. When Bella opened the door and asked her if she could help her, the other woman asked her where I was. Bella told her I was on shift. The other woman said that Bella had better not be lying and that I'd better not actually be home. Taken a little bit aback, Bella told her that she was free to go to the Station and see me there if she thought it was that important.

FALLING INTO FIRE

The other woman started crying and said she had to talk to me, that it was sort of an emergency. Bella told her that she didn't know what else to say or do, but that I wasn't home. Then the other woman suddenly got very belligerent and shouted, "Who in the hell do you think you are, bitch?" Bella held up her hand with the ring on it and said that she was the woman that was going to marry me next week. Then Bella looked the other woman squarely in the eyes, and said that she must be Melanie.

Melanie's shoulders slumped, she started crying even harder, and she fell down to sit on the steps of the porch. Bell hobbled out on her crutches and told Melanie that the past was the past, that there were no grudges, but that I'd moved on and that Melanie needed to as well. Melanie wiped her eyes a few times with her gloved hands and said that she was sorry to have bothered her and got in her car and left.

I texted Bella to call 9-1-1 if Melanie ever came back for any reason and not open the door to talk to her. Bella said that it was clear to her that Melanie was clearly in love with me still and had some issues, and didn't see the need to have the police involved. I told her to at least watch out and be careful. I was scolded and Bella told me that she was a big girl and could fend for herself relatively well. She reminded me that she didn't have my brawn, but she had lightning fast mental skills and could think and talk her way out of most situations. I did have to give Bella that. She was sharp, all right.

I told Bella that I'd see her in a few hours and that I loved her. And that I had a present for her. She asked what, and I told her she'd find out when I got home. We spent the rest of the evening doing general cleaning around the Station house. We even took all the dishes and silverware out and cleaned the cabinets and drawers, then the same with the drink cabinet and the pots and pans bins. Just a slow, leisurely cleanup. Moving at about half speed, waiting for shift change, hoping we'd already earned our pay for the day and didn't get called back out.

Neither Station 9 nor Station 17 has a Ladder, so right before shift end, when an alarm went out, we had to send Ladder 7 out to help out Station 9. Although trained on all apparatus, everybody basically has a primary assignment. It rotates periodically but for now I was on Engine duty. I was relieved not to have to go back out. I would really rather get back to Bella.

I knew it would become easier as we were together longer, but we hadn't even known each other a month. Wow, I thought. Not even a month, and I was getting married in five days. And I never felt like it was a spur of the moment thing. I felt like it had been planned for the last ten years. I do know that Bella is what I'd been searching for the last ten years or more. She was it, she was the one. There was no doubt in my mind. None whatsoever.

I went out to my truck and put the photos, assuming that's what was in the envelope again, on the dashboard. Going back inside I went into the bunk bay and lay down in my bunk. I was going to take my bunker gear and put it by my bunk at first but I thought why? I was going to have to move it back into the apparatus bay in less than an hour and a half. When you're not on shift, your gear lines one of the walls in the big bay.

Ladder 7 was still out when shift change came up. Every shift change there's a brief/debrief session for a few minutes for both incoming and outgoing shift, then the incoming shift will do safety briefings, news, changes in procedures, information from City Hall and Human Resources, etc. I got our debriefing and then B shift worked its way out of the building. The Ladder 7 crew from C Shift got geared up and their Lieutenant got the second Suburban fired up and they got in to go relieve B Shift. I drove home.

I went inside, took off my cold weather clothes and boots, dropped my bag, and took the envelope upstairs. Since we'd worked a fire, I'd already put on a clean uniform after a shower to get the smell of smoke off of me as best as possible. After my shower at the station I'd laid down a fresh coat of lip-gloss. Scott had jokingly said that he wished he'd met me before he'd met his wife. I reminded him that I was gay. He said he was man enough to turn me. I told him that more than likely I would have turned him. We laughed for a few.

I went inside the bedroom and Bella was sitting up, propped up on pillows, reading a book. Both Tinkerbelle and Ivan were curled up on her.

"Look, I have a pair of shadows."

"So, they get along alright?"

"They've been following each other around all night. You'd think they were littermates."

"Are you okay with Melanie having been here today?"

"I'm fine. You were the one that seemed upset."

"I was. I mean, I still am. I truly don't ever want to see her again. For anything. If her house is on fire I'll extinguish it. If she's hurt, and

I'm dispatched as a paramedic, I'll stabilize and transport her. But that's where it ends. Right there. Not one step more."

"Calm down. Don't let her get to you. Just relax. Now where's my present?" asked Bella.

I held out the manila envelope to her.

"Oh, goody, goody, goody. Is it pictures again?"

"How would I know? It's addressed to you so I wouldn't open it. And it's sealed. It was clearly meant for you, I'm just the delivery girl."

Bella ripped the envelope open. She took out the photos, but this time without any note. And this time there were photos of my handling hoses, adjusting the foamers and valves on the engine, spraying with both fixed and adjustable nozzles, sometimes in the clear and sometimes enveloped in smoke. But in all of them it was very clear that it was me. Even when my back was turned you could see 'Pope' on the back of my bunker coat and helmet.

"Oh, baby, you're so gosh darned cute!"

"Whatever you say. If it makes you happy, then it makes me happy."

"I'm not kidding. I'm not sure whether the photos make me go 'aww' or get me wet. Could go either way."

"You pervert."

"I'm entitled. It's my wife we're talking about here. I've got to say, you have definitely moved firefighters to the very top of my list of uniformed service."

"What are you going to do when I make Paramedic?"

"I guess then I'll have to rethink my paradigm. I guess then I'll go for the jumpsuit with cloth tape and tuff cuts. I love these photos. These are much better than the first ones. These really show you in action. Right out in front of the flames and the water and the steam... Jesus. I can't wait to scan them and send them to Mama and Daddy. And to Bryce and Nancy, too, of course. And maybe even a couple of my friends from school. I still email a couple of them once in a while.

"How do you know about tuff cuts? Oh, never mind, father and brother are doctors. My bad."

"I'm sleepy. Get undressed and turn out the light."

Bella rolled over where she was facing the back wall. I took off my clothes, then turned off the light on my side of the bed. I crawled in behind her, put my right arm under her neck and wrapped my left arm around her waist. She pulled me in tight and we drifted off to sleep very quickly.

CHAPTER TWELVE

    Bella had set the alarm clock to go off, since she needed to work on Friday, as well as next Monday so that she'd be able to take off after the wedding for the rest of the week. She leaned over me and gave me a kiss, and I didn't move more than I had to in order to kiss her back. I fell back asleep immediately. Bella got dressed and went downstairs to get busy. Today would turn out to be spent almost all day on the phone with other managers. Most of the lower end staff was taking time off for the holidays, but even the managers that were officially taking time off were taking one-hour conferences here and there. And Bella ended up being the coordinator for many of the meetings, along with Courtney.
    I woke up around eight-thirty and did my morning routine in the bathroom. I put on some shorts and a tee to work out in. I walked downstairs and went to the office and gave Bella a quick kiss. She looked at my tee shirt. It was a St. Paul Police Department shirt. She didn't miss a beat with the people on the phone, but she just shook her head at me, smiling.

I went down and ran for forty-five minutes at a pretty slow pace. Then I did the weight bench first at fifty kilos, then one hundred kilos, then back down to fifty. I sat on the bench and did both inward and inverse curls with twenty-kilo free weights. I was really burning today. I ran up the stairs, which took me right by the opening to the office.

"Hey, baby, come here for a minute," yelled Bella.

I turned around and walked back to the office.

"What?"

"What are you going to do next?"

"I think take a shower and then go to the grocery store. Anything specific that you need or want while I'm out?"

"Yes. I want some new ponytail holders. Grey if you can find a card of black and greys. If not, black. And some allergy tablets, without decongestants. A bottle of ninety if you can find them. And before you go bring my weights to me so I can use them while I'm stuck on these stupid calls."

"Now that's a great idea. Nothing says you have to do it all at once, either. Do one set while you can. Wait a little while. Change the exercise and do those reps. And so on."

I took the weights to Bella and went looking for the cats. I hadn't seen them this morning. I looked all over the house. Finally, I looked under the bed in the second bedroom. They were sitting side by side underneath the bed. How totally cute. I pulled the bedspread up and out of the way, then pulled out my phone and took three photos. Then I texted them to Bella's phone.

I pulled the bedspread back down and went on my errands. I went to the department store first and found a card of fifteen ponytail holders in black, charcoal grey, medium grey, light grey, and white. Several of each in monochrome. I also got the decongestants. I paid and headed over to the grocery store. I got meat, vegetables, some cold cereal, more coffee, some hot chocolate, two loaves of bread, some chips and some cheese puffs, non-stick spray for pans, milk, orange juice, some frozen vegetables, some eggs, and several bananas. It cost more than I thought it would, but then I remembered that I was buying enough for two people to eat, not just me.

I also went to an outlet store and bought Bella a new acrylic scarf to keep the chill off her neck and a matching beanie even though she already had one. After all, didn't most gay chicks have a thing for beanies? I laughed to myself. I went by the pet store and bought a cat bed. I didn't know if they'd use it or not, but it only cost fifteen dollars. And I got cat food. Finally, I headed home.

I took everything inside and put it all up. I put the cat bed in the master bedroom along the outside wall so it was out of the way. I grabbed my mp3 player, my study guide, and headed for the couch after getting a glass of milk. I heard the noise of the postman and got up to get the mail. After I grabbed it I went over to Bella to remind her we had a two-thirty appointment with the orthopedist.

"Shit, I forgot about that. I better message Courtney and remind her I'm going. Ha, that's funny. She just this second sent me a message to remind me of my appointment this afternoon. I'm telling you, she's my life blood at the company."

I went back over to the couch and sat down. I started going through the mail. Bella already had her mail forwarded here. I made three stacks. Hers, mine, and ours. I picked up my stack and immediately threw three of them in the fourth pile, circular file number thirteen. Trash. I had an insurance notification. Then I had something from the department. I opened it, unsure of what it was. Probably wanting money for another departmental charity or some such. But when I opened it I was stunned. I was to report Tuesday, April Second to Medic 4, a little way southwest of Station 7. I was finally getting my practicum and possible assignment. I was at least going to be licensed even if I would have to wait up to a few years for my permanent opening.

I walked into the office where Bella was talking on the phone. I lay the letter in front of her quietly. She talked for another couple of minutes and then told the person at the other end of the line that they should both think about the changes and they'd get back together later in the day to see what they had come up with, then she hung up. She read the letter carefully to make sure she got it right.

"Where is Station 4?" asked Bella.

"A mile and a half southwest of my current station."

"Wow! That's great!"

"I'm thinking, yeah, it is!"

"Did you get my allergy pills?"

"I did. You want one now?"

"Yes, please. With a glass of iced tea."

"When are you going to stop for lunch?"

"I'm not since we have to go to the doctor's office this afternoon. Just make me a sandwich and bring it in. I'll eat while I work."

"Okay. Give me a minute."

I took Bella a sandwich, some chips, a glass of tea with some freshly pressed mint leaves, and her pill. I went back into the living room. I called Pops to see if he was available. He didn't answer his phone so I left a message. I started to go get a refill for my tea and my phone rang. It was Pops already calling back.

"Hey, Kitten. What did you need?"

"I got my letter. I start my EMT II Paramedic practicum on Tuesday, April Second with Medic 4. And I think I'm going to take the written test before I start. That way half of it will be out of the way and as soon as my practicum is over, I'll be fully licensed."

"Not a bad plan. Did you just get notice today?"

"Yeah, I got a letter in the mail. Out of the blue. Never got any clue from the Lieu about it at all."

"I have to tell you being the Lieu isn't any great reward. The pay jump is minimal and the paperwork increase is staggering. Plus, I hate meetings and now I have more meetings that I have actual police work. I should have turned it down. I knew better. I really did. I think I'm going to put in my paperwork the day I'm eligible. Truly."

"You never know, Pops. You might make Captain by then and things will change again."

"Oh, God no! Captains don't do any police work at all. Totally administrative. Completely."

"Okay. I'll let you get back to work. See you, Pops."

"Love you, Kitten. Bye."

Bella and I walked into the doctor's office about twenty minutes before our appointment time. We still had to wait a half hour after our scheduled time to be taken back, and twenty minutes after that for the nurse to come in with a technician. They cut Bella's cast off and carefully cleaned her ankle and foot. They put her in a wheelchair and took her back to get a current x-ray to check on the progress of her healing. Bella came back a bit tired of waiting endlessly.

Finally, the doctor came in.

"I've got good news and I've got bad news. The bad news is that you're not going to be able to get a walking cast like you asked about last time you were in. I just don't want to take a chance on your ankle, since it was so badly broken. Let's not tempt fate, shall we? The good news is that your ankle is healing just about like I thought it would. And the x-rays confirm that we won't have to go back in and put in any pins in your ankle. But I wouldn't fret. You'll heal completely. My only concern at all is that we can't judge if there's any ligament or tendon damage until you can walk again. There's no way to take a scan of that. No reliable way, anyway."

"Crap," complained Bella.

"It'll heal. Just give it time and try and have a little patience. I'll see you in three weeks then. Make an appointment at the desk on your way out."

"Thank you, doctor," I said extending my hand for a shake.

"No problem."

A little bit later the technician came in and put on a new hard cast for Bella. She was not a happy camper, and she let it be known.

"Be nice, sweetie. It's not his fault."

"I know it. I just hate it. And Sir, I am sorry for being so short with you."

"Don't worry about it. I get worse than that all the time. I'm used to it," the technician said.

"Still, it's no excuse. And I'm terribly sorry."

The technician patted her knee to let Bella there were no hard feelings. After he left the room, I looked at Bella and took her hand.

"I'm sorry, sweetie. Like the doctor said, you'll just have to have patience."

"It's not that. I just wanted to be able to stand on both feet when we got married. It's no big thing. I'll just have to deal with it."

"We'll manage it. We'll do the ceremony and when we take the pictures we'll set your crutches down for a minute, like we did at the Christmas party."

"Can we go out to eat tonight? At a real restaurant?"

"Of course we can, as long as you feel up to it."

"I do."

"That's funny. I do."

"I'll be saying it again before you know it," Bella offered.

"I know. I'm so glad. Because I do, too."

We drove back home and Bella lay down on the couch to get her foot up. I sat down on the end of the couch and put her feet in my lap, rubbing her legs. We watched television until about seven-thirty and then got up to go to dinner. Because we waited until so late, the wait at the restaurant was fairly short. Bella ordered a strawberry daiquiri to drink.

"What's up with that? One of your deep dark secrets?" I asked.

"No, and the only time I'll ever drink hard liquor is when I go out to dinner. I don't know why. And I may have two, so you better get over it."

"You can do whatever you want. Have more. I'm driving so go right ahead."

"Don't forget, you promised to wash my hair tonight."

"I haven't forgotten. I take pretty good care of you, don't I?"

"Actually, you treat me like an invalid. I feel so guilty at times thinking I've taken advantage of you."

"You did. The second day," I giggled.

"True. True."

We ate dinner casually and talked. When we got home, I pulled a chair over to the sink then went upstairs to get shampoo and conditioner. I peeked into the bedroom and smiled to myself when I saw Tinkerbelle and Ivan curled up in the cat bed. It hadn't been a waste of money after all. After washing Bella's hair, she went upstairs and blew it dry. I was on the couch watching television when I heard her calling down to me.

"Kathleen?"

"Yeah?"

"Come upstairs and pleasure me."

"Coming love. One minute."

I turned off the lights downstairs and headed for the bedroom. Bella was in bed with the covers pulled up to her chin. I had a pretty good idea of what she was wearing underneath the blanket. Or rather, what she wasn't wearing. I sat down on my side of the bed and reached under the covers. I ran my hand up and down her bare stomach. My suspicions were confirmed. I slid under the covers fully dressed.

"Is that how you're going to stay?"

I answered her by unbuttoning my shirt and taking it off. Then I undid my belt and slid out of my jeans. Lastly, I took off my underwear and pushed all the clothes out and down onto the floor beside the bed.

"You're actually going to let the clothes sit there? Little Miss Neat Freak?"

"I can either pleasure you or clean the house. Which would you rather me do?"

She didn't answer me but instead rolled over halfway on top of me putting her leg over mine.

"I'll be glad when you get that damned cast off, too. I'm tired of you clubbing me with it during the night."

"Whiny bitch."

"Princess."

"Stop it."

"You started it."

"Shut up and kiss me."

It was a long time before we reached out and turned off the lights.

CHAPTER THIRTEEN

Saturday was a different day than usual. Other than working out, all I did was pick up my skirt and go to the cleaners. I took it in because that was the best way to get the fold lines out of new clothes. After I got back we watched movies and ate pizza. Neither of us cared to stir for the entire day. For dinner, we had cheese and crackers and summer sausage. At eleven my watch went off.

"Well, sweetie, this is the last night that I'll go to work having a girlfriend. What do you think about that?"

"I couldn't be happier," answered Bella.

I put on my uniform and made a sandwich to take with me. I left Bella in bed reading.

"Don't stay up too late. Put on some music and relax."

"I will. I pretty much die after you're at work. I never could stay up that late."

"You seemed to our first week together."

"Stop it. That was different."

"Is the new wearing off yet?" I asked.

"Not even. I hope that never happens to us. I want us to be comfortable with each other but I never want to be complacent."

"I hear you. I'm off. I love you."

"I love you too, baby. Be safe."

As soon as I had my bunk made I hit the pillow and was out. I didn't wake up until the morning bell. I had a hard time getting started for the day. Everybody drank coffee or tea, and loitered around the canteen for almost an hour, just talking. Scott came over to me.

"So, you have any big plans for the week, Kathleen?" he said, winking at me.

"I should never have said anything."

"I'm glad you did though. I haven't even said anything to my wife. And as far as anybody knows, you're just up on the calendar as taking off a personal day. Nothing out of the ordinary for a holiday season."

"I can barely stand it, to tell you the truth. I'm not nervous or anything like that. I'm just totally anxious, you know?"

"You'll make it. It's only two more days."

There were no calls out that shift. None. During the afternoon we pulled the Engine, the Ladder, and the Chief's Suburban out in front and ran the motors for half an hour. Everybody shouted at us to hurry up and close the bay doors. It was about minus two degrees even that late in the day. You could definitely feel the inside of your lungs tighten up. I called Bella right before dinner and asked what she was doing.

"I'm sitting here on the bed, reading my book, and babysitting two funny looking little kids. They're all covered with hair and they make strange noises like a motor is running."

"Did you call them up on the bed or did they show up on their own?"

"They just jumped up here. Tinks came up first, and then about ten minutes later Ivan showed up as well. I love our kids. They're perfect."

"I just wanted to see what you were doing. I'll call you tonight before I bunk down."

"Okay. I love you."

"I love you too. Talk to you later."

The Station was spic and span. Without any response calls, we spent the whole day cleaning. And watching television. The Vikings weren't in the playoffs but there was still some interest in the game that was on. I spent most of my free time on my tablet. So much so that I got the warning that I was only at five percent charge and had to plug it in. Thank goodness the station had WIFI so that I didn't have to use my data allotment.

When I got home, all the lights were already turned off. I got out of my coat, hat, and gloves, and took off my boots. I walked up the stairs, and the lights were all off there as well. There was flickering light coming out of the bedroom, though, from two candles. Bella was lying on top of the covers without any clothes on. Even from where I stood, and in the dim light, I could see she was covered in goose bumps. I took my time taking my uniform off, folding it neatly and putting it on the chair, and putting the rest of my clothes in the hamper. I got up on the bed and crawled over Bella giving her my warmth.

"This will be the last night I ever make love to the last girlfriend I ever will have had. I wanted to make it special."

"We'll have tomorrow night, you know," I said.

"I mean, when she gets off work and comes home to me."

I didn't argue with Bella. I simply granted her wish. We slept in late since Bella had taken the whole week off. I woke up about half past eight and made some toast and jam. We ate in bed quietly. Neither of us said a word until it was time to eat lunch. We just basked in the glow of each other. It was almost spiritual. I cooked some chimichangas and we sat at the table eating and chatting. I always worried that there would be this awkward time when we ran out of things to say. But it was never like that with Bella. We rarely had a moment that we didn't have something to say, even this morning, when we didn't say anything. We were still saying volumes, with our eyes, our periodic touches.

I called Pops just to check in with him.

"You ready for tomorrow, Pops?"

"Sure we are. We're going to make sure and be at the courthouse by one o'clock since we're supposed to be in the judge's chambers at one-thirty. I want to make sure we don't delay anything. We're getting a special favor granted here. I don't want to waste it. And I surely don't want to piss the judge off. I may need something some day and judges have very long memories."

"Bella and I will be there early, too. I'm bringing a camera in my purse. I want to make sure we get good pictures. Better than the ones from my phone."

"Sounds like a plan. I've got to go. I'll talk to you tomorrow, Kitten."

"Bye, Pops. I love you."

"Love you too. Bye."

I got out my uniform pumps, which I'd only worn a couple of times, knocked the dust off of them, and polished them to a high shine. I also cleaned the brass on my uniform. I had used my American flag pin for something or other and couldn't find it. I dug through my jewelry box and found two more. I pinned one to my dress coat lapel and the other to Bella's dress. I ironed my dress shirt and ran the lint brush over my tie, dress cap, and dress coat. I also made sure my pantyhose didn't have any runs in them. Everything was ready for tomorrow. I helped Bella get her things ready after I was finished with my own wardrobe. We were all set for tomorrow.

We passed the rest of the day and evening quietly, playing with the cats and some toys, watching movies, reading, and things like that. We turned in early even though neither of us was particularly tired.

"I can't sleep. Make me go to sleep," said Bella.

"What do you want me to do?"

"Run your fingernails over my tummy."

I ran my fingernails lightly over Bella's stomach for about fifteen minutes until she said one word.

"Lower."

A little over an hour later, we actually did go to sleep.

※ ※ ※

We got up late again on Tuesday, New Year's Eve. We ate a brunch of Spanish omelets and rice. About eleven thirty we started getting dressed. Bella put on her underwear, then I helped her get her tights on over her cast, and I helped her get her dress over her head. She pulled out her normal hoops and put diamond studs in her ears and put on her new pendant. I helped her put her shoe on her good foot.

I got dressed in my uniform with everything but my coat. I even had my tie on already.

"Jesus. You're beautiful, baby. You look so brilliant in your uniform."

"I bet you say that to all the sailors," I smiled at her.

"Not anymore. There's only one sailor in the world for me now. Forever."

"Last chance to back out without repercussion. Just so you know."

"The advantage of going together is that I can't be left standing at the altar."

We finished at about twelve o'clock and each of us picked up an mp3 player and put in our respective purses. We were going extra early and find a place to just sit and hang out until time to meet up with Pops and Martha. I put on my dress coat and cap. It was fairly cold out but I didn't want to wrinkle my coat so I just put my winter coat in the truck in case of an emergency. I bundled Bella up in her knee-length wool coat and gloves, gave her the beanie and scarf, and we left for the Ramsey County office building.

The first thing I did was go to the County Clerk's office and pick up our marriage license. A lady came up to the window and introduced herself to us. She said she'd be going to the ceremony with us, and gave us the room number. She said she'd call us when it was about time and I gave her my phone number, and Pops' number too just in case. Bella went to a waiting area on the courtroom floor that had nice, soft padded chairs and after finding her, we hung out. We both listened to music and just held hands. My phone went off. It was Pops asking where to meet up. When he and Martha came up to us, I stood up and gave Pops a hug and Martha a hug and kissed her cheek, an act that didn't go unnoticed by Pops. Martha brushed my lapel and told me how sharp I looked. She looked at Bella and told her that she thought that Bella was absolutely beautiful, and she thought I was so lucky to have found her.

We finally got the call from the Clerk's office. We went to the room and were standing in the hallway. The lady from the Clerk's office met us there and introduced herself to us. She said she'd be with us during the ceremony and was just about to unlock the door, when I heard a voice behind us ask us where we going in such a hurry, to wait for them.

Everybody turned around in unison.

"Mama! Daddy! What are you doing here? How did...?" Bella shouted.

"Honey, we don't hate you. You're still our daughter. No matter what," said her father.

"But how did you know where to find us?"

"It took about two dozen calls, but I started with what was on the invitation and worked my way from there. Is it okay we're here?"

"Yeah, it's okay. I mean, I'm happy you're here. Ecstatic. But how did you get tickets and everything on such short notice?"

"It's called a Gulfstream G150. It costs a little more than a pair of first class tickets, but we wouldn't have missed this for the world."

Bella was in total shock. Then she looked at her mother. Her mother stood looking at her for several minutes without saying a word. When she finally spoke, she opened her arms wide, and Bella's face lit up with a huge smile.

"Everybody, this precious little girl is my beautiful, wonderful daughter, Bella, and she is a lesbian!"

~THE END~

About HollyAnne Weaver

Ms. Weaver has worked for many years in a scientifically-based career writing technical documents. An avid reader from a very young age, she gradually began writing poetry and fiction, one of her current passions. Growing up, Ms. Weaver was always fascinated with books and the ability of an author to write fiction. A sequence of emails with a close friend led to her writing longer pieces, eventually culminating in her first novel being completed in 2010. Ms. Weaver's main writing focus is on lesbian fiction, although she has projects for mysteries and historical fiction already planned.

⚜ LEAVING AFGHANISTAN BEHIND ⚜

If you have enjoyed **FALLING INTO FIRE**
please look for HollyAnne Weaver's novel
LEAVING AFGHANISTAN BEHIND from
Shadoe Publishing, LLC:
We have a chapter here for your enjoyment.

Amelia Gittens, a black female, has the distinct honor of being the first female to be admitted to the US Army's elite group of snipers, fighting in Afghanistan. It doesn't come without its price, though, as she comes back as so many veterans do with post-traumatic stress syndrome complete with major flashbacks. Working as a New York City police officer, she is involved with a suspect shooting. Unfortunately for her, it is the cousin of a major international drug dealer who seeks revenge on her and her partner, as well as the departmental psychiatrist. Amelia responds the only way she knows how, falling back upon her military training to keep her ward safe while the situation is being resolved. The whole while, she is battling her own inner demons, fighting with herself to keep them at bay, nearly tearing herself apart.

HOLLYANNE WEAVER

CHAPTER ONE

"Dispatch, 168. Show me 10-7 at East 46th and Avenue N."

"Roger, 168."

The thought of actually getting thirty minutes to sit and eat was particularly tantalizing to me at this point. It was pretty chilly, even having my Second Chance and my heavy coat. I should have worn long johns underneath everything. What I wouldn't give to be a weatherman. I could be wrong more than forty percent of the time and still get paid like I was a damned genius. Especially with all the forecasts coming from the National Weather Service and purchased software that processed that data.

Then again, even when it was sweltering in the summer and freezing in the winter, I got to be outside and take it all in. You couldn't get me to trade places with one of the desk monkeys at One Police Plaza for all the tea in China. Not a chance! So naturally, when given the choice to eat inside where it was warm, I was stupid enough to take my food out on the sidewalk to a table and eat there. Partially to be outside, and partially to be alone. I'm not a loner, per se. I mean, I have Theresa. She's the love of my life, but I do embrace solitude, for the most part.

⁕ LEAVING AFGHANISTAN BEHIND ⁕

"Amelia, sit your ass right back down. You'll catch your death of a cold if you eat outside tonight," said Mama. Make no mistake about it, it was her little restaurant, not the family's. "Are you listening to me?"

"Yes, Mama. I promise I'll come back in for a refill of coffee in just a minute. Let me sit down and take a load off first."

"Take a load off in here, you crazy child!" I laughed under my breath. I felt privileged. She didn't treat just anyone that way. "I don't know why I try with you. You never listen to my advice anyway."

"Not true! Didn't I listen to you when you set me up with Theresa? You were the one that pushed me to ask her out. You practically pushed me in front of a train… or should I say train wreck?" Mama laughed and dismissed me with a wave of her hand. "Come back for that refill or I'll haunt your dreams tonight."

"I don't doubt you will, Mama." I sat my food and coffee on the table and relaxed. As much as I like walking a beat (unlike most cops these days who prefer a cruiser), I do like to sit down and take a load off periodically. I'd no sooner unwrapped my sandwich, when the stupid radio went off.

"All units, vicinity of Flatbush and Quentin, shots fired. 10-32. Approach 10-39. Units in the area respond."

"Dispatch, 168. Show me 10-8 en route, two blocks out. Request 10-78 from 10-60."

I ran like the wind. Shots fired, no other information. Naturally I was the closest respondent. All I wanted was a measly half hour for a meal. Was that too much to ask? I'm not only a marathon runner, I can sprint a 5K. I'm now thirty-one years old, but have never been in better shape. The United States Army took a wiry Flatbush girl, with no experience other than the ability to play basketball, and shaped her into what I am now. I am daily grateful. My mom is so proud! She and papa came from Bermuda with little to their names after paying for college, dragging a few suitcases and me and my sister, Cheryl Anne. We'd all flourished here in the United States, but papa had died the year before I went into the army. I always wished he'd lived just one more year to see me graduate from basic training.

I don't think I ever considered being a lifer. That was brought home to me when I pulled my gauntlet in Southwest Asia. That's where you pull your fifth tour. Supposedly it means that you never have to go back, but that doesn't apply to certain specialties. My best friend growing up, Vam Dho, came back from her sixth deployment in a coffin aboard a C-17. She was Psychological Operations. I did five tours and they wanted me to go again. I would have had to extend my enlistment before I left though, since it ran out about the third week of what would have been a six to nine month deployment.

I was, officially, a military policeman - whatever - I was a sniper!

These things were running through my head while I was beating boots down the sidewalk as fast I could, toward the vicinity of the call. Just as I got there, two men ran out into the street ahead of me. I could clearly see the gun that one of them held, even in the dimly lit street. It was a large automatic pistol, either nickel or stainless steel, with light glinting off it.

"Stop! Police!" I shouted at them, which, of course, both ignored. I pulled my weapon and held it up as I ran, pushing the safety off simultaneously. "Stop! Police!" I repeated, to no avail.

Suddenly the one with the shiny gun turned toward me. I didn't know if the other had a gun, but I definitely knew this one did. I immediately got down into a crouching stance and lowered my weapon at him. "Drop your weapon! Now!" I screamed. Nobody said criminals were smart. I heard a bullet whiz by my head, then heard it strike the brick in the building behind me. I firmly pulled the trigger three times. He dropped. The other man continued to run.

I quickly moved up to the suspect I had shot. He still had a fairly strong pulse, but I knew I'd hit him three times in the gut. I grabbed my radio. "Dispatch, 168, two suspects. One down, three shots. Other suspect is heading south on Hendrickson. Send an ambulance and a squad, 10-18."

"168, 10-4. Stand by." While I waited, I tried to find the wounds through the suspect's coat, after first recovering his pistol and sticking it in the back of my Sam Browne. "168, ambulance and squad dispatched. Ambulance ETA, five to six minutes. Squad ETA, less than two minutes."

"168, 10-4." For a two minute ETA, they sure were quick. The squad fishtailed around the corner and came to a screeching halt about twenty feet from me, their headlights and both spotlights focused on the scene. They killed the siren, but left the flashing lights on.

🌟 LEAVING AFGHANISTAN BEHIND 🌟

"I've got this one. The other one ran down Hendrickson on foot. Five ten to six feet, dark hair, light complexion, jeans, dark, heavy coat. Sorry I don't have more!" I yelled out.

The other two officers jumped back in the squad. With a wave from each, they hit the siren again and screeched the tires. I had the suspect on his back. I was trying to apply pressure to his midsection, but he was bleeding too badly. I had a terrible feeling. Even when the bad guy shoots first, even when it's a completely justified shoot, you still feel it. If you don't, you should quit and find a new job.

Finally, the ambulance came lumbering up the street. They pulled up beside me. The driver and passenger hopped out with their bags. The paramedic in the back opened the door from the inside and pulled the stretcher out, joining the other two. There was so much blood! It was all over me, all over the victim, and all over the street. The paramedics took over for me. I stood back, really feeling the lack of food now.

Within four or five minutes, there were four more squads on scene. The first one had gone down the street and found nothing. Another squad close to the site, the patrol sergeant on duty, and the patrol training officer pulled up. The sergeant was there to fill out the reports on weapons discharge and the suspect's condition after a physical confrontation resulting in medical treatment. While the sarge was filling out his paperwork, the second squad was filling out the incident report and had already called in Crime Scene Investigation. The good news was that it was a relatively slow night, and CSI were expected within about fifteen minutes. Even though I was the officer involved, they had to fill out the report for the investigation. My report would be just for the record.

The paramedics had put in a mainline and gone through many pints of blood and plasma, but they couldn't slow the flow of blood enough to transport him. About thirty minutes into it, they pulled the parachute cord and bailed. They'd have to wait for CSI before they could leave, but in the meantime it took them a good twenty minutes to get everything squared away.

The paramedics had begun cleaning me up and making sure that I had no injuries. My right knee was a little out of sorts from all the pounding on the pavement getting over here, plus the chase... I'm not twenty-one any more. They gave me some naproxen for that, along with a twenty-four ounce bottle of water with added electrolytes to keep me hydrated. I thanked them for their help. They'd also given me a couple of Mylar blankets to wrap up in and let me sit in the back of the ambulance until I could get some replacement clothes. My shirt and coat were soaked with blood, but at least it was off my hands and arms now.

The back of the ambulance opened and the sarge and the reporting officer got in, shutting the door behind them. "Amelia, from what I've gathered already, it was a good, clean shoot. No worries there. Glen here is going to drive you over to the precinct so that you can finish your report while it's still fresh in your head. Then we're going to kick you loose, with pay of course, and you'll have to drive a desk for a few days until we get the official okay from 1PP." He handed me the business card of the head doctor, as required by departmental regulations. "Dr. Feynman is the duty shrink for this week. Call her! Let her do her job! Even if you feel fine. I'm not kidding!"

"No need to shout, Timmy. I heard you the first time."

"I could bust you for insubordination. Not for not using my rank, but for calling me Timmy instead of Tim. For God's sake, Amelia, you're not my parents. I could get away with kicking your ass," he said playfully, punching me in the arm. "I'm going to head home now. I've been on duty since six thirty this morning. Call Dr. Feynman. Promise me."

"I promise, Sarge. Go on home to Rita. Glen will take care of me."

"Good night, you two."

"Good night, Sarge," Glen and I said in unison.

Glen looked me right in the eyes. "Does this bring anything back? I have never discharged my weapon, but I've drawn it, and it takes me back."

Glen was in my unit at the same time, but we always deployed opposite each other, so we never met until we joined the force at the NYPD. On paper, we were the XVIII Airborne Corps, 16th MP Brigade, 91st MP Battalion, 32nd MP Company out of Fort Bragg. When we were deployed, we became the 10th Mountain Division, 1st Brigade, 10th Military Police Battalion, 1st Platoon. Officially you had to be an infantryman, a Special Forces member, a Stryker, or a cavalry scout, but since women weren't allowed in those jobs, they allowed me to be selected from an MP unit that was embedded in an infantry

LEAVING AFGHANISTAN BEHIND

division. But then, in those blurred lines that sometimes present themselves, life wasn't what it seemed.

I said nothing. He helped me into the squad he was driving and took me back to the precinct. I had a couple of spare shirts in my locker and he managed to find me a couple of hoodies to put on. They were both oversized for me, so I had no problem getting them on. I put my beat cap in my locker and picked up a snapback and threw it on. I also got my chain out and put my ID on it so that I could be identified throughout the building. After I finished filling out my report, Glen, who was about ready for his coffee break, came in where I was set up and took my reports to turn in. Then he picked up the phone, slammed it against the desk in front of me, picked up the handset, and shoved it in my face.

"I'll do it."

"When."

"Later. I promise."

"You'll do it now!"

I sighed, pulling out the card for Dr. Feynman. I punched the numbers into the phone as Glen was leaving the office, gently pulling the door shut behind him.

"This is Elizabeth Feynman. May I help you?"

"Dr. Feynman. This is Officer Amelia Gittens. I was just... involved in a suspect shooting." Dr. Feynman immediately lost the sound of sleepiness in her voice.

"Amelia, are you there?"

"Yeah. Look, I can call you tomorrow if you'd like. It's almost midnight now."

"Which precinct are you at right now?"

"67th Flatbush."

"Give me twenty-five minutes. I'll be right there."

"Really, I can do this tomorrow."

"Nonsense. The sooner we do this, the better it will be. See you in a few. Just don't make fun of me without makeup," she laughed. I tried to laugh, but it didn't come.

Next, I pulled out my cell phone. "Hi, baby. How are you tonight?"

"Knowing you're going to be walking in that door in less than an hour, how could I not be perfect?"

"About that... I'm... uh... going to be a little late. I've got to hang out here at the precinct for a while. I'm waiting on the departmental psychiatrist to have an hour visit with me before I can leave, and she won't be here for about half an hour. Then I have to get a ride home. They won't let me drive tonight."

"Baby! What's wrong? Are you all right? Did you get hurt?"

"No, I'm fine actually. It was just... well, you're going to hear about it anyway. I was involved in a shooting tonight."

"But you're fine, right? Tell me you're fine."

"Yeah, I'm just fine. I had a suspect shoot at me. He missed. I didn't."

"...So, you shot him? Or her? Or whatever?"

"Yeah. I shot him three times. The ambulance couldn't even get him stable enough to transport."

"Baby girl, are you sure you're okay?"

"I'll be fine. I don't technically have to see the shrink tonight, but I won't be allowed to do anything without talking to one of them, so I might as well get it over with. I'll see you in a couple of hours. I just wanted to let you know I'd be late. Scratch Ferdinand for me. See you in a while. Love you."

"I love you too, baby. So much."

Theresa Biancardi was almost an empath, she cared so much. Not just about me, about everybody really, but especially towards me. Her family had some trouble getting used to me. Not because I'm black, but because of my sounds-sort-of-British-but-not-quite accent.

Finally, the doctor showed up. "Hello, Officer Gittens. I'm Elizabeth Feynman. Please, let's find some place a little more conducive to a chat than this office." We found a lounge area, where she took out a large sticky note and put it on the door. She wrote on it with a big marker, 'IN USE'. "Please, come in. Sit down and make yourself comfortable."

We both got seated, but neither of us spoke, initially. I understood quickly, she was waiting for me to go first in order to judge my condition. I played it coy for a few minutes before finally deciding to speak, "So when you go out on one these little ventures, do you jump on the departmental database and do a quick dossier scan before coming out, or something like that?"

"Or something like that," she responded.

LEAVING AFGHANISTAN BEHIND

"So you already know what I did before joining the NYPD. Right?"

"You were an MP in the army."

"Does my quick record show what my TDYs were?"

"All I know is that you were in the army as an MP for thirteen and a half years, and that you retired honorably as a Sergeant First Class. It takes an absolute minimum of twelve and a half years to make SFC and yet you achieved that grade and functioned there for some time. It also says that you have a Bronze Star with two oak leaf clusters and two Vs, Global War on Terrorism medal with three clusters, a Commendation Medal with oak leaf cluster, Afghanistan Campaign medal with three clusters, Distinguished Service Medal, Good Conduct Medal, two Purple Hearts, Army Achievement Medal twice, and a Combat Infantry Badge. Christ! That's only the first quarter or so of the alphabet. And that's only medals, not to mention ribbons and awards. It doesn't say why, it just says that you have them. If you don't mind my asking, what were the extent of your wounds?"

I stood up from my chair, pulled my tee shirt up and my sweat bottoms down about four inches. That let her see the scars from four bullet holes. "Dr. Feynman, I rarely performed MP duties in the army."

"Being from an enemy weapon, those would be thirty caliber wounds, correct?"

I nodded my head at her. I was impressed that she knew the difference and the implications that went along with them.

"So what did you do?"

"I was a sniper. I was already in the 10th Mountain Division, firmly embedded in Afghanistan, but worked primarily in the forward combat brigades. I still wore my MP insignias, in addition to the ones for the unit I worked with. That's what I did for about eighty percent of my time, both at home and deployed. My rotations home were always short, and my deployments always long."

"Well, that explains the CIB. I wondered about that. Most MPs don't get those."

"You do if you're working in a forward area, actually. Glen Parsons, the officer that wrote up my incident tonight, was in my unit at the same time. Never met him until we both started working here. Sort of funny. He has a Silver Star, a Commendation Medal, and a CIB, but he wasn't a sniper."

"Let's talk about being sniper a little bit before we move on. Do you have any confirmed kills?"

"Yes."

"Do you know how many?"

"Yes."

"Would you mind sharing that with me?"

"Yes."

"Amelia, I'm not the enemy here, I'm your friend. I'm not going to be asked to testify at your review board. In fact, I'm prohibited by both licensure and law (not to mention the union), from doing so. I'm just trying to get a baseline for you. The more I know, the more I can help you."

"Who says I need help?"

"That was poorly worded. How about the more I know, the more I can make myself available to you for whatever support I can give? Is that better?"

"Much." I paused for a couple of minutes. What the hell. "Seventeen confirmed, thirty-one suspected."

"And how do you feel about that, after the fact? Not at that moment, but now."

"Whatever."

"Does it bother you? Do you ever have nightmares? Have you ever been diagnosed with PTSD, even mild?"

"Yes, yes, and yes."

"Okay. Let's move on to tonight. What happened?"

"I'm a beat cop. I responded to a call. I gave chase to two suspects. One had a gun that was easy to see, even at night. Shiny. Forty-five caliber. I identified myself twice and gave them warning to stop. Both suspects failed to respond. Shortly after that, the suspect with the gun fired one round that missed me. I did hear the bullet whiz by, so it must have been fairly close. I fired three rounds into the suspect. Guaranteed to immobilize, but not overkill. The other suspect ran away. I radioed in the situation to dispatch and immediately cleared the suspect's weapon and begin giving him first aid as best I could. The paramedics weren't able to save him."

"How did it make you feel, hearing the bullet go by you?"

"I didn't particularly have an opinion one way or another about it, ma'am."

LEAVING AFGHANISTAN BEHIND

"Please, no need for ma'am. You can call me Elizabeth if you like."

"Actually, I'd prefer Dr. Feynman."

"That's okay as well. So you didn't get upset? Angry? Scared? Nothing particular regarding being shot at?"

"No, but it was because of that I returned fire. I would never have shot first. I would have let them escape and evade before shooting first."

"Departmental policy does give you circumstances where you not only should, but are required to, shoot first if there is a safety issue for the public or yourself."

"Are you going to report me for what I just said, ma'am?"

"No, of course not. I wish I could get you to understand that I represent your interests here, nobody else's. I tell you what, I want some time to review my notes, develop a little plan of action if you will, for you to follow. We'll talk again."

"How often will I have to report to you before returning to duty?"

"Officer Gittens, I really want to see you again. At least a few times. Maybe three or four if you would consent, but as far as I'm concerned, I'll sign off for you tomorrow. I'll have your notice of record included in your jacket to go to the review board, to allow them to rest assured. Okay?"

"Thank you, ma'am."

"On one condition…"

"What's that?"

"Just once, say it. Say Elizabeth. Then I promise you, I'll clear you," she smiled.

I managed to smile back at her, even if I didn't mean it wholeheartedly. I stood up from my chair and stared her down for a minute. I extended my hand to her and said, "Elizabeth. Thank you."

As she shook my hand, she said, "You're welcome. Now was that so hard?"

"No, ma'am." We both broke out laughing then. A long, hard, belly laugh. It broke the tension tremendously. That alone made me feel better than everything else did. There was something about talking to a shrink. I kept having to do it on active duty, and with the VA for the two or three years after I got out because I had PTSD. The day you go in and talk to them, and even the day after, you feel like crud. Then you get better, better than if you hadn't gone. Maybe it was just stirring everything up that created that feeling.

Since Elizabeth was going my way, she offered to give me a ride home. I took her up on it. I thanked her again as I closed the car door and waved goodbye. I went to the door and was fumbling with the lock and my key, when Theresa yanked it open. She grabbed my hoody and jerked me inside. "Hi, baby girl. How are you doing?"

"I'm fine," was about all I could muster.

"Are you sure?"

"Yeah. I'm fine."

"Do you maybe want a little *happy time* tonight?" she asked.

"Not really. I just want a hot shower and to go to bed."

"Are you sure?" she asked, grabbing the hands on my hips, her thumbs tickling me playfully.

"I'm sure," I said, pulling her hand away. "Let me take a shower, and then we'll cuddle up together in bed. Would that be okay for tonight?"

"No problem."

"Are you disappointed?"

"Baby, I just want to do everything I can to make you as happy as I can tonight. You've had the shittiest of all possible nights, I suspect. I'll do anything, not do anything, you just tell me what you need and I'll make it so. I'll even get you a hooker if it helps," she joked.

"Now that sounds pretty darn good. The thing is, my girlfriend, she's sort of the jealous type. She doesn't snoop my email or anything like that, but I hardly think she'd take kindly to my fooling around with another chick," I cracked back at her, jokingly.

"You got that shit right! She's a whack, totally wicked bitch when it comes to that. I don't see what you'd want in another woman anyway. After all, she's so cute, and adorable, and funny, and loving…"

"Or so she thinks," I said with a grin.

"But she loves you. More than anything in the world."

"Next time you see her? Tell her that I was the one who fell in love first. I was the one who told her first, and I was the one who asked her to marry me first…"

"What?"

LEAVING AFGHANISTAN BEHIND

"You heard me. Tell her that I was the one who asked her to marry me first."

"So you're..." she started, shaking her head. "You're asking me to marry you?"

"I was thinking of the right way to tell you. I've been carrying this damn thing around with me for three days at work, thinking about it while I was out pounding the pavement. Usually, I'm pretty good at presenting myself, but this one was different." I got down on the floor on one knee, in front of the couch where she was sitting, and pulled out the ring box. "Theresa Rosanna Biancardi, will you marry me, and live with me, and have babies with me, for the rest of my life?"

She launched herself up and on me, with her arms around my neck, and began crying uncontrollably. Finally she stepped back, tears still flowing, and put her hand out so I could put the ring on her finger. It was a little difficult because she kept shaking her hand up and down. Finally, I took my left hand and grabbed her thumb to hold her hand in place, and used my right hand to slide the ring up. She kept her hand flat to see what it looked like on her. Still, she cried and cried. I wrapped her arms around my neck again, and I encircled her waist and picked her off the floor. I carried her like that into the bathroom, then put her down. She took off her night shirt and her underwear, then reached in to turn on the water in the shower. I took my clothes off and made a little pile on the floor. She stepped in first, then held out her hand, beckoning me. I took her hand, then stepped in beside her. Her tears were gone and now she was simply beaming at me with those crystal clear, blue grey eyes, so common in the north of her country of origin. We washed each other, rinsed each other, dried each other, and dressed each other. Then we crawled beneath the covers and snuggled in tightly. We were both asleep in minutes. Unfortunately, I didn't stay there.

~End Sample Chapter of LEAVING AFGHANISTAN BEHIND ~
For more go to www.Shadoepublishing.com to purchase
the complete book or for many other delightful offerings.

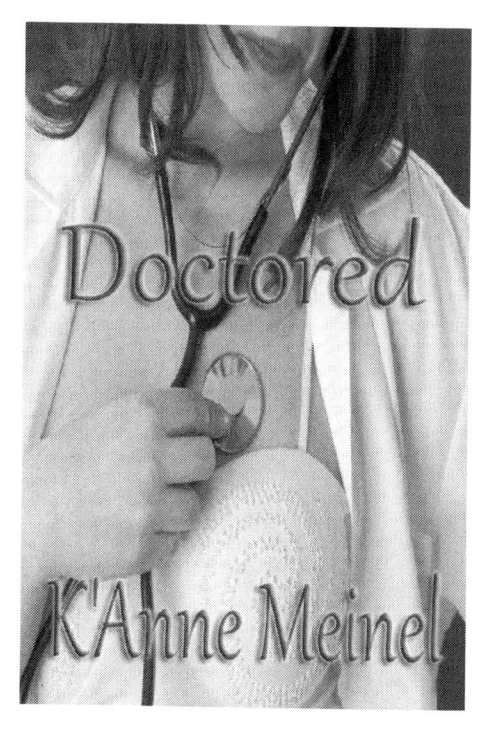

~ Because a publisher should stand behind their authors~

Doctored
K'Anne Meinel

A brilliant child protégée, she dreams of becoming a doctor and a surgeon...and accomplishes her goals. Unfortunately, her youth and round, child-like face work against her. No matter how skilled she becomes, how knowledgeable, the old school, male-dominated medical hierarchy wants to keep her in 'her place.'

Deanna has worked hard to become an expert in her chosen field, but few believe this 'child' capable. Specializing in infectious diseases, she travels the world—from the States to Europe to South America—honing her skills before winding up in Africa where her skills are desperately needed.

Meeting a nurse by the name of Madison MacGregor, she finds they share an insatiable curiosity and a love of helping others, but falling in love was not what she intended. Later, when she loses Maddie to a misunderstanding, she is haunted by the one that got away...

Ten years have passed and both the doctor and nurse have moved on with their lives, but fate intervenes when they find themselves working at the same hospital. Their friendship is revived...can their love be rekindled? Will the past haunt them or bring them closer? Will the secrets that both harbor keep them from realizing a future together?

www.shadoepublishing.com

~ *Because a publisher should stand behind their authors~*

What do you do when you meet someone who changes everything you know about love and passion?

Paige Harlow is a good girl. She's always known where she was going in life: top grades, an ivy league school, a medical degree, regular church attendance, and a happy marriage to a man. So falling in love with her gorgeous roommate and best friend Alyssa Torres is no small crisis. Alyssa is chasing demons of her own, a medical condition that makes her an outcast and a family dysfunctional to the point of disintegration make her a questionable choice for any stable relationship. But Paige's heart is no longer her own. She must now battle the prejudices of her family, friends, and church and come to peace with her new sexuality before she can hope to win the affections of the woman of her dreams. But will love be enough?

www.shadoepublishing.com

~ *Because a publisher should stand behind their authors~*

As I watch the wormhole start to close, I make one last desperate plea...
"Please? Please don't make me do this?" I whisper.
   "You're almost out of time, Lily. Please, just let go?"
   I look down at the control panel. I know what I have to do.

   Lilith Madison is captain of the Phoenix, a spaceship filled with an elite crew and travelling through the Delta Gamma Quadrant. Their mission is mankind's last hope for survival.

   But there is a killer on board. One who kills without leaving a trace and seems intent on making sure their mission fails. With the ship falling apart and her crew being ruthlessly picked off one by one, Lilith must choose who to trust while tracking down the killer before it's too late.

   "A suspenseful...exciting...thrilling whodunit adventure in space...discover the shocking truth about what's really happening on the Phoenix" (Clarion)

www.shadoepublishing.com

~ *Because a publisher should stand behind their authors*~

FAST LANE
JENNIS SLAUGHTER
A.D. CAMPBELL

In the male dominated sport of Formula 1 racing, Samantha 'Sam' Dupree is struggling to make her mark against the boys. She hears about a driver who is making a name for herself in NASCAR and goes to check her out. Little does she know that she's in for the race of her heart.

Addison McCloud wants nothing more than to drive. She doesn't care about fame or fortune; she just wants to be fast enough to get herself and her family away from her abusive father. Meeting Sam changes her world and revs her life into overdrive.

When the two women meet, sparks fly like the race cars that they drive. Will they be able to steer their relationship into something more and win the race, or will their families make them crash and burn? The boys of Formula 1 are going to learn that Southern girls are a force to be reckoned with.

www.shadoepublishing.com

~ *Because a publisher should stand behind their authors*~

HEART OF VENGEANCE

DAWN CARTER

WARNING ~ book contains graphic violence towards women

A serial killer plagues the gay community and leaves a trail of dead bodies across state lines. Agent Danni Pacelli and Agent Parker Stevens rush against time to catch their killer and stop the body count from increasing.

Agent Parker Stevens life was perfect when transferred to a new city and new location which offered her solitude from the grief of losing her partner and children to a predator. But, while hunting down her suspect, she meets Samantha Petrino who takes the once closed off Stevens and opens a world to new love. The charming advertising agent breaks down her defenses, and no matter how hard she fights to protect her heart, she finds herself falling for the beautiful and intelligent woman.

New to the FBI, Agent Danni Pacelli's struggles to balance her personal life along with the job, to save her relationship, she convinces her new partner to bring in Annabel and utilize the young detective's skills to track down their killer or risk losing Annabel all together.

The heroic efforts of two agents who hunt down a serial killer, but find more than they bargained for.

www.shadoepublishing.com

~ *Because a publisher should stand behind their authors*~

FRANKIE

PRUDENCE MACLEOD
IN COLLABORATION WITH
CRYSTIANNA CRAWFORD

Carrie flees from the demons of her present, trying to protect the ones she loves.

Frankie hides from the demons of her past, and the memory of loved ones she failed to protect.

A modern day princess thrown to the wolves, Carrie's only hope is the rancher who had spent the better part of a decade in self imposed, near total, isolation. Frankie's history of losing those she tries to save haunts her, but this madman threatens her home, her livestock, her sanctuary. She knows she can't do it alone, has she still got enough support from her oldest friends?

www.shadoepublishing.com

~ *Because a publisher should stand behind their authors~*

In a world on the verge of being told that everything they once thought was merely myth is real, can one teenage girl cope with life changes she never saw coming?

Seventeen year old Kyndle Callahan began her year as a typical high school senior. Well, as typical as a girl can be while living life as a werewolf. She wasn't bitten or scratched as most people believe all werewolves are made, no, she was born into the pack that's always been her extended family. She's never seen the people she grew up with as the monsters of myth and legend but everything in her life is thrown into a tailspin when her father springs some shocking news on her. Suddenly, reality as a werewolf is much scarier than the stories humans tell. Stunned by the prospect of spending her life bonded to someone she can't even stand sharing the same space with and devastated at the thought of losing the only love she's ever known, can Kyndle settle into who and what she is in time to set things right? Can the girl that grew up knowing only pack law stand up, embrace her true calling, and become the woman she was meant to be despite going against everything her family believes?

With the help of her best friend Abbey, Kyndle must navigate a confusing world of wolf culture, teenage drama, and coming out in a group that believes her lifestyle is unnatural. Follow her journey through pain, heartache, several states, and the fight to be with the girl she loves and take her place in the world.

www.shadoepublishing.com

~ *Because a publisher should stand behind their authors~*

THE DEATH ROOM
RACHEL MALDONADO

Roberta Pena finally has her dream job of being a Biology Teacher at the high school that she once attended, but something sinister lurks in her classroom. She begins to have unusual paranormal experiences. Is she simply losing her mind or is there a ghost trying to make contact? How will she deal with the mystery of the room that often smells of death and where she has begun to have so many unsettling and ghastly sightings? Will she solve the mystery or be forced to leave her career that she worked so hard to achieve? Might she find love in the process?

www.shadoepublishing.com

~ Because a publisher should stand behind their authors~

RIDING THE RAINBOW
GENTA SEBASTIAN

A Children's Novel for ages 8-11

Horse crazy Lily, eleven years old with two out-loud-and-proud mothers, is plump and clumsy. Her mothers say she's too young to ride horses, she can't seem to get anything right in class, and bullies torment her on the playground. Alone and lonely, how will she ever survive the mean girls of Hardyvale Elementary's fifth-grade?

Across the room Clara sits still as a statue, never volunteering or raising her hand. To avoid the bullying that is Lily's daily life she answers only in a whisper with her head down, desperate to keep her family's secret that she has two fathers.

Then one day Clara makes a brave move that changes the girls' lives forever. She passes a note to Lily asking to meet secretly at lunch time. As they share cupcakes she explains about her in-the-closet dads. Both girls are relieved to finally have a friend, especially one who understands about living in a rainbow family.

Life gets better. As their friendship deepens and their families grow close, their circle of friends expand. The girls even volunteer together at the local animal shelter. Everything is great, until old lies and blackmail catch up with them. Can Lily and her mothers rescue Clara's family from disaster? Or will Lily lose her first and best friend?

www.shadoepublishing.com

~ Because a publisher should stand behind their authors~

Dakota

KAREN E. BAKER

When U.S. Marine Dakota McKnight returned home from her third tour in Operation Iraqi Freedom, she carried more baggage than the gear and dress blues she had deployed with. A vicious rocket-propelled grenade attack on her base left her best friend dead and Dakota physically and emotionally wounded. The marine who once carried herself with purpose and confidence, has returned broken and haunted by the horrors of war. When she returns to the civilian world, life is not easy, but with the help of her therapist, Janie, she is barely managing to hold her life together...then she meets Beth.

Beth Kendrick is an American history college professor. She is as straight-laced as they come, until Dakota enters her life, that is. Will her children understand what she is going through? Will she take a chance on the broken marine or decide to wait for the perfect someone to come along?

Time is on your side, they say, unless there is a dark, sinister evil at work. Is their love strong enough to hold these two people together? Will the love of a good woman help Dakota find the path to recovery? Or is she doomed to a life of inner turmoil and destruction that knows no end?

www.shadoepublishing.com

~ Because a publisher should stand behind their authors~

To Paris With Blood
Eternity Has Its Price...

A Novel By Jeffrey Niewinski

Welcome to Paris, "The City of Lights"---where the only requirement to visit is being "Undead."

Struggling with a past tragedy and growing unrest with my sister, I accepted an invitation to visit my very close friends in Paris.

My early morning flight had just arrived in Paris. As I made my way through the busy concourse, timed seemed to stop. All my mind could register were the three friends standing in front of me. Janine and her two brothers, Luc and Jaycee.

Meanwhile, back in the States my Sister Elena had taken great joy in antagonizing me. Elena's jealousy would come to be the driving force that would lead to the culmination of a showdown that will resolve a past injustice and ultimately lead to the destruction of our relationship, and a much darker, sinister means to an end.

Would the love that Luc and I came to share, along with Janine and Jaycee be enough to overcome the deceit, treachery and betrayal we would encounter? Would the secret my friends have destroy me or renew me?

Little did I know, they would literally hold my soul in their hands.

www.shadoepublishing.com

~ *Because a publisher should stand behind their authors*~

After an unhappy marriage, Marie is lonely and wants to find love. Her old ways of searching for someone special hasn't worked. So after learning a new technique, she found the love of her life. Marie puts everything she has into this new relationship with Jada, wanting only her happiness, sacrificing all, even her mental and physical health. However through Jada's family and personal secrets, she wonders what is in it for her. Did she really find what she was looking for when she met Jada, a younger black woman?

Jada answers the call for companionship with Marie, but she's holding on to the past, unwilling to let her mother know her closely guarded secret. Unfortunately, she's confronted with some disturbing news which threatens to destroy her future.

Will her secrets keep her from happiness with Marie? Will her suspicions cause her to miss out on the best thing in her life?

Unbeknownst to Kelly, "another" answered the call for friendship with Marie was well. When Kelly's attracted to her dance partner, "Kelly" makes it her life's mission to become more than just Marie's friend, even if that means ruining her love's life.

Those that lie within the unsuspecting woman are a mystery to Kelly, but also to Marie and Jada as well.

www.shadoepublishing.com

~ *Because a publisher should stand behind their authors*~

SADIE'S REVENGE
ROSE STONE

Slim Pritchard had been Sadie's first kiss and he planned to make her his wife one day, but when Sadie meets her new neighbor, Sparrow, plans change. Sadie is in love for the very first time.

One day, while defending Sadie, Sparrow comes to blows with Slim and he vows to take his revenge. Sadie's life has already been marred by so many tragedies. Will Slim come between the lovers? Or will Sadie and Sparrow overcome adversity and be together forever?

www.shadoepublishing.com

*If you have enjoyed this book and the others listed here Shadoe Publishing, LLC is always looking for authors. Please check out our website @ www.shadoepublishing.com
For information or to contact us @
shadoepublishing@gmail.com.*

We may be able to help you make your dreams of becoming a published author come true.

Made in the USA
Middletown, DE
06 March 2019